Following My Duty

Copyright

First Edition, February 2024
Copyright © 2024 by Melony Ann

Chapter One

♡ Reid ♡

Station 28.

Home, that's what I've missed these last few months. I've been busy at the Police Academy in Austin, finally working on my promotion to Lieutenant.

Today is day one of my new rank and position, and I have to admit to myself, I'm feeling good. Nina Simone's song goes around my head as Jo greets me with coffee and a huge smile at The Cozy Bean where I usually begin the day. I nearly bump into Abi Charmichael with my coffee as she grabs the coffee order for her Firehouse squad.

Since her hen party, I've gotten to know our latest, feisty resident. What started as her sister hitting up on me, thinking I was a stripper and not an actual cop in uniform, had me making friends with her and Nick outside of the station.

She makes a thing of being Scottish, until she tears you a new one in a torrent of words with an accent no one can understand. However, while the words ain't comprehensible, her tone and body language more than make her meaning clear.

In getting to know her, I've gotten to know Nick, and he's turned out to be a great friend. He was a few years older than me back in school, a

Senior to my Sophomore, the same year as my brother. I'd heard the rumours about him at school and decided there and then that women (more importantly, girls) weren't worth that level of commitment.

I recall asking Lyndsey Tainer to the Prom in my senior year. I don't think I even kissed the girl. Which started rumours all of their own.

"Good morning, everyone! Conference room for everyone, two minutes!" Peter's voice rings out around the squad room, bringing me back to the present. "Hope you're ready for this, Reid."

"Hell, yeah." I grin back, eager to get on with things.

"We'll get your new squad issued when this video conference is over. Let's get to it." I nod as everyone grabs a coffee from the jug and makes their way into the conference room.

I notice Ethan, and we acknowledge each other. He's a Sergeant just now, but I know he has ambitions to rank up, and it makes me think of Noah. Going through high school, college and then the academy with Noah, Griffin, Matt, Caden and Mateo, made us quite a bonded team, even if we are missing a few of us these days.

I make a mental promise to go and check on his widow when today is over with; he'd be the one I'd celebrate this day with. I try not to let the bitterness of Griff's absence taint the mood. On the video screen, I see a woman who I recognise, though it's been a few years since I've seen her. She's greying around the temples now, and her no-nonsense body language makes me smirk as her image chases the demons back to their hiding places.

"Okay, settle down. Everyone, you all know Fed liaison, Federal Special Agent Maggie Forrester. She's back with us."

The room goes quiet.

"Good morning, everyone," Maggie's voice cascades over us all as the lights get dimmed. The blinds to this room are already closed over. "Sorry to drop in on you all in this way. In better circumstances, I'd be there in person, but I can't be in two places at once. However, I have authorisation for Station 28 to be briefed."

Peter nods at Maggie as he sits down in a chair.

"I'm sure you're all aware of the container incident near Waco a few weeks ago," she begins, and we all murmur an acknowledgement. "Well, it was a little more than that, as I know some of you are aware. The container in question was full of women, who blew their way out of it.

Some have escaped and made a run for it, some are in hospital being treated. Some, regretfully, didn't make it."

Again, the murmurs rise, and Peter motions for us to quieten down, now.

"My office thinks that these women are either being trafficked *to* the USA or they're being lured here with false jobs and *then* being trafficked elsewhere. Every one of them was or is a foreign national, and our Foreign Affairs Office is getting a lot of heat from their counterpart Foreign Offices, especially from our British and French friends. I understand that the British and French Prime Ministers, as well as the Scottish First Minister, have been talking with both the President and the Secretary of State, loudly and quite late. We've been ordered to end it."

There are many nods around, an understanding that this is now getting some serious attention from Capitol Hill. I can only imagine the scenes and the types of conversations. "I know that three of the missing women are Brits, one is from Scotland." *Damn, why did I pipe up with that information?*

Maggie smiles, though it shows her thin lips and fine lines. If ever there was a smile that wasn't a smile, she wore it. It makes me sit up straighter as I realise that the hunch I mentioned to Preston when this started was likely right. Damn my early days' training from my dirty-cop-of-an-uncle.

"That is very true. We have a call from one of their *husbands*," and she uses her fingers to emphasise the word, so we know she thinks that's a load of garbage, "that she went missing after an argument. What he says happened and the CCTV of that night from surrounding buildings isn't adding up." I sit back and let her carry on.

"What do you need, Special Agent Forrester?" Preston knows I've had an interest in this case since that explosion; we've talked about it the few times he's checked in with me on how the training was going. I shouldn't have an interest, but it was on the Piper Falls side of Waco, and something like that is hard to miss.

"Eyes. Ears. None of these women are experienced hikers or outdoors people. I've contacted their families via the British and French Consulates. They hardly went out into the wilderness or for walks in nature. None of them was ever a Girl Scout, and only one has ever gone camping. If they're out in the Texan Wilderness alone, they're woefully underprepared."

"Texas ain't a State to go wandering around in just 'cause you feel like it," Ethan pipes up. And that's not just because of the rattlers.

Maggie grins. "Well, not underprepared anyway. One woman, Alysia Davidson, was last seen at a service station in the hills outside of Waco. We've alerted Dallas and Austin, but there's a lot of ground to cover between Waco and everywhere else." As Maggie talks, a picture of a pretty girl with flowing auburn hair, a cheery smile and blue eyes appears on screen, and my eyes are drawn into her still image.

"Where do you think she might be going?" I lean forward, keen as hell to get stuck into finding this woman, or hell, any of them. The murmurs about how pretty she is by the guys in uniform reaches my ears, and Preston halts any further cat-calling with just a glare.

Maggie smiles and holds up a tourist pamphlet of Piper Falls. "Alysia picked this up, read it then put it back and walked out the door, into the tree line, vanishing moments later. She didn't pay for what she took, but someone behind her in the line did. Said she looked half-dead, not quite awake and almost grey in color."

Something in the bottom of my stomach knots up. "She ain't well." I murmur as I look at Peter to see that Preston's now standing next to him. He nods in agreement with me.

Maggie shakes her head. "I unfortunately agree. When I asked the elderly gentleman why he paid for her goods, he simply said: *'She looked like she needed it.'*" Thank God for Good Samaritans.

"So, what's the plan here?" Preston's question echoes my own, and I acknowledge him with a discreet nod. I see Maggie leaning forward. Her voice is quieter—not quite a whisper, but it ain't far from it.

"This is not the *only* sighting of these missing women. I'm in Dallas to see about the possible sighting of two others, so I can't be in Piper Falls to see if Alysia comes through, or help her if she does. Your station is tasked with assisting the FBI in finding Alysia *and* keeping her safe."

"Won't they try and leave the USA?" I ask, knowing that without a ticket, they'll get arrested at Austin and processed, which will then flag them up. But, Austin is huge, and once they flag up… "They *want* to get caught at Austin," I state, and Maggie nods.

"Or at another airport, yes. I can't be sure why that is the case yet, but I need all the bases covered."

"Is there anything else, Maggie?" Preston asks, and when she confirms that there isn't, Preston wraps up the call. I'm glad Maggie reached out to ask us. I've always enjoyed working closely with her; she's a good Fed and plays it by numbers, unless her intuition tells her otherwise. And when it does, she ain't wrong.

Immediately, the murmurs begin, and Preston whistles, making us all shut up.

"All right, ladies, simmer down. Here's the story. Reid here has had his nose in this case for a few weeks, something the Feds ain't too happy about. We spoke with Maggie before this; she hinted that there's more going on, and she needs someone else digging up things she can't quite yet."

Eyes turn to me, and I shrug, understanding I'm more on the mark than they'd like, and I don't like the implication that Maggie's hands are tied somehow.

"So, anything to do with this case, send Reid's way. He's going to be our liaison on this case."

I go to object, but I see the looks on Preston's and Peter's faces. I guess this is my first case.

Piper Falls. Population, 10,459, plus tourists for a few months. This quaint little town has me winding down the window and breathing in the warm air as I slowly drive through in my unmarked squad car, taking in where everything is situated. It's been a few days since the conference chat with the Feds, and seeing the case file unfold as bits have come in, has me appreciating our little community a whole lot more.

I'd taken the weekend off, heading across to New Mexico to see my brother and his family for a short time, celebrating my win. Sure, it was a short drive to Austin to fly out, but worth it. Nothing is more important to me than family, but visiting with him begins a yearning in me for my own. Driving along, seeing the Police Station next to the Firehouse makes me smile. Over the road is City Hall, the Court House and Papi's Bar and Grill. Further down, I see Cozy Bean and the Blue Bonnet Bakery.

Finding a parking space, I pull up and stretch, heading into Abuela's Outpost to catch up with Eduardo. The news is on, and the fire incident at Waco is being churned around by the news media. The Feds are milking this, adding in a little extra "news" every other day. I begin to watch the broadcast at the bar, along with Abi Charmichael.

"Hey, Abi." I smile at my friend.

"Hallo, Reid. How ye keepin'?" she asks, nursing the half beer in her hands.

I nod as I hear the broadcaster go on again. "I'm keeping good, thank y'all. And yourself?"

"I'm braw," she tells me with a wink as her smile grows wide.

"What do you think?" Ed nods to the TV as he comes over. Abi's smile vanishes as her lips go thin.

"There's far more shite goin' on wi' that than they're tellin'. That fire? Something's no addin' up." I can't help but love her accent.

"Ya think?" he asks.

"None of it makes sense."

"Oh, I hear ye, pal!" Eduardo grins at her.

"This," she says, motioning to the screen, "ain't all that's kicking aff, I promise ye."

I sip my drink and make a note of her observations. I know it ain't all of the story, and I can't enlighten them to what I know. I do know that if Alysia had come through town already, we'd know. Abi gets hugged by Essie and Sakura in quick succession as they enter, before they take their drinks and head to a booth seat.

Nothing more interesting comes to light in the next hour. I know better than to interrupt Abi when she's with Estrella and Sakura. The three of them are as thick as thieves, and only a fool would try to engage any of them. Knowing that Essie is with Sakura makes it interesting when outsiders try to hit on either Essie or Sakura. Abi just adds in a little more dynamite. As they walk past to leave, I hear them talking.

"Ready for another forty-eight, milky?" Essie asks as her black hair swishes.

"Aye, Cap, I am. Remind me to chat with the wee man, aye?" They exit through the door and out into the evening air. I can't help but wonder who the wee man is, and what Abi wants to chat with him about.

After I've eaten at Abuela's, I check in on Mallory and the kids before I grab some supplies from Bessie's and head home. I grin as I take the cookie tin I know Mallory and the kids have filled with treats and place it on the coffee table.

Home is a converted loft barn on the outskirts of town, hidden away. There was a neighbour for a while about half a mile away, some Hawaiian fella, but he didn't stay for long, and I didn't get to meet him. I park in the barn that I use as a garage and head up, unlocking the doors. The lights are off, so I turn them on and can hear the hum of the refrigerator as I begin to put the food away. Opening a window, I can hear the crickets and nighttime creatures as they start moving around and doing their thing. The filter coffee machine, a stove-kettle, a toaster and an electric cooker make up the small kitchen. I don't need anything else.

The bed is unmade, and I wish I'd made it before I left to visit my brother, but I quickly find the sheets and make it up then shave before I grab a shower. Standing by the huge picture window as the sun fully sets, the towel wrapped around me, I take the time to appreciate the purple and red hues that get taken out quickly by the tree line while I munch on a home-made cookie. Soon, darkness befalls inside the loft.

The following morning, with the coffee machine brewing a small pot, I get to go over the latest case files for every one of the women who I *think* are still missing.

The evidence of the fire sits before me with the full, unredacted Investigation Report. Five bodies were burnt to nothing but bones in the container that exploded. There must've been a barricade at the back as the back two-foot section of the container is far less damaged. What or who was in that section, boggles me. However, their DNA didn't get erased in the fire, some of their fingerprints were visible with blue light and powder. I doubt there's a section that wasn't dotted with prints.

As I look through the files, I again take note of how their looks are pretty damn similar. The same mid-length red or auburn hair, similar color of eyes too. Their build, their form. They're almost a replica of each other. Picking up the phone, I call Maggie on the secure number.

"Morning, Maggie, it's Detective Reid Flanagan, Station 28."

"Good morning! How are you?"

"I'm good! Have you a moment?"

"Give me a second," and I hear some button presses before she speaks again. "Line is secured. What do you have?"

"Was just reading your latest updates. Have you noticed that they're all pretty similar? Same build, hair, eyes? I hadn't realised how close they **all** are, until now."

There's total silence in reply for a moment. "Yes, I had. We're profiling others from different countries that match and are missing, but that's taking time."

"I'd like to show the local Firehouse the report, see what they make of it. They might see things we've missed."

"I have no problem with that, though you have the report the experts here made. Keep it to a few key members though, please? We don't need any more flies in this ointment." That has my interest, but there's no point in askin' her; she won't reveal what she means. "We have an update, which I've sent to Preston. Unfortunately, there's been no sighting of Alysia at all." I hear the frustration in Maggie's voice.

"I'll check in with him when my shift starts."

"Okay, great. Let me call you though."

I understand her implication. "Done. Speak soon." I slide the phone along the coffee table after I press the big red button, taking a moment to absorb the instructions. A few moments later, I've transferred my coffee to a travel mug, stuffed another of Mallory's cookies in my mouth, and I'm heading into town.

The Police Station, Town Hall, Court House and the Firehouse are all close to each other, making it very easy to find where this town is run from. Looking up, I take a moment to absorb the age of these buildings. There aren't many of these designs left in the bigger cities and towns like Waco; they're deemed too small. It makes me feel as if I've stepped back in time, to someplace where things are simpler, more carefree. For the first time in years, I feel something inside that I can name but hadn't dared to believe still existed: Hope. Maybe that visit to my brother in New Mexico did more for me than I realised.

"Morning, Reid!" Jo sings out as I head in to grab another coffee. I'd noticed that the engine is out on a call, so I grab my usual and head into work.

○ ○ ○

"Mornin', Reid," Preston's voice is high, and his smile is broad. He still looks fit and more contented somehow.

"Morning. Hey, do you think I can grab some input on that fire in Waco from the Firehouse?"

Preston nods. "I've already called Blake Falcon; he'll be there with Estrella. I'll come with ya; I could do with getting outta here for a moment or two. Plus, I need to brief you on what Maggie sent over." His tone tells me it's not a request.

○ ○ ○

"Captain Ortiz!" Preston calls out as he walks into the Firehouse without a care in the world. Their call clearly couldn't have been a long one, even though the engine was now being cleaned out.

"Preston!" This little Spanish lady might be tiny, but she commands respect; we all know what her temper is like. "What can I do for y'all?"

"Are you and Blake free?"

Estrella blinks and nods. "Beau, take over for me, please." A fireman much broader than me acknowledges her and takes over the reins as Estrella motions for us to head up to the office while her crew get on with the job at hand.

Blake is already in the squad room, bitching about the strength of the coffee. "Damn it, Essie, can't you have coffee that doesn't taste like tar?"

She grins. "You know me! I like my coffee like I like my men. Thick, dark and roasted."

I don't try to hide my smirk as I put the fire report for the container on the desk and grin. "I could do with your input on this."

Essie tilts her head at me. "You heard us talkin' about this last night?"

"Hard not to. Abi was talking about it with your brother when the news came on. That's the unredacted report."

Blake and Estrella look at each other and then Essie leans back against the wall, crossing her legs at the ankle as Blake picks up the report.

Preston chuckles. "We got briefed on this from the FBI end of last week. Reid got tasked with helping out from the Piper Falls end, and I feel you two might be able to give us some extra insight." Preston sits, making it clear he's used to being here. "I know what that report says. But, I want an honest interpretation of it. Something ain't addin' up in our minds."

"You're looking for needles in haystacks?" Blake asks as Preston nods. "Tell us what you were told," he commands as he begins to thumb through the report.

"Okay, so…" I go back through the incident in Waco that started all this. Then what the Federal agent shared with us a few days ago and Preston's update with that report this morning; the French lady has been found. The count is now more than five in that back section who made it out, not the three the news had been reporting of late.

He's silent for a long while as he slowly reads through the file. Everyone looks around as he reads pages of the information.

"Well, rock me gently. Hidden compartment, propane accelerant. Those women didn't stand a chance if they were in the main bit of that container."

"And we know that five somehow got out. Might be six."

"If these prints up on the wall are anything to go by, I have to agree with y'all." He hands the file to Essie, who begins to read it. "What makes ya think any of them are heading this way?"

I add on what Agent Forrester said, about the Scotswoman picking up a pamphlet and then putting it back, which makes Essie stop reading the file. She looks at Blake, her jaw slack.

"You thinkin' who I'm thinkin' of?" she asks Blake. He nods affirmation just once.

"The best person we have to go lookin'. She'd find a whisper in a whirlwind, for sure."

"Care to clue us in?" Preston asks, leaning forward.

"Your favourite Scotswoman, Abi Charmichael. She spent time with the Highland Rescue Service before she emigrated out here. If anyone can find anything or anyone up in those hills and get them down, it'll be her." I look at Preston, who nods.

"I'll make a point of droppin' in and askin' her. Though, she still doesn't like scary policemen with guns." He chuckles.

Essie smirks and rolls her eyes at me, then shakes her head. "Gimme a second," she says and vanishes. We look at Blake, who is smirking like a fox after a chicken raid. Seconds later, Essie is back and with Abi hot on her heels.

"Ach, hell, what have I dun?" she asks as she steps into the room with fear in her eyes, closing the door firmly behind her. She glances around at all of us and swallows.

"Nothin', Milky. But your skills and discretion are needed. Hear us out." Essie quickly takes her through what we've discussed. Abi nods and gets calmer as she listens.

"Okay…the hiking path to Waco is more on Jaxon's ranch side of town than by Knotts." She looks at Preston. "I'll start walking that area with the dug, see if I can find anything that might hint she's around. Are ye sure she's ill?" She looks at me to confirm that, and I nod.

"We're pretty sure. The man in the queue said she looked grey, like death warmed over, so she's either coming down with something or she'll have fought it off."

"Aye, got it. I take it that we're keepin' this on the Q.T?"

I look at Preston, then Blake, and this time, Abi chuckles. "Q.T. On the quiet."

"Yeah. I don't even want to tell this Federal agent she's safe until I have to."

Abi's eyes go wide, and she tilts her head like a dog would. "Why for?"

"We don't have all the facts of *why* she and the other women were in that container. And until we do…" Estrella and Blake share a look, and then they nod to Abi.

"They dinnae need to know," Abi concludes, taking the report Essie hands her, turning to the start of it.

Too damn right.

Chapter Two

Alysia

The sound of the river bubbling past guides me onwards, slowly. I can't recall when I last ate or when I last slept. I just know I have to put that place behind me, that I have to keep going. Piper Falls. That's the place I remember setting out for. I remember why; I have to get away.

I stumble and stop myself from falling. I've been doing far too much of that lately. I can just see the path I need to take, noticing a red ribbon tied into the bushes, and I persuade myself it's just one more step.

The cold wet thing nudges me again, then whines. I try to move, but I can't. It barks and whines a little, and I don't want it to make a noise, to attract attention to me, but I can't tell it to be quiet.

"Good lad! She's here!" There's a pause and then something snaps near me. "Alysia, can ye hear me?" It's another voice, not American. *Did I make it home?* I can't answer, and the last thing I hear is the dog whine some more.

The warm, dark space I find myself in smells clean and fresh. I timidly move my fingers. They're not cold, and they're not digging into raw, wet soil. There's a warm weight on me, and I wiggle my toes. They're covered too.

"Ah, you're awake. Take it easy, you've had it pretty rough." The voice is soft and gentle, but it's American. *'I'm not home. I'm still in danger.'* I know whoever this kind person is, they're now in the firing line.

"Can you open your eyes for me?" The warm voice sweeps over me, and I do as it asks. She's got long dark hair that falls over a shoulder, smoky grey eyes and a soft smile. "That's my girl! Here, try this." She puts a straw in my mouth, and I suck on it, gently. Water. Cold, blissful, thirst-quenching water.

"You can rest again now. You're safe."

"Naw…I'm not."

Her hand comes and sweeps some hair away from my face, whispering that I am. I can't keep my eyes open anymore, and I let the darkness fall.

Every time I open my eyes, someone is there—either the one with the softest voice, or the one with the voice of home. Slowly, I take in some water, then watered-down soup, then full soup. When the one with the soft voice leaves me alone after one of the feedings, I try to get up but fall to the floor. The decor tells me I'm in a hospital and therefore, I'll be easily found.

"Let's get you back to bed. Unless you need the bathroom?"

"You can't help me anymore."

"You can't even stand." They're both here, but the one with the softest voice is trying to get me to stand up.

"I'm putting you in danger."

"Aye, we ken. And we'll take it on and bust its chops anol. Now, ye need to dae as yer telt." There's a man behind her that I don't recognise, and while he scares me, he's not scaring them.

"You…found me."

The one with the voice of home nods at me with a soft smile. "Aye, well, it was more Buster, my dog, than me, but we'd been looking out for ye."

"Why?"

"We'll tell ye when yer able to stand up. Let's get you to the loo, then yer going back to bed." I can hardly argue with that command; she's right, I can't stand. She reminds me of my older sister, and her tough love suddenly becomes a comfort.

"Who else knows I'm here?"

"Just us. No one has told anyone anything just noo, yer filed under Jane Doe." I collapse into the nurse lady and in seconds, both women take me to the bathroom, help me do what I need to and then take me back to bed. Neither seems fazed that I can't even clean myself up.

The man is still there, silent, watching. His clean-shaven angled jaw ticks and his tattooed arms flex, but he says nothing to me. I can't help but wonder who he is.

I wake up regularly and every time, I feel a little stronger, a little more human, but nothing like I was before this happened.

"Yer a fighter," the Scotswoman says. "Now, I kinda guess ye've got questions. What dae ye wanna know?"

"You're no here all the time?" I ask, and she shakes her head. I have no idea what day it is or how long I've been here. I also find I don't care.

"Naw, I still have to work."

"What do you do?"

She grins. "I'm a firefighter."

"Oh! Where am I?"

"Piper Falls, Texas."

"I made it!" I lean back against the soft pillows, letting my eyes close.

"Aye, ye did. And ye were severely dehydrated, malnourished and goodness knows what else when yer were found. I'm gonna let Aly and Doctor Candy tell ye all aboot that."

"I'm putting ye in danger." I try to hold back the tears.

"We'll deal with that as and when. Ye said that afore, and I dinnae give a toss. I've some idea of what ye've been through, but that copper wants the whole story. Are ye up for telling him now? Or would you rather wait a wee bit?"

I pause and crack open my eyes to look at her. "Is never an option?"

The woman shakes her head slowly, and she's trying not to laugh. "Sorry, naw. I'm Abi, by the way. And I ken yer Alysia Davidson."

I sigh. "You ken more about me than I'd like."

"Aye, I figured ye'd say that. But, listen..." She waits until I open one eye and look at her. "That copper, he's wanting answers. He wants to know. Needs it so he and a Federal agent can stop whatever the hell it is you've been through from happening again. Ye need to be brave."

"You cannae stop them."

Abi raises her eyebrows at me. "Maybe no on my own. Neither can you. Combine our forces, and we can." I pull in a breath, but it doesn't stop Abi from talking. "Ye can trust this one. For a copper, he's no too bad." She seems to be chuckling.

"They're all in on it."

Her silence is deafening, and I open my eyes again to see her eyebrows are raised. "Ye need to tell him what ye ken. It cannae be fixed if ye haud yer whist." Abi's gaze is intense; she's not going to let me avoid this.

"I just wanna hide."

"Ye'll get chance. But, ye cannae keep silent. If ye dinnae tell him for yerself, tell him to stop the next lassie getting hurt, like in that container fire." She pats me on the arm, but I barely feel it.

She knows, she knows! I can't hold it in anymore and burst into tears. I have no idea how long she's holding me, or when I pass out. When I come to, he's there, holding my hand, not saying a word.

"You need to eat."

I take a few mouthfuls of the soft vegetable soup he offers before I lay back.

"You're doing great! Try and eat another spoonful for me." When I do, he praises me: "Good girl." Then I get to rest. When I try to get up, he just helps me. I have no idea who he is or why he's helping me. I want to ask Abi who he is; didn't she say he was a copper? His short hair, days' old stubble, tattooed arms and biceps make him at least appealing to the eyes. The same kind that got me into trouble not too long ago.

When Abi does visit, the man vanishes. I see them whispering outside as I get stronger, and Abi scolds him for something, though I can't tell what. Her face contorts, she wags a finger at him, and another man, who she kisses passionately, takes away the man who has watched over me.

"Can ye tell me something?" I ask as Abi helps me into a chair after making me visit the bathroom. I can at least use a walking frame now. With a grin, Abi pulls out several packs of soft protein bars and hands one to me, then leaves the others on the bedside table.

"If I can," she replies, sitting back into the other chair.

"Who is he?" I nod towards the door.

"Reid? He's the copper I was tellin' ye aboot. The one that wants to know what happened to ye."

I sigh. "He's barely said a word to me."

Abi grins. "I've just telt him off for not even tellin' ye his name. So, he'd better introduce himself when he gets his arse back here."

"Who was the other guy?"

"That's my husband, Nick." She smiles coyly, and her eyes soften. I suspect she's not been married to him for long; she's all dovey-eyed over the mention of his name.

I decide that eating the chewy protein bar was better than asking more questions. Abi doesn't push me though; she just sits and waits patiently. Finally, I get through the bar and feel a little better for it.

"This care is going to be expensive," I state.

"When Aly says you're good enough to walk out on yer own, ye will. You'll just get up and walk right outta the hospital, into the tree line and vanish again."

I blink at her, aware that she's not only let me eat, she's told me my escape route.

"Yer awfully quiet," I comment. Abi shrugs.

"I learned long ago that my opinion doesn't matter a fig. If ye want to ken it, ye'll ask. Otherwise, I'll no volunteer it."

"You're not judging me?" Everyone in my family has an opinion about my looks, height, lack of weight, how I act and voiced it. The silence Abi is giving me is strange but very welcoming.

"Naw. I could." Abi shifts in her seat, leaning forward. "But, naw. I've no been what ye've been through, so…" She smirks as she shrugs.

"You're verra different," I murmur, making her smile.

"Aye, I ken that. So are ye. But, *ye are* a Scot. Mind that, aye?"

We hear men's voices on the other side of the door, and Abi grins.

"Dinnae fash if I smack him upside the heid." She grins then winks at me, and I have to smile back. It's nice having someone from home to talk with, something familiar in this very unfamiliar time. I need the banter, the directness. It's been a long time since anyone was just plain honest and nice to me.

The men walk in, and Abi watches the door as if her life depends on it. She only relaxes when the door is closed tightly behind the man I now know as Reid.

"Alysia, meet Nick Charmichael, my husband, and Reid Flanagan, a Lieutenant here in Piper Falls PD."

"Hallo." I smile at them, and Nick walks over to shake my hand.

"You gave us quite a scare," Nick tells me as he gently shakes my hand. "Abi and Reid had been searching for you for about a week." I look across at Abi, who just shrugs and winks again. I look at Reid, who doesn't speak.

"Reid," Abi's voice cautions. She's glaring at him, and her arms are folded across her stomach. "Are ye gonna introduce yerself?" she demands, scowling at him. However, it makes me chuckle, and he shoots me a glance, then he grins as his eyes fall fully on me.

"Yeah, okay," he replies, frowning at Abi. Then he turns to me. "Hi, Alysia, I'm Lieutenant Reid Flanagan with Piper Falls PD."

"Nice to meet ye, properly, at last," I respond, taking his huge hand. For the first time, I pay attention to the man. He is clean shaven again. One arm, his right, has tattoos running from the wrist up and beyond his t-shirt sleeve. The left arm tattoo only begins at his elbow. His dark green t-shirt compliments his whisky-coloured eyes and tan, while his jeans hide just how huge his legs are.

"Yeah, I've been trying not to push you."

I look deeply into his expressive eyes. Somehow, I forget to breathe, and it's only when my eyesight begins to merge into colours with no form, do I remember I need to do that very important, basic thing.

"Hey, are you okay?" Reid's brow is furrowed, but I manage to nod.

"I seem to be forgetting basic things right now," I admit. As Reid moves back, Abi comes into focus.

"Breathe, yer okay," she reminds me, stroking my hand. I can't tell her that seeing him made my brain and body go on the frizz. "Ye okay?" she asks, and I nod, managing a weak smile.

Nick taps Abi on the shoulder, and she nods. "We need to get going," Nick says. "Buster will need seein' to."

"Thank you," I breathe out to Abi.

"I'll see ye the morrow!" Abi assures me, before giving me a huge hug. She hugs Reid before the guys say their bye-for-nows and then, they're gone. I sigh and lean back in the chair, closing my eyes once the door has softly clicked closed.

"Are you tired?" Reid asks, and I nod. That's not the only reason I'm keeping my eyes closed though. "Let me help get you back into bed. Aly will be around soon."

"Dae ye all know each other?" I ask, and it makes him chuckle.

"Piper Falls is a small place. About ten-and-a-half thousand people. Most of the civil servants know each other. Can't have each other's backs without it."

I grin. "Piper Falls is about nine times smaller than Sterling," I remark as Reid offers an arm to help me up.

"I read that your folks are from Livingston. That's where Abi is from."

I nod, and he helps lift my legs up into the bed. "I couldnae wait to get away from my parents and siblings. They're..." I pause, looking for the best words to describe my over-loving, nosy family. "Full on."

"In y'all's business all the time?" he asks.

"Aye. They mean well, but..."

"You can't breathe," he finishes. I can only nod.

"My parents moved outta town, down to the coast, but I live on the edge, in a loft of a converted barn. Think *Roadhouse*, but more modern."

"I love that movie," I confess. "It's a shame what happened to Patrick Swayze."

"Yeah, that was a terrible way to go though."

"Aye, it was." I lean back, making that comment the last thing I remember.

When I see Aly again, it's the following morning. She looks tired when I finally open my eyes. Reid's not around.

"He's at the station," she shares as she sees me looking around.

"I'm putin' you all in danger," I tell her quietly as she helps me into the shower.

"You need to stop talkin' like that. And you need to tell Reid what went on when he comes to visit you in a while."

"He'll be here?" I ask, and she nods.

"Sure will be. Has been every day since you were found."

"Abi said that I was dehydrated and other things?"

Aly nods as she sits me on a chair and warms up the shower.

"You were. You're lucky we didn't have to transport you up to Waco or down to Austin. We gave you medication for bites, sepsis and other things. Dehydration was your worst complaint. Does your back feel sore?" I give a half-hearted shrug, which makes Aly smile at me. "Shows you're still dehydrated. I need you to take on some more water, okay? But, slowly though," she encourages me to stand, "Too much will have you back in here, and we'll have trouble keeping you under wraps another time."

"How have you managed it this time?" I inquire, and she grins knowingly.

"Reid hasn't told the Feds yet."

"Why not?"

Aly looks around, her eyes sparkling. "We may not have recorded the fact you're awake, or that we know who you are."

I gasp. "There's gonna be hell to pay when they work it out," I state. Aly shrugs.

"We'll come clean. But we need to know if we can do that by you telling Reid what went down in that container."

I sigh as Aly guides me into the warm water. After a thorough shower, I prepare to do what she and Abi have been asking for days. Tell Reid what happened. The idea of it makes me twitch.

Chapter Three

♡ Reid ♡

(Eight Days Prior)

My older nephew's birthday and a promise to my brother to be there took me away to New Mexico for the weekend. A weekend I didn't know I desperately needed.

When I get back, Preston briefs me then he gives me the okay to go looking for Alysia. When I inform Abi and Nick, they tell me to leave it with them, so I do. I soon wish I hadn't.

They might be used to being up and in work for 6 am, but that's a time of day I don't often see anymore; unless the proverbial hits the fan or I'm on call. To top it off, we're at Jaxon's ranch. The horses aren't even out of their stalls, which I'm kind of glad about; these beasts make me nervous. Nick and Abi are gathered near a set of quad bikes when I arrive. They've got their dog and four bikes out. Another firefighter is with them, someone I kind of know.

"Morning," I whisper to them as I walk up to them. It's too early to be hollerin' at folk. Abi said not to wear stuff that was too new; we'd be out for most of the day.

"It sure is! Are ye ready?" she asks as she claims a quad bike.

"I…hell, why are we on these things?"

Abi chuckles, shaking her head. "There's a lot of trail up that way. Dae ye wanna do it on foot? Or do ye wanna cover more ground, fast?" She raises her eyebrows at me, and I smirk.

"Fast," I reply as Nick motions for which bike I'm to have. Beau comes over and gives us the thumbs-up. Abi pats the quad, and Buster jumps up behind her. The dog is wearing a harness that she straps to the quad and then to her. In seconds, she's got the thing started and she's off, leaving us guys in the dust.

Nick and Beau just chuckle and copy her, leaving me to play catch-up.

Higher up on the trail about half an hour later, we stop where the path splits. Abi went slow at certain points and navigated these trails like she knew them. She probably does.

"Okay, what gives?" There was no time for pleasantries back at the ranch, which is unusual, but she's keen.

Abi's smirk turns to a scowl, and she nods to Beau. "Jaxon thinks that the security at the ranch is compromised."

"Oh?" That news makes my stomach sink.

Beau nods. "He ain't sure why, but the cameras aren't always focusing on the steers or the house, even if he's moved them back. They're focusin' up here, the woods and trails."

I fold my arms. "Has he reported it?"

Beau nods. "The security company is coming in today to take a look, but Caleb was taking the cameras offline while we rode out."

I blink. "Okay." I nod before turning to Abi. Chances are it'll be one of Caden's brother's companies, so I leave the subject alone. "You've been up here before?"

Abi nods. "While ye were away at the weekend, I walked up as far as here with Buster and realised that we need to cover more ground. Hence why I hired the quads from Jaxon and asked Beau to come with us. We can search in pairs."

"I can search on my own."

"And if ye find her? What are you going to do? Did ye bring ropes? Harnesses? Are ye used to freeing people outta shitty situations? How ye gonna get her doon? Cause the three of us are capable of a' that." My friend's prickly wife calmly lays her hands on her thighs and simply waits, staring me out. I pull in a breath and acknowledge their expertise in this area over my own.

"Yeah, okay, you've got a point."

Abi just grins at me. She ain't being mean; she's just right and she darn well knows it, the sassy Scot. "Course I do! But I doubt we'll find her today, or at all. But, that's no the point."

"So what is the point?" I ask as Beau and I prepare to head off in one direction.

"To cover ground to find the lass. Now, ye ken how to tell if someone's been up on the trail?" she asks, and I nod confirmation. With a smirk, she, Nick and their dog head off in one direction while Beau and I go in the other.

That first day of quadding wasn't as successful as I had wanted it to be. Abi though, isn't perturbed. She was tying red ribbon on bushes where we'd checked, so we knew where we'd gotten to.

Nick is back on shift the next day, and Beau and Abi repeat the same thing, this time accessing the trails from a different entry point, not from the ranch. I'm stuck at my desk, but I'm not being idle. I profile every woman who died in that container. They're all petite little women, with varying shades of red hair and blue eyes, and if they're wet, they might weigh a hundred-and-ten pounds.

I quickly start checking missing women who fit that description, and my list grows quickly from the ten I had to over thirty possible women who were in the USA at the time they went missing.

I doubt any are over the age of twenty-five; they're mostly early twenties, and a few may have been mid-twenties, but not all their details are available to me yet; they're still being identified through various medical records.

I sit back in my chair and focus on Alysia's image. These women are young, girls still almost. *How did they get into this situation? And why?* They're mostly from middle-class, working families, girls with careers, jobs and lives. None of them seem to be engaged or have serious boyfriends. I have the feelin' that they were targeted. I'd love to access their mobile phones and see how they were lured into whatever mess they've landed themselves in, but I know my clearance isn't high enough.

By the time I check my watch, it's time to clock off. Abi hasn't contacted me, which means today was another bust. Preston catches me on the way out.

"Still looking?" he asks, and I nod.

"Abi spent another day up on the trails," I remark. Preston chuckles.

"She is determined."

"Yes, sir, she is. You know, I am kinda glad she's with us right now."

Preston nods. "I'm also glad I'm not the one tryin' to keep her in line."

I snort in reply. "Amen! Nick does have to whisper in her ear at least once a day." Preston raises an eyebrow and smirks.

"I can only imagine what those comments are like," he says, patting me on the arm as he leaves. "Go home, Reid. Carry on tomorrow."

"Yes, sir!" I reply. I could do with a beer.

Piper Falls is small enough that you can pretty much walk everywhere, and I love the town for it. I glance down the street to see the soft lights from the Cozy Bean and the Blue Bonnet Bakery reflect on the cars that are parked. They'll be open very early tomorrow, but I have no intention of catching the rush that early.

The smell of food from Abuela's entices me, but the noise from that and Nautical Grill makes me head for Papi's. It's a little quieter, though not much. Some of the Firehouse squads are taking up their usual corner, while my crew seem to be gathered on the other side.

"You up for a beer, Reid?" Matt offers me a cold one, as if my presence was anticipated. We shoot the breeze, talking shit. We watch as Engine 49 goes out on a call, our colleagues accompanying them. We might be off duty, but we're never really.

Others come and go. Abuela's is rockin', but that's not my concern, not tonight. I have another beer, then saunter home. As the noise of the bars and the high street gets left behind, I take in the quietness of Piper Falls. The town won't be partying for too much longer, which makes me smile. I also feel it's too quiet, like there's a calm before a storm. *Why do I feel like something is coming, and it ain't gonna be good?*

The following day begins just like any other. Preston calls me aside, and Peter is with him, which means that there's trouble.

"How's the search going?" Peter asks, and I look at Preston before I answer.

"Enlisted help from the Charmichael's. Not found anything yet." Peter nods, and Preston shrugs. "What's going on?"

"Feds seem to be gettin' antsy. I don't like it when they start getting this inquisitive and impatient."

"Let me go out and find her," I suggest. "I'm feelin' useless stuck behind a desk. Nick's not on shift, he can come with."

Preston and Peter look at each other, as if in code.

"Or, did you have someone else in mind?"

"The Feds suggested they'd be down tonight."

I grimace. "Then hope that we don't find her while they're in town." All I get in response are noises of agreement.

"Call Nick, get his help. I'll brief Blake and Estrella," Preston states as they head in one direction, and I head back out.

At Nick's, he's busy fixing a screen on their front porch. It was opened up, so I wonder why he's closing it down again.

"Hey, Reid! You not on duty today?"

"I am," I state as I help him hoist the frame up. "How come you're puttin' this back up?"

Nick grimaces. "Seems the little insect critters like Abi's blood, and she can't keep them off her, no matter what she does."

I hold it in place as he screws the frame on one corner. I wait until it's semi-secured before I take a step back.

"Ya'll okay? You look tense." Nick grabs a few screws but looks at me as he does.

"Feds say they'll be down in Piper Falls tonight."

Nick scowls and fastens another screw. "We've not found her, yet."

I push against the screen frame. "I know. I'm kinda hoping we don't, and they clear on out."

Nick shakes his head. "This is their investigation. They'll be here for as long as they need and want to be, and they will pull rank on ya."

"I know. But something about this feels off. I can't put my finger on it."

Nick tidies his tools away. "Abi's of the same mind. She's gotten hyper-focused on it; her problem-solving brain won't switch off from this."

"Does she have ADHD?" I ask; it would explain her attitude. Nick shrugs.

"She's never been diagnosed, at least not that I know of. Frank was the same though. Seems she got a lot from her daddy that she's slowly figuring out."

I know that her daddy died rescuing a family from a house fire. The station mood was sombre that night; even though he hadn't served with us, someone in our emergency family breathed his last that night. It sent Mallory off into one of her really quiet phases.

"Well, while you two do that, is there any chance we can search more of the trails?"

Nick grins at me and motions around. "Help me pack up, and we'll go. Abi has another trail in mind that might be fruitful. I'll tell her we've checked it when I stop in tonight with Buster." He calls the dog, and in five minutes, we're heading up the back trail in Nick's old blue truck.

That day was a bust, and it's when I'm out again with Nick and their dog the following day that the Feds show up. Preston calls me, and I tell him I'm up on the trails, searching. After a quick conference call with him and the Feds, they leave me to it.

When we come down, I head for the station to check in. Preston is waiting for me, working on some paperwork.

"Feds would like an update when we find her. They appreciated us looking." He pulls up the video surveillance we have, and I watch the interaction with Preston, Peter and the two Federal agents. Maggie, I recognise from our video call.

"Who is the other fella?" I ask, taking a dislike to him just from his body language.

"Her partner, Grant Esse." Preston smirks. When I repeat his name in my head, I can't help but join in the smirks. It sounds like "grand ass." I watch as Maggie and Grant talk with Preston, but something about Grant feels off. He's caught the camera view directly twice already; Maggie hasn't, not once. *Why is he being particularly aware of the cameras?*

"Did you know Jaxon has issues at the ranch with his security cameras?" I comment as we watch Grant again, looking directly at the camera as they leave.

"No. I'll swing by, check it out."

"His security company were there the other day."

Preston nods. "I'll go and check on him after I've asked Caden. That sounds very out of sorts."

"Don't it?" I remark. "The Feds haven't got any warrants out for security system hacks, have they?"

Preston shakes his head. "Even if they had, we wouldn't hear of it." He throws me a weird look. "I hope you're wrong." I somehow doubt it, but I can't say anything. Fate has already been tempted by me speaking it out aloud.

Abi is now on shift, so Nick and I head up again the next day, coming in at a different point again. Abi has highlighted the whole area on a map, and every trail has a different colour marked out. The key next to it is all crossed off; trails we've checked. Nick pulls me aside on our quads and shows me something interesting.

"Motorbike tracks," he tells me, following them down a distance. The ground is soft, and while the weather today is decent, it had rained overnight. "These weren't here the other day," he points out. "I came up with Abi and Buster," he says, fussing the dog's ears.

The tracks are quite a ways into the mud too. "Heavy person on the bike," I comment. Nick nods. "Or, there are two people."

His scowl says it all.

The following day, I check in with Preston, heading straight to Nick and Abi's place after I've updated him. I know that this was her daddy's house, and they've taken progress pictures since she moved here, though Preston was the first policeman in Piper Falls to meet her. She still calls him the *"scary policeman with the gun."*

Abi doesn't answer the door, Nick does. "Abi just finished a forty–eight. Want to head up, just us? She said she'll follow later on, when she's had some more sleep."

I nod and wait on the porch, admiring the pair of Adirondack rockers. The last time I saw them, they looked pretty beaten up. Nick smiles at me as he comes out, Buster at his heel.

"Abi and I did them up." He looks so proud. "She's got her daddy's knack for fixin' things."

I nod and smile, fussing their retriever's ears as Nick sits down and pulls on some heavy walking boots.

"Which trail do we go on?" I ask.

"Abi mentioned we should check the trails we started out from. But, avoid the ranch."

"Preston said he'd go out and check with Jaxon."

Nick nods. "Beau said Caleb and Jaxon were talkin' with him. So they'll take it from there with what he needs to do." Nick grins as he grabs the keys, and quietly, we head back up the trails.

♡ ♡ ♡

Later that afternoon, Abi finds us.

"Hey, you pair," she calls out as she joins us, hugging Nick.

"You okay, darlin'?" he asks, his face showing concern for her.

She pulls in a huge breath, lets it go, and she nods. "Aye, I'll be fine. Shite night."

"I know," he says, hugging her close again. Buster has run off somewhere, then he appears, darting back and forth, bouncing at his owner's feet, whining and dancing. That pulls Abi from Nick's embrace.

"Show me then," she encourages, motioning the dog onward. Clearly, she understands what her dog is telling her better than we can. He whines, and Abi gasps.

"Guys, I think we have her!" She scrambles down the side of the path and right enough, there's a body in torn jeans and covered in mud; we hadn't looked over the path edges, and I could kick myself. I can only watch from above as Abi sweeps her hand over the hair. The part of her that I can see is caked in mud, but the auburn color beneath it is unmistakable. Buster whines a little, reminding me I need to breathe. *Why did I forget to breathe?*

"Good lad! It is her." Abi bends down, her cheek to the woman's face. "Alysia, can ye hear me?" I look at Nick as he runs back to the quad bikes we've used and the uneaten lunch pack Abi brought up for us. In moments, he's got ropes out, and I can only watch as they get Alysia onto Nick's back and tied to him, like a mannequin.

Then, he slowly mounts the quad bike, Abi helping to get Alysia's legs over before she and Buster jump onto the other as I pick up the backpack. Abi's on the phone, and in two sentences, I know who.

"Aye, back entrance, that'll be fine, cheers! Aye, we'll need a gurney. And some physio for Nick, she's oot cold, shallow breathing." There's a pause. "Aye, see ya soon, Aly!"

Nick nods then gives a thumbs up, and we head down the trail, slowly, with Abi leading us back to town.

Chapter Four

♡ Alysia ♡

I did walk out of the hospital, but it was out the front door after Reid persuaded me to be brave, that my being found hadn't been broadcast so there was no need for any further subterfuge.

Sitting in a police station though, wasn't what I had bargained for, even if Reid needed what I was about to say for evidence.

I must look horrible, and while I care, I can't be arsed. Aly and the very nice lady doctor told me that I had been drugged and assaulted. Raped. I have no recollection of it, but added to the drugs that I was getting out of my system that I still had a trace of, the malnutrition and the dehydration, I'm on strict bed rest after I've recorded this with Reid.

"Hey," he says as he comes into the rather informal room. I always thought interrogation rooms would be pokey, windowless rooms, like on *NCIS*. This room is a far cry from that. It's not an office, it's more like a small conference room. The camera in the corner though, reminds me why I am here.

"Hi," I sigh, trying to smile. I want to go and hide and never speak to anyone ever again. Reid places down a brown bag and motions for me to look inside. I do and see there is a mountain of food. Well, it might not be a mountain, but there are four foil-wrapped items in the bag and two takeaway cups. Reid pulls one of the foil-wrapped items out and passes me one of the cups.

"That's tea," he explains, his smile making me soar.

"Thanks! You know how to make a tea?" I ask, taking the huge cup. Reid chuckles.

"Abi said you might prefer tea, but Jo knows how to make it. Oh, the teabag might still be in there," he points out, and I check as he sets up. Moments later, he's ready.

"Shall we do this? Then it's done and dusted," he says, his voice gentle and low. I hear a small beep, and I know the camera is recording.

"I don't want to. But I get that I can't keep quiet," I confide.

"It'll help others if you can tell me what happened. Shall we start in Chicago?" I draw in a huge breath and begin.

I recall going out for a meal with colleagues; being a low-ranking employee of a marketing company that won a contract for a large pharmaceutical company, coming to the USA on a week-long jolly was a dream come true. My colleagues raised the alarm when I didn't come down for breakfast the following morning, and when they checked my room, everything I had was gone. There was no trace of me, and the CCTV had been messed with, so the local police had no idea what had happened. I was the fifth young woman on the Western Seaboard with auburn hair to go missing, and that's when I'm told the Feds got involved.

I go through what I learned this morning, but I don't remember much.

"Do you remember getting married?" Reid asks, and I go wide-eyed.

"I am not married," I declare, my voice becoming clipped and forceful.

Reid walks me through a conversation the Feds had with my '*husband*,' and when Reid shows me a picture, I forget to breathe as the image quickly comes out of focus. It's when he's kneeling in front of me and reminding me to breathe that I realise I fazed out again.

"What were you thinking when you saw the image of that man?" he asks, careful to not use the word '*husband.*'

"He was at the bar at the hotel. I felt funny and said goodnight to my colleagues, then I went to my room. When I woke up, I was in a dark room, the bed smelled and I…" I begin crying, and I'm a full-on-howl as I reveal I was handcuffed to the bed. I could recall the man from the photograph visiting, injecting me, and I begin to rub my inner arm as I talk.

Hours later, Reid's walked me through so much that I'm exhausted. The extra food was most welcome, and I slowly nibbled at it as he made me remember and talk. He didn't force me, but he did prompt me, reminding me.

"We can go through the container part tomorrow," he says as he packs everything away. "I can see you're exhausted."

I nod. "Where do I go?" I blurt out, and he smiles.

"Where do you want to go?" He stops packing things and sits on the edge of the desk. His thighs are threatening to rip his trousers apart, so I focus on his face.

"I don't know. I don't know anyone, apart from you and Abi," I admit.

"We've both made space for you. The choice is yours." He leans forward. "I feel responsible for you though."

I look into his eyes and can see the amber swirls staring back at me; his lips are slightly parted, and suddenly, I want to kiss him.

"Why?" I ask, noticing my voice is quiet, barely there.

"You're not out of the woods yet, and I have a gun. Abi's great, but Nick and her just don't do guns."

"Neither do I."

Reid smiles at me. "I figured, since you're a Brit like Abi. But I don't think this is over quite yet, darlin'," he admits. Hearing those words makes me shiver.

I sigh. "Me neither. Can I stay with you?" I request, making it about him protecting me. *I mean, I can't fall for him. He's now my protector. Right?*

◡ ◡ ◡

Outside of the police station, I take in the town. Right next door is the fire station, and the Town Hall is opposite. My stomach growls when I smell the fried food coming from the nearby eateries and bars.

"What do you fancy?" Reid wants to know. I realise now, he stands a full foot taller than I do. He's huge, and I can hide behind him. Without thinking, I duck in behind him, not wanting to be seen. When he stops, I run into him, and he turns, scowling.

"Is this too scary for you?" he questions, and I can only nod like a mechanical dog. He grabs my hand and takes me across the road. We pass a lawyer's office and turn. Soon, we're at a dog park and parked alongside the dog park is a food truck. The smells from it make my stomach growl. I chuckle as Reid's own joins in.

He motions for me to sit at a picnic bench, and I watch as he walks up to the food van, has a quick conversation and then comes back to me with a can of cola. Here, the loudest sounds are the birds in the trees, dogs barking as they play with each other or demand the ball be thrown one more time.

"What did you do?" I ask as Reid hands me a full-fat cola. I open the can and take a long slurp from it. *The cold bubbles taste so good!*

"I just ordered some food. Why?"

I blink at him. "Some food?" I lean to glance past him and watch as various skillets and things are used to cook the food Reid just ordered. "Or did you order enough for the whole office?"

Reid laughs. "I ordered enough for two, and they have selection boxes, so I hope you like Greek food."

I purse my lips, not wanting to tell him that I'm not adventurous with my food. Or with much of anything.

"You've never tried it?" he asks, guessing my hesitation is because I just don't know.

So, I shake my head. "This will be a first."

He smiles in a way that I cannot fathom. *Is he surprised? Disappointed?* I can't tell what he's thinking, so I take another drink and wait until he's called over, enjoying the quietness. When he comes back, he's carrying a huge pizza box and opens it, revealing grilled meats, sauces, flatbreads, salad, dips…there's so much, I just stare at it. Then a paper plate appears before me, and Reid waits for a moment before taking one of everything and placing it on my plate with throw away cutlery.

"Try it. I promise you'll like it." Unsure of what else to do and with a sudden inability to speak, I do as I'm told.

Half an hour later, I'm stuffed like Pooh Bear after a pot of delicious honey. I don't tend to eat a lot in general, but Reid has made sure I try every meat that was on offer (lamb and chicken, mostly) with the flatbreads and salad. I even tried the dips and sauces.

"Do you feel better?" he asks, and I nod.

"I don't think I can move," I tell him honestly as I pat my stomach. I now think I look pregnant, I've eaten that much.

"I'm sure you can. We don't have much by way of clothes for you," he says, rubbing the back of his head. "So, I err…I texted Abi while you were eating. She said she'll have Nick drop us some stuff."

"I never thought about any of that," I admit.

"We can head to Twice As Nice and Unique Boutique tomorrow and pick up some other clothes for you."

I look at the table and my drink can, rather than him.

"Alysia? Look at me," he instructs, and I do. "Don't worry about what it costs. They're thrift stores. Abi said to tell you that." I nod and begin to breathe. I know what she means. Charity shops, so she's not spending a lot on me. Not that I asked her to. But I do like the idea of recycling clothes.

"I'm sorry," I whisper and look at my hands again. "I'm just…" *Not myself? How do I tell him that I just don't want to talk? That I want to curl up in a cabin somewhere and forget about the world? And let it forget about me.*

"I get it. You're dealing with a lot, trust me, I get it. Ah, here's Nick." An old blue pick-up pulls up at the dog park, and Nick gets out with Buster. The dog bounds up to me and sits beside me, whining for fuss and nudging my leg. I can't help but smile at him.

"Hallo, puppy!" I fuss him, and in seconds, I feel I can breathe; I can think. "It's good to see you again," I tell him. He just nudges me and whines a little as he rubs against me more, as if repeating the same words back to me.

"Alysia? It's time to go." Reid reaches out for me to take his hand, and I suck in a breath. Nick is by the truck, just waiting. Buster, his dog, is by my side, and he nudges me again, as big dogs do. His coat is so soft. The food box and utensils have been cleared away, along with the napkins. As soon as we leave, no one will know we were here. I nod and take his hand, and as Reid walks me to the pick-up, Buster walks on the other side of me.

"You're a ladies' man," Nick teases the dog. "In," he commands with both his voice and a hand signal. "You like Abi more than me," he says, semi-laughing.

I can't reply, I just hug the dog in the backseat as Reid gets in, and Nick drives us to Reid's loft.

I love the quietness here. Nick dropped us off, and Buster started whining, but with a quick call to Abi, he perked up. I guess he can tell us apart after all. Nick didn't leave until Reid turned a light on in the loft. It really is like *Roadhouse*. There's a staircase up to the rooms with a huge oak door barricading your way in. When Reid opened it, he did so easily. I try to shut it over and need to push it: Hard. It is also a few inches thick. Then, Reid bolts it with three huge bolts. One at the top and bottom and a huge square one in the middle.

"We'll be safe," he assures me, and I take in the flat.

There's a huge corner sofa facing a wood-burning stove. Behind that is the kitchen area which is mostly down the same side as the stove and a little across a window. Then there are two doorways: one to a bedroom and one to a bathroom. Everything else is pretty open plan.

I stand still in the middle of the flat, unable to move or think. *Are we sharing a bed?* He didn't mention *that*. The world starts going black, and when I realise where I am, my head is between my legs and Reid's coaching me to breathe.

"There you are. What got you unable to breathe?"

I daren't tell him that being this close to him does it. That thinking we'd be sharing anything beyond the same four walls caused me, again, to just faze out. I need to sort this out. *Why am I doing this? What is wrong with me?*

"Alysia?" I look up and realise that he's been waiting for an answer.

"We'll be…together?" I mutter and can just hear my own words. Reid smiles.

"I'll sleep on the sofa. It turns into a double bed that's quite comfortable, trust me." At his words, I visibly relax. "Alysia, have you ever had panic attacks before?"

I shake my head, knowing I hadn't. "Is that…what I'm doing?" My voice is tiny, especially for a Scot; it isn't me. It's not my normal.

"I'm pretty sure that's what you're doing, and it ain't your fault. I'll try not to trigger any more for you, okay?" I nod and as he smiles, my insides contract.

"Thank you."

"Stay there and let me sort out the sofa bed." I nod at his command and watch as he heads into the bedroom to find bedsheets and the things he needs. It takes him about ten minutes, and all I can do is sit and watch him move.

When I visited the zoo as a child, I was always in awe of the big cats, my favourite being the tiger. That's how I see Reid move. With grace and surety. By the time he's finished, I imagine him prowling over to me and…my eyes go fuzzy again, and I blink when I hear a whistle, then realise Reid's making a hot drink. The whistle was the stove kettle. As he handles it, I look around and spot a musical instrument in the corner that's wrapped in a case. I'd guess it was a cello, but I can't be sure. It's not huge, but you can't put it on your shoulders, of that I am certain.

I watch him try and open a box of tea bags. I didn't know Americans liked tea, but apparently, they do.

"I can help," I offer meekly as I walk towards the kitchen area. He's got it divided off with a large Ikea box grid unit, which creates a soft divide. The models are interesting; they're not all *Star Wars* figures.

"Would you? I've seen Abi make tea, but…" I smile as his huge shoulders sag.

"Do you have a tea pot?" I ask, but he shakes his head. "That's okay, here," I say, putting the tea bags into the huge mugs he has, then pouring hot water from the kettle on it. The stove kettle is quaint.

"Do you not have an electric kettle?" I ask, and he shakes his head.

"Don't need one. And this was from a yard sale."

"They're real things?" I ask, and he nods with a grin. They're always things you see on the television shows.

"They are. Abi's run one, clearing out her dad's things when she and her sister first came back."

"Why are ye so friendly with her?" Not that Abi's not likeable, but if she's with Nick, why is Reid often talking about her?

He straightens his face and sucks in a huge breath. "On her hen do, her sister and Estrella organised a policeman stripper party. Only, we got complaints, and I was in uniform at the time. I had to attend. Her sister thought I was a stripper and got very handsy with me. I had to arrest her."

I laugh and hide my face in my hands as he tells me.

"Ach, that's hilarious! What happened after?"

Reid grins as he motions for me to sit at the small kitchen table he has.

"She spent the night in the cells, sobering up. I had never witnessed someone so drunk before. She apologised the morning after, but the stripper uniforms were a little too authentic lookin', and Preston thought it was just hilarious, so he didn't want to press charges. Neither did I."

"But, you're friends now?"

He nods. "Just friends. Nick was a few years above me in school, a senior when I was a sophomore, same year as my brother."

I frown. I know those words mean something, but I can't recall why.

"Alysia…what went through your mind?"

"Those words… They seem familiar."

"Not just TV show familiar? But, you've heard them in a conversation before right now?"

I nod. *Why do I feel that they're important, and why can't I remember?*

"I hope you like spaghetti," Reid tells me much later. I've been curled up in one of his chairs for ages, dozing, resting. The other, he has been sat in. When he was reading, he had glasses on. I've never looked at anyone with glasses the way I have him. I can't help but wonder if he's noticed me staring at him. If he has, he's not said anything.

"I do," I repeat when he comes around to check.

"That's good. I'd appreciate some help though, if you don't mind?"

"Okay," I reply and forget I've been sitting in one position for so long; my legs are now numb. "Oh!" My body doesn't want to work, my leg feels dead, as does my bum.

"Did your legs go to sleep?" he asks, and I nod, which makes him smile. "Take your time. It'll be a few more minutes."

I grin and slowly work the circulation around my body, and then I come to help Reid set the table.

While Reid serves up, I find the cutlery and placemats where he tells me to. Minutes later, we're sitting and eating.

I take a bite of the food, then another. And another. My portion was smaller than Reid's, but I finish it all before him. And I could happily eat the amount he has.

"Nice to see you enjoy my food," he remarks as he finishes up his spaghetti and meatballs.

"That was delicious, thank you!"

The smile I get from him makes me smile back at him. And for the first time, I'm content with the moment to eat.

I hadn't realised Reid had bought an apple pie for dessert. When I ask about it, he tells me it was in his freezer, and that Mrs. Bunn has a habit of baking lots of pies for the Firehouse and Police Station. When she does bake, everyone makes room in their freezers or eats it that night, and she encourages the local kids to climb the trees for her to fetch the apples.

"She seems like a nice, old lady," I comment, and it makes Reid laugh, hard.

"She's a feisty one, don't let her old lady demeanour fool ya. She's ruthless."

I raise my eyebrows. "Really?"

"Oh yeah, don't you believe she's all sugar and spice with everything nice. That old lady was a spitfire in her day, let me tell you."

I chuckle; she sounds a lot like my great-grandmother. "Not to be messed with?" I confirm, and Reid just gives me a little nod in acknowledgement.

"She ain't. How do you feel about washing up? I need to bring up those bags of clothes for you"

"What bags?" I confirm, trying to hide.

"Clothes. Abi went shopping for ya, remember?"

My mouth drops into an "O" and I nod. Sure, I can wash the dishes. I look around for a dishwasher, and Reid pulls out a plastic tub with the dishwashing stuff in it. A set of marigolds, washing up liquid, brushes and a sponge. "Got it," I comment. As he heads down the stairs, I get on with the task he's set.

When I'm done, Reid calls me through to the bedroom. It's sparse but tidy. A bed and a dresser. "Where do you keep yer clothes?" I inquire, and Reid opens up the door I can see, which is a huge built-in wardrobe.

"In the closet, where else?" he asks, and I purse my lips.

"I didn't see that," I admit, and he just shrugs his huge shoulders.

"I've made some room for you to hang your stuff up," he says and motions to the bed. He folds up three huge black bags that held the clothes, and I gape. Jeans, t-shirts, jumpers, skirts: everything I can think of is here. None of it is mine, they're not things I brought with me from home.

Without warning, I burst into tears and lean heavily against the wall, sliding down it as I finally understand that my life, as I knew it, is gone.

Huge arms surround me, and all I can do is cry my heart out.

Reid held me as the tears dried on their own. Just having him there, holding me, letting me break, was something I hadn't benefited from before. No one has ever just held me; I'd always been told to stop, suck it up, put on a brave face. He did none of that.

"Alysia, darlin', we've gotta move."

"Hmm?" I'm cosy where I am; I don't want to move.

"I need to visit the bathroom, darlin'." I suck in a breath as my cheeks get warm.

"Oh, erm…sure." I get up off his lap and in seconds, he's up and in the bathroom, leaving me staring at all these clothes. When he's back, I still haven't moved. "How much did Abi spend?"

He shrugs. "She went shopping, but the Firehouse, the Station and some of the hospital staff had a whip around to get it all. Some of the locals who own shops on the high street added to it. You'd have to ask her, but I don't think she spent half of it."

I can feel my jaw slacken. "You're all too generous."

He chuckles. "You've met Abi, ain't ya? We all know she's a force to be reckoned with, and I've seen that. Add in her Captain, Estrella, and there's a tornado of retribution right there."

I can only chuckle in response. "Not met her Captain yet. Wait…" I turn to him. "Abi's Fire Captain is a woman? Wow!"

"Sure is. Aly's her younger sister."

I frown for a second. "The nurse from the hospital?" I ask, and he nods.

"Erm…I started running you a bath. I assume you'll want one of these?" he questions, holding up a huge bath bomb.

"You only need half of one of those," I tell him.

"Well, let's get it cut in half then," he responds, heading to the kitchen. With a sharp knife, he manages to cut the tennis ball-sized bath bomb in half.

"It took me ten minutes the last time I attempted to do that, and it went everywhere."

"Did it now?" He smirks as he hands me one half. "I'm glad it didn't go off." His joke makes me chuckle. "Come on, let's get you into a warm bath. Abi wanted to know what your bra size was; she says it was the only thing she couldn't figure out for you."

"Oh! In British terms, 30 double-d." Why I just blurted out my size, I do not know, but it doesn't faze him. He pulls out his phone and sends a message. Then he squints, before he smiles.

"Abi says she'll look for nice bras in that size tomorrow."

"She disnae have to do this," I comment.

Reid tries to suppress a laugh, but his shoulders shake and his eyes water. It takes a few moments before he can speak. "As I said before, she's a force to be reckoned with." He motions to the bathroom and puts the other half of the bath bomb away before he shuts off the water. I throw my half in and watch as the water turns pink; the half-bomb melts and suddenly, the bathroom smells divine.

Chapter Five

♡ Reid ♡

Today took its toll on Alysia. After the second panic attack, I suspected what was going on. Abi's clearly seen it before, given the replies to my queries after seeing how she dealt with it the first time. Alysia thinks I didn't notice, but I could tell when she was staring at me what she was thinking. The rest of the time, I just let her chill out, and if her mind wandered away, that was fine by me. It's like every little thing she does, I see. *How is that even possible?*

Sometimes, she napped, and I took the chance to check in on Mallory via text. Now, having fed her, and had her break down on me again when I showed her the clothes, I ran her a bath. I put away most that we'd whipped around to get her once she was in the tub to stop her from being overwhelmed, but I left out a set of PJs that I think she'll like. Thanks to Harper from the Blue Bonnet Bakery, we had a rough idea of what sizes to get, then Harper and Abi teamed up with Essie, Sakura and Aly. No way were the guys getting involved with those hell-cats raiding the thrift stores.

While Alysia takes it easy, I finish tidying up. I'm not surprised she's disengaging from life; the fact she can't remember being raped is perhaps both a blessing and a curse. It'll mean whoever did it, and I doubt that it's one person, will unlikely ever be found. I know exactly what I'd like to do to them if I ever find them; a bear might be kinder. And I don't understand why I'm being overly protective, or why my thoughts turn violent when I think of her being hurt.

I breathe in and out twice slowly, focusing on the plant my sister-in-law gave me that loves a sunny spot. *Goodness knows how I haven't killed* that *yet!*

She'd started healing from that damage before we found her, from what Aly and Doctor Candy said. I recall the drugs that the toxicology report shows she was riddled with: at least two date-rape drugs, along with a bunch of others, but no alcohol.

Thinking about it makes me angry again, and I have to try and remember not to let her see it. At least for now. It isn't her fault; she didn't ask for that. Or any of this. Hearing how she was so easily taken from that hotel in Chicago without a trace has me thinking of Cartels, drug running and a whole lot of underground nonsense I'd like to put into a coffin and burn. Why I suddenly think of Jack Green boggles me.

I hear movement from the bathroom before I hear the plug being pulled and the water draining out. I turn as she comes out of the steamy bathroom, wrapped in nothing but a couple of towels. One is wrapped around her hair, the other around her. Just.

"I'll let you get dressed," I tell her, walking past her and closing the door behind me. I daren't look at her. Right now, she doesn't need me letching after her. And I need to keep it professional.

I watch Alysia as she settles into what I've come to call her chair. As I work on wording my report, I glance across and realise that she's asleep. Not a dozing sleep, but full-on, deep sleep. Smiling, I quietly put my work onto the coffee table and turn down the bed before I pick her up and tuck her in for the night. I don't know how she prefers to sleep, with the curtains open or closed, a light on or just nearby. So I set it so that she can see she's not in that container, that she's safe. Then I turn myself in, and remembering that there's a vulnerable woman in the house, I wear some jogging bottoms.

I wake up a few times through the night and check on Alysia when I do. She seems to be resting, though she's fitful at around four am. By the time dawn is peeking above the tree line, her nightmare seems to be over, and I'm asleep again.

It's later than usual when I wake up, but we're not on a strict timetable today. I stretch and tuck an arm behind my head. On hearing a noise, I turn to find Alysia standing in the bedroom doorway, like a deer caught in headlights.

"Hey, you okay? How did you sleep?"

She blinks a few times, and I can't help but wonder, *what she was looking at. Me? Maybe.* She might be twenty-two, but in many ways, she's still a child, and she's almost a decade younger.

"I slept, I think. Shall I make some tea?" She heads off to the kitchen area and makes herself busy with the kettle and the tea bags. I focus on the bathroom door, my morning routine—anything that isn't her in her PJs, showing me that ass and her chest. By the time I come out, there's a coffee on the counter, and she's back in the bedroom. The door isn't shut tightly, which makes me smile a little.

I knock on the door. "Alysia? I need to come in and grab some clothes, sweetheart."

There's a pause. "Okay, I'm decent. I'm kinda hurkle-durkling."

When I push open the door, Alysia is back in bed, propped up with pillows, she's got an old book of mine in her lap, the lamp on with the tea on the bedside table. It's endearing somehow to see she feels safe enough to get comfortable. *So that's hurkle-durkling? Going back to bed when you should be getting up?*

"I don't think I've read any of those. My sister-in-law gave me those books." Those books are old Mills and Boon novels from, I think, the eighties. Their covers are certainly dated.

"You've not read them?" she asks, holding up one that my mother would call 'a bodice-ripper.'

I shake my head. "No, ma'am, not at all."

She giggles, properly. I don't think she did that at all yesterday. "You should."

"Is that so?" I ask, pulling out clothes but not looking at her. When I do turn to look at her, she's bright red in the cheeks and her eyes are glued to the page, but they're not moving, so she's not reading. She thinks she's foolin' me, but she ain't. However, I let it slide. "I'm going to quickly shower and dress. There's some stuff for breakfast, or we can go and eat at the Cozy Bean."

"Why do I wanna get outta bed?" she asks, her accent stronger. I watch her drink some tea, envious suddenly of the cup she's drinking from.

"Because," I lean in, hating that Im about to burst her bubble, "we need to finish off your statement."

Her face falls just like I knew it would. "Oh, I was hoping you'd forgotten."

I shake my head. "I wouldn't be a very good cop if I did that, now would I?"

As she looks at me, I wink and head to the bathroom. Now I need a cold shower.

In the station a good while later, Alysia looks like she's had enough, and we've not even started from what happened from the time of the explosion to when she was found. She's curled up in the chair as the video recording starts and slowly, I ask her what happened. Turns out, my suspicions were pretty darn close. Someone had given them the means to cook some cans of food—but there was no ventilation. They turned that into getting the hell out of the container, dead or otherwise. From what she says, there were twelve women in that container. Five survived, meaning eight women didn't make it.

"Some of them, they'd had enough and they were going to die trying. Some of us wanted out, away from there. We made a makeshift barricade as best we could and left the others to it." She goes on to list some names, one of which I know hasn't either been identified or made out without being detected or leaving a single strand of DNA behind. I'm beginning to think that one of the women who did make it out is a part of it. How they got the equipment and were trusted with it, doesn't add up.

I listen, noting down the voices she heard, accents. She won't know the subtle differences from a Seattle accent to a Floridian one, but I do. However, she describes the guttural sounds and high pitches pretty well.

After a few hours, we take a break, and again, there are food parcels in a bag from the Cozy Bean and Blue Bonnet Bakery. How Jo and Harper know, I don't fathom, but since Harper is Preston's cousin, it ain't too much of a leap.

I grin as Alysia unfurls herself from the chair and stretches before changing seats to eat. In seconds, I wrap it all back up, grab her and take her to the kitchen area, causing looks of surprise on my colleagues' faces as I march us by, but I don't care.

"Eat in here. Not in there."

I place the food on the table and unwrap it again so that she can eat.

"Why'd we move?" she asks, hesitantly taking the wrap she's claimed.

"I don't want you associating food with that room, with what we have to go over."

"Oh."

"Think about it. You're eating and talking about a harrowing event in the same place. Somewhere along the line, you'll associate that food with that moment. And then that food is a trigger, reaching back to that moment. It'll take a long while to undo such a tenuous link."

She tilts her head and gives me a weird look. "Did you do psychology as well as learn how to be a detective?"

"It's all a part of it." I smile at her, seeing her eyes widen a little and a soft smile appear on her lips.

"Well, thank you. And I don't like being in that room."

I shrug. "For me, it's a part of work. But," I bite the pastrami on rye that Jo made for me and chew it as I decide how to say what I want to, "For you, I know it ain't gonna be."

"It's bearable because you're there," she comments, before stuffing some of her wrap into her mouth. She forgets to chew and starts coughing. A couple of the uniformed guys come in, and they think about saying something, but a glare from me means they don't squeak a peep.

We chill out for a while as we eat, then I suggest we take a walk up and down Main Street, so she can get some air before we carry on with the last session.

The smile from her is brighter than the overhead LED lights.

"Have you always lived in Piper Falls?" she asks as we leave the station. Preston knows we're getting some air, but we'll be back. The day is warm for early April and already, it's a little humid. Perfect sweater weather, but Alysia is hardly dressed for it, and when I comment she might be cold, she laughs.

"Ye ken, I hail from Scotland? This is positively summer-like weather." She grins at me. She's not being sullen, she's dancing around as she walks, twirls and lifts her face to the sun. "There was a time I didn't think I'd get to feel the sun on my face again."

"And here you are." That's a fact.

"Aye, I am. But, I dinnae know if it's this small town, another Scot being here or you, but I'm falling in love wi' this wee town."

I grin at her words. Somehow, the trees are more vibrant today.

We walk down to the bakery and pick up yet more sweet things. Alysia is probably as thin as my leg, so I have no idea where she puts all the calories she's consuming. However, she doesn't look as hollow as she did the day we found her.

We walk back to the station on the other side of town, taking into account the traffic, and she oohs at all the shops. "I think I'm going to need to ask Abi to come underwear shopping with me," she says, and I grin.

"I can text her; she can meet you when we're done with this last session."

She turns to me and beams. "You'd do that?" I nod.

"Sure! Why wouldn't I?"

"Just…well, ye dinnae know me."

I can't help but lean in and whisper, "Not yet."

Then I remember, I'm supposed to be protecting her, not leading her on, and I pull back but let her decide when we move off. I don't get why I like teasin' her, or why on earth I'm on edge with her all the damn time. Even when we're talking about her situation, I'm aware of every breath she takes, and the Police song comes to mind as we walk back. Yeah, I'm watching her. Far too closely.

The last session of the day is the most harrowing. Hearing how she just decided on Piper Falls because of the flier in the gas station and how she kept on going, makes me believe that there might be something to this Fate nonsense I've heard others talkin' about. Abi and Nick have mentioned it. Even Jack Green has uttered the phrase "Damn Fate" a few times recently. I'm just glad I'm not his partner in any capacity.

That Alysia managed to eat what she could carry out of that gas station and into the woods over a week stuns me. For most, that wouldn't last a day.

"I need to pay them back. I kinda stole it all."

I grin and nod. "You did, but there was someone else in the line who covered your bill. He paid up, said you looked like you needed it."

She covers her mouth with her hands, and I think she swears behind them. *What I wouldn't give for her to whisper dirty words like that in my ear.* I draw in a breath when I realise my mind is, again, in the gutter and focus on what she's telling me.

She goes on, telling me how she slept out in the wilderness, as unprepared as she was, and I'm amazed by her strength. How the hell she did it, is beyond me. She missed the reason Piper Falls has its name, and it makes me smile that I'll get to show that to her, but I listen as she tells me she can't swim so avoided the river.

As we finish up with the last session, there's a knock at the door. I turn, and Preston smiles at me. "You did well," he praises Alysia, then he looks at me and gives me that small nod of his. He means I did too, which pleases me.

"Maggie's been on the phone," he tells me. "She said she'll be down tomorrow to go over the video evidence."

"Dae I have to meet her?" Alysia asks as she helps tidy up the office. She looks half scared.

"Not unless she needs to meet you. I think it'll be good if you do, but not here at the station. Maggie's our usual FBI contact; she's one of the good ones."

"Oh," is all Alysia can say as she tucks the last chair under the table while I put the cable away.

"We got the recording saved?" I ask, and Preston acknowledges my question.

"We do," he replies, adding. "Code Amber." And I breathe easier knowing he's backed it up to a cloud, an external drive and other areas I wouldn't think of.

Chapter Six

♡ Alysia ♡

As we finish up, his phone pings a few times. When he reads the message, he laughs. "Abi, Harper, Aly, Estrella and Sakura are all waiting to take you shopping again," he says, and his face changes as he looks at me. "You don't have to go with them all, or at all."

How can he read me so well so soon? "I don't know most of them. Who are they?"

"Harper is Preston's cousin; she runs the bakery. Estrella and Sakura are Abi's best friends here in Piper Falls. There's safety in numbers, and I'm sorry, but I need to spend some time here with my notes and things before we can head back home."

I can feel my face fall. "So I'd be stuck here until yer done?" I ask, already missing him paying me attention, and he nods.

"'Fraid so, darlin'."

I bite my lower lip, deciding on what to do, but knowing that Abi and Aly are going to be there, it helps. "Okay, I'll spend some time with them. You don't mind?"

His face gets to be unreadable for a very split second. *Does he mind? Is he going to suggest I sit and wait for him to do some paperwork?* "Doesn't matter if I mind, I need to finish work, and you," he says, as he guides me out of the room, "need some more fresh air and other company. Trust me, if anything was going to happen, they'd hit a truck-load-of-trouble with just Essie and Abi."

I giggle at the image he's now painted in my head. *I know what Abi's like, so what's Essie going to add?* "How will I know yer finished?" I ask, and he holds up his phone.

"I'll call Abi."

I sigh as a thought hits me. "I've no called home, yet."

He nods, his slight smile gentle. No one has been gentle with me before. "I know ya ain't, darlin', but I figured we could do that tomorrow. We'll get word to them via the Feds that now you've been found and since you're recovering, you're able to talk. But I am gonna have to ask ya not to go into too much detail yet as the case is on-going."

I smile at him. If only he knew just how much of an inquisition he's just saved me from. "I can live with that. Work hard." I wink as I head out, but he grabs my arm.

"Hang on, darlin'," he cautions. "Let them come to you. They'll be here in a minute."

"Oh…" I fold my arms over my waist. "Am I still in danger?" I ask, and Reid shrugs.

"Until I check in with the Feds and they give me the all-clear, yeah, I consider you to be in danger." His look goes dark, broody. I suck in a breath and hold it for a moment.

"Aye, okay," I relent and turn towards the front waiting room.

"Huh uh," Reid says, guiding me past desks to his office. "Where I can see ya," he tells me, pointing to a small sofa in a room with windows on two sides. I'd roll my eyes, but his look says I might be in trouble if I do.

It takes Abi about five minutes to appear at Reid's desk and as soon as I see her, I want to hug her.

"Ye okay?" she asks as I stand, her brow furrowed, and I shrug. "Need a hug?" she offers, and I nod, then I'm wrapped up in Abi's strong arms and can just take a moment to centre myself.

"I needed that," I tell her. She smiles at me before she turns to Reid.

"Gimme a call when yer ready. Until then, we've got her."

"Make sure you do," he says.

"Aye, sir," Abi sasses.

I give Reid a little wave with my fingers as I leave, and I swear he growls.

Outside, the evening air is lovely after being inside the station for most of the day.

"Ach, it's so *good* to be oot!" I declare as I stretch, and everyone around laughs, making me self-conscious.

"Aye, it's a braw evenin', for sure," Abi agrees as she leans over to me. "It's no you they're laughing at. They thought how I say things was just for fun, ye ken?"

I chuckle. "They've nae idea," I agree.

"Okay, you two, let's go shoppin'," declares a woman who looks like Aly, but isn't.

"Let's get the introductions done. That's Essie, Sakura, Aly, Harper and Bentley." Abi ensures I shake hands with each of them as she introduces them. Then, suddenly, Harper has me in a huge hug, then it's a group hug. With women around me, chatting and being themselves, they drag me out of my mind funk and bring forth someone from within I haven't seen in years: someone who was happy and content. Someone who is sociable but allowed to be quiet and not the centre of attention all the time.

"You and Nick got plans for kids?" Essie teases as Abi looks yearningly after a woman walking by with a baby in a pram.

"We're enjoying the practice," she smirks at Essie, making everyone laugh.

Twice As Nice is the closest thrift store, but there's nothing in there that I need or like; certainly no underwear or bras. Unique Boutique has a few and only one in my size, but there isn't another clothes shop in town, the town is that small.

"Well, one is better than none," I emphasise, looking on the brighter side of things. The Bakery is closed, and I sigh, commenting about the chocolate muffins I saw in the window earlier, only to see Harper unlocking the door.

"Well, I do own it," she says when I ask if we're gonna get into trouble. Then Abi asks that since Harper has a key, how would we get into trouble? Lass has a point!

With giggles, we head in, and Harper vanishes into the back, then brings out some boxes of cake.

"Abi, as requested! Ya'll have to let me know if this is better than the last attempt."

"Harper, yer an angel, and they're always divine, yer too much of a perfectionist!"

I sit and watch as she puts the other colourful boxes to one side. Then, Harper pulls out smaller boxes and hands us all one. "I made some cupcakes earlier, all new recipes with the frosting."

I look into the boxes and see different coloured, swirly icing on the top. Harper grins and hands me a box.

"Ach, ye dinnae," I begin, and everyone laughs. "What?" They're confusing me, and I'm feeling like I'm missing out on a joke. It makes me want to hide.

"See! Ye all thought that I make these phrases up! It's how we speak, so ye can all start gettin' used to it," Abi states, hugging me, and now I get it. *Poor Abi!*

"You don't have any cupcakes?" I ask as I notice that there's a pie in Abi's box.

"I'm lactose intolerant, so those, as nice as they are, would make me quite ill unless I've had a pill to combat it. Even then, it's not guaranteed to work, so I just avoid it." Abi grabs her box and grins. "Harper's been trying out different key-lime pie recipes that don't involve lactose. Some are better than others." She grins. "Harper's determined to find something that's astounding, not just 'good.'"

Harper grins. "To be honest, the anti-lactose cakes are getting more popular. Are you sure they're not just turning up at your house?" Harper's eyes go wide, as if there's some teasing going on.

Abi laughs. "No, but funny enough, there's always one of your cakes at Mrs Bunn's! And Lila's when we go over."

"Isn't she on tour?" Bentley asks.

"I think so… We'll know if she turns up to poker night. Or not."

"Ye play poker?" I ask, my interest piqued. "Ma taught me how to play; I love that and bridge."

Estrella's grin gets wider, and her face lights up. "Guess we've got ourselves another lady for poker night," she announces. There are cheers as we get into discussing when and where, and as we're wrapping up, Abi pulls me aside.

"We did a wee whip-around for ye. Reid says he's told ye, but we ken ye've not got any funds with ye right now," she says and hands me an envelope. "So, that's for ye to spend, cash-in-hand. Wanna go through and order yer size?" She offers me her phone with a browser tab open to a ladies' lingerie store.

"Are ye sure?" I ask, and she nods.

"Aye. Ye can use that fund to get them, they're for ye anyway, but it can get delivered to mine, and we can meet up when it's here. For now, ye've got the few soft ones and that nice one we saw earlier to get ye by."

I nod and hug her, making everyone group hug. Again.

As we break apart, Abi's phone goes and so does a few others. "Oh, fuck," Abi swears, as do Bentley and Estrella. Abi grabs me, and we head off with boxes etc. in hand. Then she answers her own phone when it rings.

"Aye, we got the message. We're heading out there now."

Everyone stops on the high street, and Estrella opens up a huge pick-up as Bentley does the same. Despite Abi being on the phone, she ushers me into Estrella's truck as Harper jumps into Bentley's with Aly. In seconds, we're all in vehicles that reverse and then head off. The direction is towards Reid's house and just as I'm about to ask what's going on,

Estrella pulls over and a Fire Engine races past us, as does a squad car, sirens blaring.

"What's happening?" I ask as Estrella pulls back onto the road. There's a huge crevice appearing in my stomach.

"Someone's tried to set Reid's house alight. They've failed, but the automation systems have called us out."

I gulp, curling up to be as small as I can and hope against hope that things are okay.

We pull up, and there are firemen walking around with policemen here and there. There doesn't seem to be any damage that I can see. I wait by the car as I'm told to. Estrella strides off, and Abi settles next to me.

I can only wrap my arms around myself as I watch. Hoses get rolled up, and water spurts around as a result. Estrella comes back with Reid in tow.

"Someone tried to set fire to the barn." His voice is low, and there's an angry demeanour coming from him that makes me shiver.

"Did yer cameras get who it was?" Abi's voice is low and calm. *How can she be calm in this situation?*

Reid shrugs. "Not looked at the footage yet, so we'll see."

"It's still standing," I comment, making Reid smile weakly at me.

"The barn is rented, the owner had it treated with an anti-flammable paint and installed a sprinkler system, so what they started didn't take. And I added in extra cameras." His jaw ticks, and Abi simply nods at him once, an understanding between them that I don't fathom.

"What do you need?"

"The asshole who did this and time to go over the footage."

"Dae ye still have power? Amenities?" Abi checks, and Reid nods in affirmation. "I dinnae like the idea of ye both being here the night. If whoever it is tried to set yer place alight once, chances are they'll come back and dae it again. Wi' ye both in it." There's a cold sweat happening at the small of my back, and I swear my heart-rate just doubled.

"I ain't putting you at risk either."

Abi raises her eyebrows, and Nick comes over. "You won't be. You know fine well if the shoe was on the other foot…"

"And who else better than a guard dog and another firefighter to help protect ye both? Now, enough of this nonsense. We can sort something out long-term the morrow. Cap, are they clear to grab some stuff?"

Estrella nods and together, Reid and I go and pack up some things. I can see where they tried to start the fire, and there's no damage to the rest of the structure and barely anything to that post. However, Abi's words ring true. If they come back and we're in bed, we might not get out. The thought that it's because of me, what I ran away from, just won't shift.

At Abi's, Reid and I get taken to a spare bedroom. With one double bed.

"I'll take their sofa," Reid whispers to me, but I shake my head.

"After what happened, I doubt I'll sleep."

"Same here."

"There's a bathroom over there. I'll make the bed up and prepare the sheets for the sofa bed, unless ye wanna share? Nick's on duty until six tomorrow, then we swap over. Dinnae fash when I leave with Buster at a quarter-past-five. Nick'll walk him at the dog park afore he comes back."

"Abi, who does your security cameras?" Reid asks as he places his bag in the closet.

"Jason's brother, Troy, did it. Ye work with Caden, don't ye?"

"Yeah, we work together, but we don't often socialise. Caden's gotten a little…private." Abi grins at that comment.

"Aye, well, Troy installed it after the wedding. Ye ken what happened with *her*."

Reid's jaw ticks, and he nods. "I'll ask him. I installed my own, and it'll be good to have him look over that footage too."

Abi smiles. "I hear ye. Right, let me go get dinner sorted." There's a woof at the back door, and Abi goes to let the dog in who leaps at her before he spies Reid and me, leaving Abi standing there with a huge grin on her face.

"Buster, yer a treacherous dug!" She's laughing, so I can tell she doesn't mean it. Buster's tail is beating like a big base drum against the wall and my leg.

"He just likes the fuss," I echo, fussing him as Reid puts his phone to his ear. His voice is so low and strained that I can't make out what he's saying, or to who. But my stomach knots and I can feel the bile in the back of my throat begin to rise.

After a few moments, Reid hangs up and sighs. When he turns, he looks at me.

"Did you hear much of that?" he inquires as I shake my head in response.

"No. But, I don't think I needed to."

He smirks. "That was Caden, he's tried to find my camera footage, but it's been wiped."

I can feel my eyebrows are somewhere in my hairline. "How?" I ask, and he growls.

"It's a closed system. They shouldn't be able to. I do have a secondary recording system in place, and he's checking that out. In the meantime, I need to make a few more calls."

"And ye dinnae want me to listen," I state.

He smiles at me. "It ain't that…the less you know, the less you'll have to lie."

"Who would I lie to?" I ask as I stand. "What aren't ye telling me?" The look on his face says it all. "It's because of me, isn't it? I *am* putting ye all in danger."

I don't notice him grabbing me by the shoulders and sitting me on the sofa, until he makes me sit.

"The fire might be, I don't know. But I need to talk with the Feds, Preston and a few others. I would leave you back at the apartment, but that's compromised. I ain't that keen on leavin' ye here either, but I ain't got any choice."

I nod, understanding that he's dealing with one problem at a time—all because of me.

"I don't get why they want me. Surely I can't be that important to them?"

"Until I work out who *'they'* are, I'm working on the basis that you're more important than we thought." I gulp and try not to show just how much I want to run, hide and pee my knickers right now. "I get you're scared, but I will do everything I can to make sure you're safe, okay?" I nod and pull in a breath. "Are you able to carry on, to be brave for me?" Taking in his whisky-coloured eyes, I slowly nod. For him, I think I'd walk through Hell itself.

♡ ♡ ♡

Five minutes later, Reid says he's gotta go into the station and leaves me with Abi. She locks the door behind him and presses some things on her phone.

"What ye doin'?"

"Setting the alarm system. Troy set up a few nice surprises for me. We had…trouble, with Nick's ma on our wedding day. Unfortunately for her, she encountered *my* mother, Mrs Bunn and half the aulder women of the town who knew her."

I gape at her. "Really?" I ask. Abi gives me an overview of what Nick's mother did about twenty-years ago and what she tried last year at their wedding.

"Yer no joking?" I confirm, my voice high, and Abi shakes her head.

"Naw, wish I were. The aulder women turned into a huge gangster crowd and saw her off. She's been by once afore since, so I took out a restraining order. I'm expecting her to violate it."

Abi cuts up the sausages she's fried off with gusto, as if the sausages are someone in particular.

"Strong imagination, aye?" I ask, motioning to her knifework. Then, she laughs.

"Aye, very much!"

"Can I help?"

"Aye, ye can." I get on with helping Abi prepare dinner, even though it's still light. I love the kitchen, how it opens up into the living space, making everything connected. I love that's the plan at Reid's too.

We talk, and I learn about some of Abi's family and how her dad owned this house before she had to sell it to fulfil her father's will, and it was sold it to Nick; something her father orchestrated. Her story is intriguing.

"Are ye allowed to talk about what happened to ye, with me?" she asks, and I shake my head.

"Reid asked that I don't. We're going to call my parents tomorrow, let me speak with them."

"Ye've no spoken aboot them much. Dae ye no get on?"

I shrug. "I'm the youngest of five, so if Mum and Dad aren't asking me what I'm doing, how I'm eating, what I'm eating, who I'm seeing and the rest of the inquisition, one of the other four are."

Abi smirks at me. "I used to do the same to Charlie, my wee brother. Ye dae realise it's 'cause they love ye?"

I snort softly. "Why can't I just be allowed to live? I took this marketing job because it was in Stirling, away from them in Livingston."

"Tell me more," she encourages as she fills up the kettle.

"No wine?" I ask.

"I'm working tomorrow, so, no. And if anything happens the night, we're gonna need oor wits aboot us." I gulp when I realise, she's right.

"So, tell me more," she insists. And as she makes us both a cup of tea—both with oat milk, and I decide I like it better—I reveal to her a few thoughts and feelings I've daren't revealed to anyone else.

It's not been easy, talking about my emotions or how I'm feeling. With Abi, it seems to just flow from me, like a tap I can't turn off. Abi just listens, sipping her tea or nodding when she understands where I'm coming from.

An alarm on Abi's phone goes off, and as she's checking it, there's a knock at the door. Buster's loud bark makes me jump.

"Aly, Essie and Sakura." She winks as she gets up to open the door. Once she's let them in, she locks us back in and resets the outer alarm. Then, she answers a call from Nick, and I can hear her telling him who set it off. Once she's done that, we all gather around on the huge L-shaped sofa and chill.

Hours later, after pizza and wings, which Essie ordered because she was hungry, the girls leave. We had a few rounds of poker, playing for matches, and I lost every time. Essie and Abi really have a poker face. Sakura and Aly wear their hearts on their sleeves, but it was Aly who won the most tonight.

"We'll leave you both to it," Essie says as they leave, everyone giving me a reassuring squeeze to the arm or a hug.

Abi nods and smiles, despite being made to play host. It's around nine pm and Abi checks in with Reid when he's likely to be back. When he says it won't be for a while yet, I help Abi make up the guest bed and the sofa bed before we both shower and retire for the night.

Lying in the dark, I finally let the possibilities of who could get hurt because of me play around in my head. And I can't shut them down.

Chapter Seven

♡ Reid ♡

I hated leaving Alysia at Abi's, but there was no other way; I need to get this resolved and keep her safe. When I get to the station, Caden is milling about at the front desk, which is unusual as he's either out or in his office. Seeing me, he pulls me aside.

"Your backup worked, but whoever it was, they didn't take a chance. They wore a hoodie that hid their face, and I'm pretty sure they knew where the cameras were."

I curse, making Caden smirk. It takes me a moment to articulate my thoughts before we part ways. "Thanks. I appreciate the help."

Heading to my desk, I pull out my chair only to have Preston come up to me before my ass hits the cushion. He motions for me to follow, and I do. He takes me to the small interview room I thought I had seen the back of, but I hadn't. Sitting and playing with a hot mug of coffee, looking like death warmed up, is Maggie Forrester.

"Maggie?" I question as Preston shuts the door behind us.

"Hey, Reid. Thanks."

"What for?" I take the seat Preston indicates I should.

"Coming in."

"Did you call me?" I look at Preston and then back at Maggie.

"I didn't get a chance to call and ask him, he appeared."

Maggie nods and lets out a sigh. I can see her shoulders deflate.

"I've got paperwork to file about my apartment fire," I begin, and Maggie holds her hand up.

"Yeah, it was attempted arson, likely because of Alysia. Look, I'm not technically here." She looks at Preston, and I notice that there's no recording equipment on; the hum from it all is missing, and I breathe in the air-conditioned air. "I found some worrying things when I was digging around, and I am having to tread carefully."

"Go on," I encourage. I watch as she sucks in a breath and holds it, as if steeling herself to deliver a truck-ton of bad news.

"I think my partner and few others from the local office are in on this container business. I need more time to gather some evidence, and I've had my higher-ups talking to Chief Charmichael; I've requested to put together a task-force on this, quietly. And I want you in on it."

I lean back. "Okay. Why?"

Maggie sighs. "You digging around the international missing women, for starts. My colleagues only started doing that *after* you found three of them. Every one of the women who I've spoken to *was* willing to make a report, as Alysia has done. Now, they won't or *can't* remember." Maggie looks at me with eyes as cold as ice. "I need her to make a stand, take the stand, and I don't want her intimidated."

I look at Maggie then Preston before Maggie slides over an envelope. I take it and open it up. There's a map, some simple instructions and very little else.

"What's this?"

Maggie draws in a huge breath as she looks at me with pleading eyes. "I need you to keep her safe. You can't do that and do your job, so I've asked for you to be on this task force. I need your priority to be Alysia."

If she's taking down colleagues as well as these guys, she's going to need all the help she can get, so I'm in. Dirty cops bug the hell outta me, thanks to my uncle. He was found to be hiding people who liked indulging in little girls when I was around two, as well as 'indulging' in them himself. The law caught up with him when a colleague hunted him down without him knowing.

66

"I need your help, Reid. Please. I ain't too sure who I can trust on my side, beyond the few already in on this. I've got my house to clean and these trafficking assholes with it. My one ace so far is Alysia. I've got some Rangers trying their damndest to keep the others safe, bring the other witnesses around."

I look at Preston who just gives me a nod. "Henry's already cleared it. Mayor Parsons is behind it."

"Okay. I said she could call her family tomorrow, speak with them and let them know she's alright, but she can't answer questions about the case." I need her to touch base with her family, to let them know she's okay. I also feel she needs to hear from them; when was the last time she heard that they loved her?

Maggie nods. "I wouldn't tell her about heading out to this place until she's done that." Maggie taps the papers. "The less they know and get told, the safer they *all* are." I get the implication. Nick and Abi can't be in on the plans either. We're going to be cut off, unless they're related to this task-force.

I sit back and let the tightness in my chest settle. Maggie's drawn up battle lines; and I'm more than playing on her side.

Sitting at my desk later, filing the paperwork, I begin thinking of ways to track Alysia should we get separated. And I need it to work over a few thousand miles. Checking with Nick, I get the distance from Piper Falls to Livingston, but I doubt any tracker can work over the Atlantic.

Hearing a noise from the door, I look up to see one of my best friends, Matt Bradley, leaning against the frame. We're the same height, but the ladies like his fairer hair. He refused to follow the path his father laid out, and we can tell when he's had discussions with his father about his career choice. Now if he can get over Amber Connery, the one we know who got away, I reckon he'll be happier.

"Hey!"

"Hi ya."

"Where's the girl?"

I sigh. "At the Charmichael's. For now."

Matt nods. "Good idea. They might not do guns, but I reckon she's safe there." I nod. Then, Matt shuts the door behind him and sits on the sofa. "You're taken with this one?"

"I ain't…" I begin to protest, but Matt's shaking his head and smirking.

"I've seen how y'all look at her. Don't let the job come between you both."

"The distance will do that. And isn't that the pot calling the kettle black? I hear Amber's back in town."

Matt shrugs. "She is, I'm gonna drop by there later. Don't try and deflect here, Reid. I'm sure Nick and Abi can tell you how they managed it. Abi's here, so it can't be that hard, just might take some time."

I pull in a sigh. "True. But, Alysia *is* the job right now."

Matt raises his eyebrows. "True. What are you going to do when she's gone home? Scotland is a good six thousand miles away."

I scoff and nearly give him the exact distance, but his question is valid. "More like four and a half thousand." We've been watching out for each other since kindergarten, especially more so since Noah was killed in the line of duty a few years back and close to his damn anniversary too.

"I ain't got that far," I admit. "My mind started wondering the same, being honest."

Matt rubs his face, the tiredness showing.

"I have an idea, but I ain't too sure how practical it is."

"Go on."

I explain my concerns.

Matt pulls out his phone and shows me a charm bracelet.

"Get a charm with a GPS tracker in it that she can activate."

"I was thinking along the same lines, but I ain't sure if they'd work across the Atlantic. Where would we get one of those?" I don't discount his idea. Matt can put a GPS tracker on any motorised vehicle in minutes. Something this small though, I know is out of his remit.

"Caden, most likely."

At that moment, the man himself opens my office door. "Just heard my name. What can I do for you *fine ladies*?" I roll my eyes at his question and tease. I don't think I've seen him this chilled in years.

"Caden, you're an asshole."

"And you know it, Bradley. But I heard my name."

"You did. How easy would it be to get a GPS tracker put into a piece of jewellery?" I ask, showing him Matt's idea. Caden looks at some of the charms, his brow furrowing a little.

"Getting a GPS tracker small enough is the trick, but try to get a charm that's got some size to it. A cube or something." He pulls out his own phone and scrolls through, then he shows me the image of a police car charm. "Something like that, we can get a GPS device into. It'll last about ten hours when they're activated."

"Do they work four and a half thousand miles away?" I ask.

Caden smirks, then nods. "They work anywhere the GPS satellites cover. So, not the Pentagon or a mile underground, but otherwise, it works anywhere else."

"What's the cost?"

"Let me check with Evan and Troy. How soon can you get a bracelet like that here?" Caden hands me Matt's phone and in seconds, I've pulled up the Etsy store on my phone, ordered that specific charm with a few other items it says I need, as well as the bracelet.

"Five days."

Caden nods. "Sure. Let me know when it's in, and I'll have Troy make it work for you." I ask the cost again. "An hour of Troy's time and the cost of the GPS, so about a hundred, if we can still get one that small, but I need to go and ask."

I nod in agreement, and Caden heads off like we've just arranged to have beers. Matt winks at me and makes his leave. When they've left me in silence, I find that the words I want for the attempted arson report come quite easily.

Hours later, I head back to Nick and Abi's. I can hear the crickets chirping and night animals moving around. I even manage to scare a few cats that have been put out for the night. As I approach the door, Abi's there, wrapped up in a bathrobe that might be Nick's; it's dark and far too big. It's around three am.

"How did you know I was here?" I whisper as I take off my shoes. Buster doesn't bark, but he does wag his tail a lot on the floor. The swishing sound is hypnotic and welcoming.

"Proximity alarms notified me." She winks at me before locking the door behind me. After the break-in when she first showed up, there's far more security on that door and around the house than is normal, but I can't blame them. Right now, I'm glad they invested in it.

"Sorry."

"Dinnae fash. Yer stuff is in the bedroom. Alysia didn't want it left out here."

"Ain't you working this morning?"

Abi nods and yawns. "A few more hours. Away ye go. I'm goin' back tae my bed." She clicks her fingers in a pattern the dog recognises, and he trots off after her without so much as a backward glance to me. With a grin, I make my way as quietly as I can to the guest bedroom.

I open the door, and the figure in the bed turns, then sits up.

"Reid?" Alysia's voice whispers to me in the darkness, and something within me leaps. I'm glad she can't see the smile that's appeared.

"Yeah, it's me. Why ain't you asleep?"

"Meh." I can see her shifting in the bed and throwing back the sheets. "I cannae sleep. I was worried aboot ye."

I grin, her accent is strong, tellin' me she's tired, so I go and sit on the bed. I can't climb in with her. I can't let her know what she does to me, especially when I work out she's only wearing a tank top and panties. Keeping her safe is my job; I can't indulge.

"I'm back and safe," I confirm, needing to break the silence.

"Well, that's good."

I smirk to myself. "Now, why ain't you asleep?" I needed her to be sound asleep.

"I was worried," her voice hitches, and I don't need to see she's crying, the dark form of her arm wiping away the tears is enough. I pull her to me. *Lord, give me strength!*

"Why were ya worried?"

"In case that ejit came back." She sucks in a breath and then calms. "This is because of me, isn't it?"

"Not just you," I confirm and regret it as soon as I open my mouth. "It's all a part of what went on when you were in the woods, and before that. The other survivors too."

"Can I tell ye something? I need ye to no laugh at me." Her voice whispers up to my ears from my chest, and I loosen my grip just a little.

"Ya sure can."

"The doctor, the one that looks like Mrs Santa Claus, she telt me…telt me I'd been raped. But I dinnae remember that. And afore I went oot to Chicago, I was…" My mind puts the word '*virgin*' into the gap she's made as she continues her statement. "Well, I've never been with anyone that I recall."

I close my eyes and swear to all that is holy: whoever took her innocence is going to die.

"I'm so sorry, Alysia. I swear if I find out who, I've got a bullet with their name on it."

She snorts, then sniffs. "That's no why I telt ye."

"Oh?" I lean back, and she looks up at me. Even in the low light, I can see she's wide-eyed. I don't get why.

"Since I woke up in the hospital, I find it hard to be alone in the dark." *That I guessed, but I hadn't seen much evidence of it.*

"Do you need a light?" I'm sure I can turn the light on for her, or use the closet light. She shakes her head.

"I slept better when I knew you were around, or when I saw you or someone sitting in that chair. I dinnae ken who ye were, but I felt safe with ye aboot when I learned ye were police, even if ye scared me. Last night, I slept better, knowing you were only a room away, but only for a few hours at a time." I love how she says '*po-lis*' and not just 'police.'

"I'll just be in—" I begin, but she cuts me off, pressing a small finger to my lips.

"Stay. I don't want anything from ye, or for anything to happen. Just, stay in here. With me. To sleep." Her voice breaks, and it takes her a moment. "Please?" she begs softly.

"Are you *sure* that's what you want?" I confirm, knowing where we're going after we've called her folks. Not that I'm gonna tell her that right this moment.

"I just want a really long hug," her sullen voice murmurs to me, and I want more than anything to chase that away. I never have before, and I freeze as I work out that this is what I *want* to do. "I feel safe wi' ye aboot."

"Come here then," I encourage, easing her back into the bed. As I spoon her, because, frankly, anything else is going to cause as much of an issue as this position already is, she drops off. I'd leave, but her head is on my arm, and the bed is soft and warm. So is she. My last thoughts are about how I'm going to Hell because of her.

We awake hours later. It's daylight, and I can hear someone moving around, then a man's voice quietly telling Buster to behave. A door opens, then closes and silence falls. I need to find out what time it is, but I'm still wrapped around Alysia. She's hugging my arm to her, but she's not as curled up as she was at three am.

I close my eyes and breathe in her hair, which smells of apples and something else sweet, vanilla maybe. Alysia stretches and curls back into me before going rigid. She relaxes when I whisper good morning to her.

"Oh, hiya." When she turns, she's smiling at me. Then she stretches again.

"Good morning, kitten." She pulls back and throws me a very clear '*what the hell?*' look, which makes me laugh. "You stretch out like a cat," I tell her, wanting to explain myself.

"Aye...okay, if ye say so," she grins. "I think Nick's hame." I guess she means 'home'.

"That would make sense. Let's go and get breakfast, then we can go and see about callin' your folks." She huffs, then pouts. "Something I need to know, kitten?" That is going to be my name for her going forward, especially if I get a sassy response like this.

"Ye dinnae ken what they're like." Her face is sullen, crest-fallen, and her voice is low.

72

"You don't get on with them. I remember you sayin' they were in y'all's business all the time."

"Aye… Have ye ever felt…claustrophobic?" I nod, wondering where she's going with this. "Well, imagine that, but with yer family. Da always has a comment about me being too skinny, too big," she exaggerates her larger breasts, "that no one is going to…ach, it disnae matter."

"It does." My reply comes out as a growl, unbidden, not-thought-out. I can't recall a single time I've been real with a girl and just, been myself. "Look, I know your family ain't easy. Mine are scattered, so I don't have the things goin' on that you do, but they *do* deserve to know you're alive. Just don't tell them where y'all callin' from. Or anything about the investigation."

"Please tell me ye'll be there with me?" I nod once, which makes her smile. "Well, that makes it more bearable. Let's get up then!" she declares, and before I can do or say anything, she's grabbed her stuff and hightailed it to the bathroom. I shake my head, wondering which side of her I'll get next. And what do I have to do to get her to be more herself.

Nick comes in from the back porch with tools in hand. "Oh, mornin'!" he calls out as Buster comes in, his tail thumping from side to side in that happy, retriever way he has. He's not a big dog, likely the runt of the litter, but he is such a happy hound. He makes a bee-line for Alysia and that makes Nick laugh.

"You, Buster, have a thing for the ladies in this 'ere house! Ya'll a treacherous, lovable mutt." Buster just looks at him before pushing into Alysia's legs a little more. It makes me chuckle.

"We'll head down to the cafe for breakfast," I state, and Nick raises his eyebrows at me.

"Abi catered for y'all," he says, heading to the fridge. "She said she'll get some more later this week for us."

He pulls out a tray of goodies that I cannot recognise. Alysia, however, does in a heartbeat.

"Is that…tattie scone?" she asks, her eyes going wide. Nick laughs.

"Abi said y'all recognise that in a second. And yeah, it is. Now this…"

"Haggis, black pudding, square sausage," she says, pointing to each of them. "How the heck did she get them o'er here?"

Nick puts the plastic board down and pulls down a skillet. "Abi's made friends with the local butcher. He spoke with another she and Vicky know in Scotland and started selling these in the grocery store in town, special order." The grocery store has a butcher section at the back, selling all the meats you could possibly want. I'd seen these, but hadn't an idea of what they were.

"So they traded secrets?"

"Looks like," he agrees as he begins to fry up everything. Alysia's dancing with a huge smile on her face. Well, hot damn, feeding the girl gets her to grin at ya.

"Alysia, darlin', could you set the table for us three, please? Stuff is over there." She bounces off, and I smirk. Nick leans into me. "The best way to a Scotswoman's heart is through her stomach. Trust me."

"Hey, we're not…"

Nick shrugs and winks at me. "She's taken with ya. I can tell you're liking what y'all seein'."

"This is just me, following my duty," I state, keeping my voice low.

"Uh huh…" he says. Yeah, he sees right through that lie.

The breakfast was huge, and Alysia ate every scrap of it. I have no idea how someone so slight can pretty much out-eat me.

"Abi's gonna have tae teach me how to do the tattie scones!" she says as she sips a large mug of tea. "They were home-made." She catches me lookin' at her and grins, then rubs her stomach. "What ye starin' at?"

"How can someone so petite, eat *that* much? I think I need to have a nap!" Honestly, my gut is bursting, and if I don't move, I'll end up in a food coma. I stand and help Nick clear the kitchen down. It's the least I can do.

"Easy. I'll no eat until later on, then it'll be something light, like a sandwich or soup. Maybe a yoghourt. Likely nothing at all."

I turn to Nick who shrugs. "When Abi and I eat like that, it is an all-day thing. We might eat in the evenin', but as Alysia says, it's a light meal. We've eaten like that when we've done trail days and know we're going to be out for fourteen hours or more."

"Abi will burn the calories off today, no doubt." I know she's working.

Nick laughs. "She was on breakfast shout with the squad this morning. She'll have cooked that for them too. Trust me, they'll hardly eat the rest of the day."

I check my watch and smirk. "Speaking of the rest of the day, we need to go and call your folks," I state. Alysia nods, grinning at me with a light in her eyes.

"After that breakfast, I feel I can take on anything! Or," she stands and pushes her chair in, "anyone."

Nick grins at her comment, but he ain't the only one. "I'll finish tidying up, you two best get goin'."

I don't ask him if he's sure; his tone tells me he ain't takin' no as an answer. With one more fuss to Buster, we head to the station. I just hope she'll forgive me when we don't head back to Nick and Abi's.

The station is buzzing, as usual. The traffic misdemeanours, the patrol guys doing their job, it's all the same as usual. Today though, it feels different. I sign Alysia in, then we head around to my desk past the bull-pen. With a wink and a grin at Alysia, she takes a seat on the sofa and for about twenty minutes, I send over my workload to different colleagues. She yawns and then chills out, but that sofa is not designed for reclining. It makes me hurry up, and when I get the last file, I press that enter key with gusto. I take my glasses off and rub my eyes, adjusting to the need to wear them when I'm using the computer a lot.

"Let's head to a small conference room to make that call." She nods at me, but the looks she's giving me are slightly worrying.

"Have I got something weird on me?" I ask as we head down a corridor. She goes red and bites her lower lip.

"Naw. Just…well…ye look cute in the glasses," she confesses and dives into the small interview room. It takes me a couple of seconds to understand what she said. *Hot damn!*

"Okay, kitten, we need to practice some answers. Just remember, we will be recording this, okay?" I look at her as she curls her hands up under her chin and looks at me through fluttering eyes, before she gives me a little nod and a smile. I can't push her up against the wall and show her what she does to me. Not here. "Where are you?"

"In a police station, in Piper Falls." I shake my head, and she smirks. "In a police station, in Texas." Her tone is starting to get sassy, and I give her a look that makes her purse her lips together. The windowless room is small, about as big as the bathroom at my own place. I try not to imagine her at my place, in my shower. I bring my mind back to why we're in this dingy little room on a bright, warm Texan day. The air-con takes the edge off the heat, but I don't think it'll touch what we seem to have going on.

"When will you be home?"

"When they've finished their investigation."

I nod in approval. "Good girl. Have you got all you need?"

She shakes her head, but her eyes are brighter. So, she responds to being praised; that's interesting. "No, but they're sorting it."

"Are you safe?"

She smirks at me. "Safest place I have ever been." Her voice lowers in volume, but she doesn't take her eyes from mine.

We go through a few more likely questions, and I somehow don't stumble on my words. This little room is quite warm all of a sudden.

"Just tell me we have to go when I do this, will ye?" She makes V signs towards the phone, making me chuckle.

"You got it, kitten."

I dial her parents' number, making our phone pretend to be somewhere else in the USA, thanks to some tech Maggie left behind. Alysia shifts in her seat, putting her feet on the floor squarely.

"Hallo?" The voice is male and deep.

"Hi, Dad, it's me," Alysia says, her voice is very quiet.

"Alysia! Is that ye? How are ye? Let me shout on yer ma! Freya!" Her father bellows loud enough for people outside the room we're in to hear him, and he ain't on loudspeaker. Alysia moves the handset away from her ears and shakes her head.

"Sorry," she whispers. I can hear her mother walking towards the phone.

"Hamish, what's aw the commotion aboot?"

"Alysia's on the phone," he says, his voice raised. He seems at least pleased to be hearing from his daughter. There's some crackling, and I can hear the moment they put their phone to loudspeaker, at least at their end. I can hear her parents clearly without the need for the speaker.

"Alysia! Alysia, hen! Where are ye?"

Alysia laughs. "Hi, Mam! I'm in Texas, but I cannae tell ye where, exactly."

"Why no?"

"Because the case is still open, aye? Just in case there's anyone listening in that shouldnae be."

"Oh! But, yer being looked after, fed? Are you alright?"

"I'm…getting better." She sighs. "They hurt me, Mam!" She starts to cry, and I silently reach out for her hand. When she grabs it, I squeeze it a little, gaining a small smile in payment.

"I'll find them," her dad promises.

"No, ye'll no. I cannae tell ye what I told the police fae same reason I cannae tell ye where I am. But, I'm alive, I'm being looked after, and I'm getting better. I dinnae know how long I'll be here though."

"How will ye get home? They said they couldn't find any of your belongings at the hotel."

She looks at me, her eyes wide, and I wink. We'll get her passport and everything sorted when this mess is cleared up.

"That's being taken care of. I'm no sure how, but I ken they will."

"That's good! Your company just said you'd vanished. To be honest, they're bawbags. Dinnae seem to care ye'd gone missing, wernae frantic aboot it."

I frown, and it's enough to make Alysia nod.

"Da, what did they say?" I nod, indicating that she was good and clever to ask. We're recording this anyway, but she knows that.

"Ach, just that they'd handed it o'er to the police, then we heard nothing for bloody weeks. The police wouldn't tell us anything, not even an update. We went to the First Minister, and then the press started."

Alysia smirks. "You talked to the bum-rags?" The scoffing sound that comes back suggests he might have.

"They keep wantin' to talk to us, but all we wanted was to hear yer were safe."

"I am now, Dad." Her voice goes soft, and she inhales a breath very quietly.

"Wish I knew where ye were."

Alysia rolls her eyes. "I cannae be tellin' ye, but I am safe. And if I dinnae tell ye, ye cannae be tellin' the press or anyone where I am." Smart cookie. Alysia glances over to me, and I smile, gaining one back.

"Fair enough."

"Are ye eating enough?" Alysia shakes her head, and I shift, ready to call a halt to this conversation.

"Aye, I am. I ate a huge breakfast this morning."

"Bet it wasnae like mine!" Her mother's voice rises.

"Nae, it wasnae, but it was just as good. Very much needed."

"I'm glad! Can ye bring some of that nice weather back wi' ye? It's dreach here."

Alysia laughs. "Da, yer in God's country. Scotland isnae in the Pyrenees!" Her papa laughs, and I roll my fingers. "Da, I've gotta wrap this up, aye?"

"Why for?"

"Because I've nothing else I can tell ye, and the Polis here need to do their job. I've still got a statement to finish off." I nod. She doesn't, but if they think she's safe in a police station, all the better.

"When will we hear from ye again?" he asks. His voice carries a tone of desperation.

"I dinnae ken. They've no told me when I can contact ye again. But, I will. Might no be for a few weeks mind."

"Aye…" Her father huffs. "We just want ye home."

"Aye, I ken, but there's stuff that's gotta be done, Dad. But I'll contact ye when I can, okay?"

"Bye, honey! Sending our prayers!" Alysia tears up at that, though I'm not sure why. She says bye-for-now, which I've heard Abi use a fair bit. Then, the call is over.

She looks at me and physically deflates. "That…went better than I expected."

"Your momma worries," I clarify.

"Aboot the wrong things."

"Them asking if you've eaten, shows that they care. They might make it all about the weight because that's something obvious to them. Or has concerned them in the past."

She brings her knees up to her chest, resting her feet on that chair. "Go on."

"Replace the words 'Have you eaten?' with 'I love you. I care for you. I'm concerned for you.'" I smile at her. I heard it in their voice, in their tone. They love her, and they express it the best way they know how. The words though, are what she's focusing on; not the meaning behind them.

"Not everyone uses the phrase 'I love you.' Food for them might be their language of love. Abi's was today."

"Hmm…" She doesn't seem convinced, but I heard it as clear as day. What she's hearing and what they're sayin' are two different things.

"You can think about it as we get outta Piper Falls."

"Why? Where are we going?"

"My place is a little too obvious; it's already been attacked."

"Aye, I know." Her voice sinks like a stone in water.

"So, we're heading on out."

"Our stuff is at Abi's."

I nod. "It is. We can go back and pack, then when it's dark, we'll move on out." The idea to move at dusk hit me while she chatted with her folks.

"Where are we going?" she asks, uncurling herself from the chair.

"Kitten, I'll tell you when we get there, okay?" She gives me a half shrug and follows me out of the station to the car-park, then I take us back to Abi's.

It doesn't take us long to pack, and Nick is with us for most of the day. While we wait for dusk, I help him cut some planks for the deck. Alysia is sitting on a deckchair on one half of the porch, in the sunlight but hidden from view. Buster is calmly laying at her feet, sunning himself and letting Alysia's feet rest on him. I comment on it to Nick, who just chuckles at me.

"He makes Abi do that to him all the time too. She usually sits and reads a book on the front porch at night, but he makes sure he is touching her, somehow."

I recall when he got Buster, it was before I went back to the Academy for my Lieutenant training, and we'd been called to an abandoned animal truck that had about fifty dogs in it. The local vets were first on scene, then us, then everyone who could house an animal got roped in. Caleb, a ranch hand at Jaxon's ranch, secured Buster for Nick.

The Rangers did find the company that hauled the animal trailer out to Piper Falls, but I hadn't heard what happened to them.

"Did Brad Morgan ever update you on what happened with that trailer?"

Nick stands and stretches for a moment. "Can't recall, but I haven't gone out of my way to ask him. I shall, next time I see him."

"Oh, was just wonderin'." I glance across to Alysia, who still has her feet on Buster. Her eyes are closed, and she's turned her head. I motion to Nick who grins, then he leans over.

"Abi does the same. I don't think the Scotswomen can take the Texan humidity."

I chuckle, and we get on with adding in more decking. By the time the daylight wanes, the deck is finished.

Chapter Eight

♡ Alysia ♡

It was peaceful to be around Nick and Reid. While Reid helped Nick nail down boards and cut wood, Buster decided I was fair game and insisted on laying *under* my feet. With the sunlight on me, my feet warm and resting on the dog, along with the noise of the wood being cut, I fell asleep. When I awake, it's because my footstool is moving, and I smirk as the pup stretches. Now I know what a downward dog looks like side on. Yoga used to be my go-to to relax, and for obvious reasons these last months, I haven't done it. For the first time, I pang that I'm missing something from home.

There are many things I already regret doing, or not doing, in my life. I didn't know that people trafficking was still happening or even a thing. I contemplate how little I knew of the real world, and I'm afraid for the world I have found.

"Hey. What's going on in that pretty little head, kitten?"

I turn and smile as Reid comes and crouches down before me. If he were in a kilt, I'd get quite the view. *How did he know I was contemplating life?* "I just got to thinking about yoga, about regrets and how little I actually knew of the world afore…any of this."

Reid stands then sits next to me in the other mismatched chair. He's not touching me, but I can smell his sweat, see his muscles flexing. I forget for a moment just how much younger I am compared to Reid, and I contemplate wondering what it would be like to be with someone you wanted and who wanted you.

"It's not a pretty world at times, that's for sure. We have good guys, like my colleagues and I, tryin' to make it a better place."

"I just didn't realise the bad *actually* existed. You hear about it, but it's removed from you. On the box that's just spouting stuff at ye."

"The box?"

"Goggle Box, the TV." I smirk, forgetting Scottish slang terms will be lost on Reid.

"Yeah, well, sometimes, you need to ignore what's on that screen. Sometimes, you need to take stock and decide what side of the line you're on."

"I'll bet you think I'm some stupid wee lassie, don't ye?" I regret asking him that as soon as the words leave my mouth, but I cannae take them back. He frowns and his jaw ticks, then he sighs and rubs his hands together.

"You're not stupid. And by wee, I guess you mean small? Kitten, dynamite is small, that's why you should still handle it delicately."

I chuckle at his view, but I somehow like being compared to dynamite. "I need you to go and pack while Nick cooks us some steaks." I am about to ask where and how when I smell it. Nick's lit the BBQ, and there's a wonderful smell coming from it.

"I dinnae think I can manage a steak." To be honest, I'm still stuffed from breakfast.

"We thought you might not. But we've been working," he motions to the deck flooring that's now finished. "So, Nick has thrown on a small steak for you. What you don't eat, he says you can give to Buster, provided it doesn't have any onions on it."

"Okay, I can do that. Dae I need to help with anything?" I offer as I shuffle my way off this huge deckchair.

"There's a salad in the fridge he says, but there's that packing to do too."

"Aye, okay, I can do that." With a grin, I go and do as I've been asked. But not before I cast Reid a backward glance. And I catch him watching me. I like the look I get.

Dinner was simple. Steak and salad, and while Nick only gave me a small steak—well, small according to him—I couldn't finish it. Buster must've thought all his Christmases came at once as he got mine and the few scraps from the guys' plates.

It's dusk, the stars are starting to shine when Reid loads our bags into his truck, then thanks Nick.

"We'll be here when it's all over." Nick calls Buster to him, making him heel by his side. Like a good boy, the pup does as he's told.

"I wanna say bye-for-now to Abi." I look at Reid and try to appear confident as I make my demand, though I'm anything but. He simply nods.

"We can do that. The Firehouse is next to the station, and I need to call in there for a few things anyway."

"Oh, okay! Braw. Nick," I turn and offer him a hug, "Cheers, pal! See ye again and soon?" I question before I fuss Buster behind an ear.

He nods then grins at me. "As my wife would say, bye-for-now."

Before I contemplate letting the waterworks loose at that very familiar term, I take the hand Reid offers to me, and he helps me up into his huge truck. Then, we're off.

Reid parks behind the Police Station, and there's a double-chain-link fence that divides the yards. Standing at the gates between the yards is Abi. I love her dark blue t-shirt with the Firehouse logo on it, her surname is printed beneath it and the station number is on the back. The floodlights are the only reason I can see her.

"Well, there ye are! I hope Nick fed ye?" she asks, and I return her grin, remembering what Reid said earlier. I nod.

"Aye, he did! Just, who the hell dae ye feed?"

Abi motions to the Firehouse with a huge grin. "This squad, who dae ye think?"

"I need to go and…" Abi nods and shoos Reid off with a grin.

"I've got her, she's safe. Away ye go," she tells him and then she's shutting the gate, ushering me across the yard and inside the Firehouse, up some stairs to the breakout room.

"Can anyone just walk in here?" I ask as she tucks a wee gadget away into her trousers, and she shakes her head.

"Not anymore. Ye used to be able to, afore I came. Things…changed."

I frown, not understanding if she had anything to do with the changes or not.

"They needed to," a huge man says as he comes up to us. "Don't tell me there's another one of y'all joining us?"

Abi grins at him. "Naw, Tiny, ye couldnae cope man! Alysia here is just waiting for Reid Flanagan, then she'll be off."

"So no more of your colleagues are coming in on this squad?"

Abi turns to look at this huge guy, and he baulks for a moment as she does, as if she's going to strike out. "No yet…why? Dae ye want mare Scots in yer life, pal?" Abi smiles sweetly and sips her drink, never taking her eyes off him.

"Just checkin'," he gruffs

"Huh, huh…" She smiles sweetly at him.

"Tiny, don't you be rattling Milkybar, she's likely to prick ya, *again*," their captain warns as she comes through. Estrella looks very different in uniform. Her hair is braided back for a start; it's not flowing down as it was when she was off duty. She also wears different labelling on her t-shirt, and her expression is more *'do not mess with me'* than anyone I've ever seen before. The huge guy behind her just shakes his head at Tiny, before throwing a smirk at Abi.

"Hey, Alysia! Reid dropped you off at us for a spell?"

I nod. "Aye, he has. Ye ken how he is, disnae wanna let me be alone."

I wink at Tiny, not really implying anything but letting him make up his own mind. "Aye, he asked. Yer good! Stay with Abi, even if we get a call, y'all with us."

I nod, understanding I have my instructions. Abi motions for me to follow, and we head to a smaller break room. With a grin, Abi gives me a guided tour of the Firehouse, the communal bedrooms, and the fire engines, cars and kit themselves. I've never been so close to an emergency vehicle before, and I hope I never need to be in real-life.

I can't believe the time when Reid comes to fetch me after what feels like five minutes, but I've slid down the firepole (Abi dared me, and she was laughing as she did) and tried on her kit. How they can move with such heavy clothing on, beats me. But she says it's what they need to stay safe. With hugs and more "bye-for-now" statements than I'd like, Reid takes us and drives us away from the station, but not in his car.

As he guides this new car through town, then out of it, I notice the *"Thanks For Visiting Piper Falls"* sign and note the *"haste ye back"* comment that looks newer. It makes me chuckle; that's a Hogmanay greeting given to guests who first-foot. Another call to home.

"Did Abi have a say in the sign?"

Reid chuckles and shakes his head. "No, there were a few Scots who settled here in Piper Falls with the Clearings, according to what Abi's found out. That statement has been on the signs out of town since forever. Abi got the town to replace the more broken ones though and explained why. Seems that quite a few of us in town have ancestors that go back to Ireland or Scotland. Myself, my great-grandaddy was Irish."

I smile. "Flanagan, aye. Northern Irish, if I recall? Flanagan is a popular name." It is, I can think of a few broadcasters back home who have that name.

"Yeah, if I remember my family history. My brother is more into that than I am. Apparently, we came across because of the Great Famine and stayed."

"There's a lot of reasons why people move, migrate, change. It's a good strong name," I state. He gives me a glance and a funny look that I can't decipher. For me, he shouldn't be sitting on that side of the car and driving, but it means I can turn to look at him as he drives.

"Alysia, kitten, please don't look at me like that."

I stop daydreaming and turn to face the window, wishing I hadn't started daydreaming about him with him there. Well. Damn.

♡ ♡ ♡

After about half an hour, Reid pulls up a dirt road. The gravel crunches under the wheels as he slowly makes the car climb. The headlights illuminate what looks like a log cabin. It's dark, so I can't see much of it.

"I need you to stay here for a moment. Can you do that?" I nod. "Good girl. Get down for me and stay there until I come back, okay?" He motions down into the footwell and waits for another nod from me as he gets out, drawing his gun. He vanishes into the night, and I rest my head on my arms as I hide in the footwell, wondering what he's doing and why.

His statement earlier confused me. I hadn't realised I had been watching him, letting my imagination run away with me, and I felt bruised when he called me out on it. When the car door opens, I jump. My imagination was running away with me again, and I'd become absorbed in how he'd acted. *Had I really upset him by looking at him?*

"Easy, I was just checking out the area. You wanna get out?"

I nod and when he offers his hand to help, I shake my head, and he steps back, letting me push myself up onto the seat and then out of the car. I wrap my arms around myself, which makes him scowl.

"You're cold. Let's get in, and I'll get the fire started. Come on."

He stalks off to the front door with our bags and lets himself in. I follow and close the door behind me, and after he's dropped the bags, he goes to the door and pushes the bolts home. The door seems quite thick, thicker than the door at my flat back in Scotland, but not like his. I find my bag and look around in it for something warm to wear. I spy a hoodie that I know isn't mine and wasn't a part of what we packed at Abi's, but I shrug it on anyway.

It's a dark-coloured Texas Ranger baseball hoodie, and I grin. It smells like it belongs to a woman, so it's likely Abi's. I find the sofa and sit as I watch Reid build a fire, first with the wee curled up bits, then thin twigs and small sticks, then the logs. In about ten minutes, he has quite a good fire going, and he turns. When he sees me, I can hear his breath hitching, right before he goes to sit on the other single chair.

"I didn't realise you liked baseball." He motions to the hoodie.

I shrug. "It was in the bag. It smells like Abi though."

He grins. "You can give it back to her when this is all over."

I pull in a breath. *How can I tell him that I don't want it to be?* "I'll do that." I smile at him, watching his reaction.

"Let's get unpacked. You can take your stuff through to the bedroom."

I go to find it, and there's one vast bed. I thought my king-size bed back home was huge. This is bigger.

"That's…big! I can't keep warm in that massive thing!"

"I'm sure you'll be warm enough."

"Where's the door?" I ask, and he stands, then slides the door across. There are no handles, and I can't see how it glides, but it does. "Oh!" I mutter, impressed. When he slides the door open and motions for me to take my bag through, I do exactly that.

"I'm just going to get the groceries out of the pick-up," he tells me, leaving me alone in the bedroom. I can only watch as he swings out of the cabin to the pick-up and starts bringing in bags of supplies. I guess we're not going anywhere for quite a while.

I unpack, focusing on what I've put where. There's a walk-in wardrobe and two simple dressers. "Reid!" I call out as I open up the bottom drawer. I back away from the contents, and he comes rushing in, gun drawn, which makes me scream and scurry backward quicker. I fall over the bed and collapse onto the floor.

"What's happened? What did you see?"

I motion to the dresser I was using, and he turns, pointing his gun at the dresser drawer. "Oh!" He leans in and takes out the offending article. Another gun. Bigger than the one he is wielding. And a box. "That shouldn't be in there."

My throat feels tight, my lips are dry, and the world stops spinning.

"You really haven't seen a gun that closely before?" he asks, and I shake my head vigorously from side to side.

"Okay, let me go and take this out your way." I nod, which makes him huff as he heads off. I don't care where he's put it, and provided I don't come across it again, I couldn't care less.

I manage to crawl to the bed, not caring I've still got to finish unpacking, before I curl up on the covers. I don't need to eat, but I could do with some tea. Or something stronger. However, I didn't like the alcohol I was given in Chicago...and I suddenly remember more of what happened that night. Rising, I go to find Reid. I need to tell him.

I find him, sitting out on the back porch in a wicker rocking chair that could do with some TLC, but not from us and not right now. The cabin is warm now, and the air outside is still a pleasant temperature, but I close the door softly behind me.

He turns as I come out and shifts, then motions to the other rocker.

"Did something else happen?"

I gulp and try to form my words. He doesn't push me; he just lets me get there on my own. "I remember..."

He leans forward. "What do you remember, kitten?" His voice is soft, warm, velvety. I know I have to trust him with this, but I don't want him to laugh at me.

"The night they took me? I was with colleagues in the bar, but I had ordered a cola. I don't drink...dinnae like the taste. But this one tasted a wee bit funny. I was told I needed to *'loosen up'* by an American female colleague I'd spent the day with."

He leans back, and his long legs reach out into the darkness. "You didn't have alcohol in your system when they did the tox reports."

I shake my head. "I just remembered. The gun..." I look up at him. "They had a gun, but I was shaky on my legs from the cola and whatever else they'd given me. I remember seeing the gun and the rest is black."

He reaches out a hand, and I take it. I don't want to be alone, then again, I do. When his huge arms wrap around me, and he hauls me up onto his lap, I find I can't stop the tears from falling.

It's light when I awake. I'm in the huge bed, and I turn to see that the other pillows have an indent in them, meaning I didn't sleep alone. My top half is still covered and my bra is still on, as are my knickers. But my hoodie and jeans are on the chair by the door.

I stretch and sigh, wondering what else I'll remember and when. The door slides open softly, and I turn to look at Reid. He's wearing black plaid pyjama bottoms and sweet nothing else. That V and that taunt stomach with abs just pop…

"Eyes up, kitten!" I lift my eyes to meet his, and I don't care that I just stared at him. "Good girl. I'm cooking some breakfast, so it's time to get up. The bathroom is this way." He motions for me to follow, and I do. The bathroom is right next door, and it's rustically beautiful.

"Is that copper?" I ask, walking over to the bath, admiring the claw feet and the higher end where you'd place your head. Then I notice that the sink is copper too; both bounce warm light around the small bathroom.

"It is. Restored from who knows when, but beautiful, ain't it?"

I turn and smile at him. "It is! How do you get water up here to fill it?"

"There's a water tank for flushing the toilet, that's rainwater that gets piped down. The drinking water is from the well, and the hot water gets heated if the fire is going."

"Oh! So we have hot water?"

Reid nods. "The Rangers thought of everything." I cock my head to the side, not understanding. "Texas Rangers. This is one of their remote stations."

"Oh! We didn't seem to take long to get here," I remark. He motions for me to follow and then takes me out onto the back deck.

"See that dip in the tree line over yonder?" He points and guides my sight down his muscley left arm. There's like a low-flying V in the tree line off to the left that's so far away, I can't see anything specific.

"Aye, I see it. Why for?"

He chuckles. "That dip is where Piper Falls is."

I turn and blink at him. "Really? We didn't move states or anything?"

He shakes his head and grins.

"The Ranger that works out of Piper Falls, Brad Morgan, secured this base for us as he's a part of the task force Maggie's forming. It's off the record, so anyone hunting for you will have a job to find out, but we're close enough for Brad or Station 28 to support us if we need it."

I can't believe we've done nothing more than hide right where they know I am. I scrunch up my face as I try to work out why.

"They'll be hunting for my car, which is now somewhere on i35, heading north." I blink.

"It's a decoy?" I guess out aloud, and he nods.

"Sure is."

"How long do we have to hide here?"

He sighs. "I don't know. I'd like to give you a rough idea of the plan, but you can't lie if they find us and try to make you talk, when you don't know." I pout, but I understand why he's not telling me. "Come on, let's get fed."

We head in, and I quickly freshen up before breakfast.

The rustic island is beautiful and long. I take the time to admire the cabin we're in. It's quite open plan, save the bathroom and bedroom. The huge fireplace sits against the back wall, angled up with bricks and stones to the ceiling. The kitchen island divides the living and eating area. The floor is warm, even though it's a dark wood. There's a sofa and two chairs facing the fire without a television in sight.

"Hope you like it," Reid says, placing a plate down on the island where there's a stool. On the plate, he's cooked hash-browns, bacon, eggs, mushrooms and toast. He puts a huge cup of something down in front of me.

"Thank you." I sit and wait for him to join me before I start eating.

"I may have forgotten how to make the tea," he says. "I wasn't told when to take the bag out." His lips are thin as he motions to the huge mug he's made my drink in.

"Is it still in the mug?" I ask, and he nods. I quickly lick my fork clean and fish out the bag, squeezing it against the side of the cup, and then stir it. I quickly take the tea bag to the compost bin, breaking open the bag and letting the tea drop into the bin, before binning the bag.

"It looks like the right colour." I grin as I come to sit back down.

"Why didn't you put the whole bag in?" he asks.

"Those tea bags are made with a composite material that likely contains plastic. Ye cannae compost them."

"Even ones made here in the States?" he questions, and I shrug.

"Dinnae ken aboot them, but that's what I do at Mum's. The bag goes into the bin. I usually have loose tea and use a diffuser at home, so I don't have that issue most of the time."

He nods in understanding, and we carry on eating.

I smile as I finish off the food. I swear I'm going to have gained a stone by the time I get to go home. "Thank you! Cooking for one is a pain," I admit. I never would have done this back home. I'd maybe have had a granola bar or made some slow-oats, but never this.

"It can be, I know."

"Let me clear up." I suddenly need to keep busy, this moment between us is giving me butterflies; my mouth is dry, and I swear there's something buzzing around me.

"Alysia…" Reid calls out as I take his plate, but I ignore him as I begin to fill up the sink. He turns the water off and grabs my hand. "What's going on?" I swallow, not able to tell him what he does to me. "Is this about last night? The gun?"

I focus on a speck of dirt on the beautiful counter; anything to not look at him. I can't even shake my head.

He sighs and takes my hands, both of them, and guides me back to the island. "Look, darlin', you're going to have to talk. I can't keep guessing what's going through that mind of yours."

"You guess? You…" I stop myself from spitting out that he runs warm and friendly one minute, then cold the next. *I don't get why he's bothered about what I think.*

"I…what?"

I shake my head. "Dissnae matter," I whisper.

"Oh, it does. I notice how you look at me. Darlin', as much as you entice me, I just can't. You're on my watch; I'm meant to keep you safe and stop the bad guys from gettin' to ya."

"So that's it? You remind yerself all that I've been through, so ye dinnae wanna touch me?" His arms drop to his sides, and I get up. "Sorry I disgust ye." I head to the bedroom and slide the door shut. The other boys in my life were never worth the breath it takes to cry. *So why am I crying over the American cop?* The same one who's just told me, I'm nothing more than a job.

Chapter Nine

♡ Reid ♡

As Alysia slides the bedroom door shut, I sigh. It takes me a moment to realise she's crying, and I feel like a dumbass for causing it. She's the perfect package; something I've known since I first saw her, but she *is* my responsibility, my duty. I can't indulge, can't cross that line. I repeat it to myself as I clear away breakfast, but I can't feel that statement echoing in my bones.

Standing at the kitchen sink and looking out towards the trees, I remember how she fell asleep in my lap last night, just sitting on the back porch. How she has done that every time I've held her. When I removed her jeans, I refrained from exploring her sleeping body. She was tired, and damned if I even sniffed at a woman without her consent. My momma would have my hide, and I was raised better than that. It was hard though not to wake her and ask with her scent filling the air.

Somewhere in the middle of the night, she turned to me and cuddled into me half-way through what I'm sure was a nightmare. Slowly, she's remembering details; important ones. I've already sent a message to Maggie, asking that her work colleagues be checked out and that footage from that Chicago hotel bar be obtained, though we've probably missed the window of opportunity there.

When I did hold her, she settled, which in turn, sent me to sleep too. I don't recall ever sleeping so soundly, or being so warm. Damned if the little kitten doesn't have some teeth too; her hissing at me about not wanting her shows they ain't killed her spark.

I wish I could take back what I'd said, but I can't. If it wasn't for her situation and my job, I'd want to show her a good time, take her out for sure! I also know, she'll have to go home. To Scotland. Away from me. My chest tightens up at that thought, and I wonder why. I haven't even kissed the girl…

And I know, in that moment, that I want to do a lot more than kiss her. She can't recollect when she lost her virginity; it was taken from her, and she'll never get it back. That was a first that was lost to her. But there's a first time for her to *consent*, for her to give permission, her first time with someone *she* wants. I kick myself for realising, perhaps too late, that she's fixin' for it to be me. Those looks last night in the car were testament to that desire, and it took all I had to not pull over and make out in the car.

I learned about Stockholm Syndrome in training, something that might well affect Alysia. It's not officially recognised as a disorder here in the USA, but we're made aware of it as a lot of it displays as PTSD. I'm not her captor; I'm not holding her against her will. *Or am I?* Less so perhaps than the assholes who took her from that hotel, drugged and raped her. I ain't as bad as them.

I realise I've finished washing the dishes as I set my mind on what I have to do next. Partly because of the training I've received, but also for my own foolish reasons. Drying my hands, I go to the bedroom and knock gently on the door.

"Alysia, can I come in?" I don't want to call her kitten, not this soon. The usual "darlin's" and "sweethearts" I've been raised to use are going to confuse the poor girl, so I need to avoid using them right now too.

I know I need to help her move forward with her life. I have no idea what plans she has, if she has any. I wait a moment more, then slide the door open. She's on the bed, hugging a pillow and still crying. I kick myself for hurting her like that.

"Alysia, sweetheart, please…" My voice catches. Darn, I failed at the first attempt. *How can she bring my defences down so easily?*

"Please, what?" She sniffs, and I go and fetch a box of tissues before sitting on the bed again.

"Please, don't cry. I'm sorry it hurt, but, darlin', I can't take–"

"You dinnae wanna, it's okay."

"I don't want to what?" I check in, thankful I got a crash course in Scots from Abi, though half of what she says is lost on me, even now.

"Disnae matter."

I sigh. "It does. I don't need to remind ya that you've been hurt."

"Aye, I *do* remember being told that."

I pause for a moment, picking my words carefully. "You're remembering a lot more as the days go by. You didn't recall the evening in Chicago until you saw the gun." She sniffs and wipes her nose. "And you'll hopefully remember a lot more as the days go on. I don't want–" She turns to me.

"What don't I want? Ye gonna tell me what I want now too?"

I move back a little; I wasn't expecting this! "What *I* want, is for your memories not to be tainted or mixed up by anyone or anything else; especially me."

She blinks, like someone who is just waking up after being asleep.

"I think I'm pretty good at keeping those monsters apart."

"Yeah, I'm just your big ol' teddy bear," I state, before I realise what I've said to her. She smirks and tries to hide her grin, which makes my comment worth it.

"Nae teddy bear of mine was like you." She's still smirking, which is a good thing.

"Honestly, Alysia, darlin', I was raised to respect women." She goes to speak, but I hold up my hand. "Let me finish, darlin'. You've been through absolute hell, and you've come through the other side. Give yourself the time to heal and sort out your own mind, okay?" She nods, and I smile at her. "Good girl." I push the box of tissues her way then leave her to it. I need some air.

About half an hour later, I can hear movement inside the cabin, so I know she's up and about. Her getting her head sorted, understanding that those assholes are very different from me, is important and key. I turn and grin at her as she comes out. It's a warm day—well, warm for me, but Alysia is still wrapped up in that hoodie.

"I'm sorry," she mumbles as she sits down on the rocker next to me on the back porch. She looks out towards where I told her Piper Falls was.

"What are y'all sorry for?" I ask, and she shrugs.

"Makin' assumptions."

I lean over to her. "I see ya lookin', and it don't bother me none."

"Why doesn't it?"

I smile back. "Because of who is doin' the lookin'."

That makes her sit back, and her mouth drops open ever so slightly. If she wants to look, I'm happy to let her; it'll help take her mind off the situation she's been through. It takes her a long moment before she smiles softly at me. "I can keep lookin'?"

I nod slowly. "You sure can."

"Ditto," she says, rising and struts her way back into the cabin. As the door closes, I look up at the sky, asking for strength. These weeks are going to be long.

Later that night, after we've eaten and cleared things away, the fire is roaring, a scented candle is lit and the two small lamps are on; until they're not. Alysia jumps as they go out.

"What happened?"

I grin. "Probably lack of power in the batteries for the lights, or there's a timer." It's about ten pm, so it ain't that late. The sun went down a little while ago.

"Oh. So, it's bed time?"

I grin. "It can be."

She nods and puts the bookmark into the book that she's been reading. Somewhere along the line, someone dumped a lot of romance books into this Ranger cabin. There are two shelves of series that just makes me think of late-night shows from authors I've never heard of. I took a look earlier when she picked one out. Books about werewolves, shifters, rock stars, the mafia, billionaires, age gaps…everything that could be romantisised, is probably on those shelves.

"Have you thought about writing down your thoughts about what happened?" I ask as she tidies our things away. There are various notebooks and stationery around that she can make use of.

"Naw. Dae I really need to?"

I rise and bank the fire for the night.

"It might help sort your head out, let you process things." I know this sounds lame, but she needs the time to get things figured out.

She sighs and nods, as if relenting on my idea. "I'll see how I feel aboot it tomorrow."

"Yeah, we'll see. I'll go check around the area, then lock up."

She nods and smiles, then heads off to the bathroom. I avoid smacking her ass then grin as I hear her begin to run the water, then it shuts off. Taking my gun, I head outside and check the perimeter. The traps and layout I set haven't been disturbed, which makes me feel better. Another thought occurs to me, and I make a note to ask Alysia about it tomorrow. When I think she's in bed, I head in, bolting the doors and securing the place for the night.

Alysia is, indeed, in bed, but she's not asleep. It would be too much to ask for that, but I did hope. I did admit about being her teddy bear earlier; that she trusts me just to hold her, *has* to be enough for now. That I want to do more is on me, and something I just have to control.

With a grin, I undress down to my boxers, then climb into bed.

"Wanna cuddle?" I ask, and she nods, then scoots over and cuddles into me. For a long moment, I hold her, letting her settle on me. "I wanted to ask you something," I begin, and she lifts her head. It's hard to miss the swell of her soft breast touching me, but I try to focus on her eyes, her face. That cute nose she has or those lips…I grin as she lifts her eyebrows at me.

"Ye likin' what yer seein', pal?" It takes me a moment to understand what she said to me, and I can't help but snigger when I do.

"Sure do! But, my idea…"

"Hmm?" I need to make this fast, she's nearly asleep.

"I want to teach you some self-defence, is that okay?"

She yawns and nods against my chest. "Aye, sounds like a good idea. We can start the 'morrow."

By the time I think to look at her for an explanation of what she said, she's asleep. I reach up and turn off the light, plunging the room into darkness and me into sleep.

"No!" Alysia's scream pulls me from my slumber, and in seconds, I'm awake, looking for the threat. But, it's in her head. Her ordeal is making her relive moments, and it hurts me that she's so scared. She's a typical Scot though; she ain't backing down.

"I said no!" She falls to the ground and from her actions, she's struggling with someone. I could go to her, but she'd end up fighting me and confusing me with them; I need her head clear on who. But she *can* help me. In seconds, I am on the floor with her, not touching her but within reach.

"Tell me who, Alysia, describe him to me, kitten."

"He's got dark hair, stinky breath and crooked teeth with beady dark eyes."

"Good girl. Tell me more."

"Tattoos…he's got a few, but I can't make them out. It's dark, he made me swallow something, and I feel sleepy now."

"It's okay, kitten, you'll be safe soon."

She stops fighting him, turns and curls up into a ball, and I rein in my anger so I can pick her up as gently as I can. I realise, she's physically reacted to that threat, and I take her to the bathroom. Damn, now I need to wake her up.

"Alysia, honey, I need you to wake up." When she doesn't react, I say it again, a little more forcefully. She stirs, and I hold her up as she comes to.

"What happened?" she asks as she tries to leave.

"You had a nightmare, a memory recall. But, you need to wash yourself, darlin'." It takes her a moment to realise that her lower half is all wet.

"Oh, bleedin' nora!" She shucks everything off as I turn my back to turn on the shower. Grabbing her stuff, I throw it into the machine that's on site. I'll work out tomorrow how it works, then I find her clean pyjamas. Letting her dress, I clean the floor, then we head back to bed.

It's late the following morning when we awake. The sun must've been up for a while, the room is warm. I grin as she squirms in my arms.

"Good mornin', darlin'! How did you sleep when you finally got back to sleep?"

She yawns and stretches, trying to come to life. "Think I did okay. I was glad I had my teddy bear." I smirk at her remark. "I'm sorry I…err…"

I shrug. "It happens. You'd have stayed there, I think, if I hadn't tried to bring you back to bed."

"Cheers, Reid." Her voice is soft, loving.

I wait until her eyes reach mine before I gently tell her she's welcome.

Chapter Ten

♡ Alysia ♡

I sigh as I once again pick myself up from the woodland floor. When Reid said he'd teach me some self-defence, I didn't think he would be brutal in its execution. What's not helping is that I relived a night that I can't fully recall, but Reid got me to describe the attacker, someone who drugged me and clearly had his way with me. When Reid woke me, it quickly became apparent why he had, and I needed to shower. I don't recall having wet myself since I was two.

Now, Reid's trying to teach me to *"drop and roll"* away from any assailant that might capture me while we're together. A technique I'm not very good at, even by my admission.

"Let's try again, darlin', you're gettin' there!"

I humph in response, being intentionally sassy, and he goes to grab me again, my frustration getting the better of me. On instinct, I drop and roll away, bringing myself to my feet as he instructed.

"So all I had to do was annoy the hell outta ya?" He grins and then chuckles. I blink and realise, I did it.

"I did it!" My voice is high and bouncy, making him laugh more.

"Ya sure did, darlin'! How about we get some lunch? It's way past time for that."

I grin and dance away as he tries to grab me. With my voice sounding out in laughter, we head in and wash up.

After lunch, Reid hands me a pen and a blank notebook. I have so many pretty notebooks like this at home, but I never write in them. I love the plain pages so much that I can't bring myself to ruin them with the mess that lives in my head.

"You need to sort your head out, sweetheart," he instructs as he gets comfortable in a chair, picking up a book that isn't a romance novel.

"What can I write in this?" As I look at him, I can feel my eyes widen, and my breath becomes shallow.

"Lots of things come to mind. What you remember. How they made you feel. How you feel now. What are your goals? What do you want to achieve?"

"That's a lot of questions," I begin, finding that I can breathe a little better now, and he nods.

"True, but they're answers you need to start formulating. As much fun as it is to be holed up here with ya," I feel my cheeks go red as he smirks, "At some point, life will take over again. You had ambitions and dreams before, didn't ya? What were they? Have they changed after what's gone down?"

I blink, and Reid offers me a hug. "I know, darlin', you hadn't thought about it. I get it. But you've got the time while we're here to decide, to make a plan. How ya get there can change; getting to them is something I want ya to do. But, you need to set your destination."

I turn and smile at him, feeling tiny sitting so close to him. "Experience is a memory, darlin', and you control that memory going forward. This will help." I focus on his words with my ears, but the sound vanishes the more I focus on his lips. Without thinking, I lean in and press my lips to his, climbing into his lap. For a moment, he freezes, and then our tongues are dancing. He tastes of what we ate for lunch, of the coffee he made on the French Press. I swallow his groans, and then his hands are in my hair, holding me as he wants. After long moments of sheer bliss just from a kiss, he pulls back and rests his forehead against mine. Our breathing is ragged, shallow.

"Darlin', I sure will go to Hell for that."

"Least it'll be warm!" My retort comes out unbidden, something my Nana says, and it makes him laugh, which makes me grin too.

"Yeah, and you'll have to be there too."

I grin back. "Wi' bells on," I concur.

"Now, go on. Let's get your ambitions set, darlin'." As I move away, he shakes his head, but he doesn't hide his smile.

The following day, we go through yet more self-defence after a healthy breakfast. Not just dropping and rolling, which I think I'm getting better at, Reid teaches me hand signals; cues that only we know, as well as how to get out of a neck lock.

"Good girl! Again," he commands as he again makes a grab for me. I tuck, turn and twist my way out of his hold. We go through this until it's almost second nature to me.

"How do you know all this?" I ask when we take a water break, and he grins.

"My brother and I used to try and beat each other up. One of us would torment the other and that often ended in punches. Mom decided we would be better off if we knew how to beat each other up, but in truth, she thought it was a way to focus our energy. If we learned how to hurt each other, we'd stop. Add in the sports, baseball and football and music."

I grin, knowing football isn't the same game in both countries.

My grinning makes him laugh. "I know what y'all thinkin'; I mean American football, not soccer." My mouth doesn't say what I'm thinking, which is that he's talking a lot of nonsense, but I realise in a heartbeat, my face is. "Hey, soccer ain't football." I can feel my eyebrows rise.

"American football isn't football. You can catch the ball in that sport, so that's basically rugby wi' paddin' on."

He laughs so hard, he has tears running down his face. "Man, you and Abi have the same take on the game! I just hope you like baseball as much as she does."

"Rounders," I mutter, calling baseball for what it is. To me, anyway. That just makes him laugh a whole lot more, and I have to join in.

"Come on, kitten, let's get you some more claws." And with that, we're back at the training. From being choked from behind, the side, Reid shows me how to get out of it, how someone as small as me can break a man's leg. Not by sheer force, but by forcing it to an angle that cannot support their and my weight. It's all rather empowering.

♡ ♡ ♡

When we take another water break, I ask him to continue his story about his brother and their antics growing up. Antics I somehow missed with my family. His face lights up when he speaks of his brother and parents. It's strange to see.

"Oh, yeah… So, my brother Jon and I got signed up for Brazilian Jiu-Jitsu. When it didn't work, Mom and Dad made sure we were too tired to do much to each other when we got home, beyond eat, do our homework in our rooms, practice our instruments and go to bed. For a while, it worked, until puberty hit us both, and then we realised, our fitness attracted girls. In his case, it worked, he's married to his high school sweetheart. He's in the same year as Nick, which is how I heard his stories."

"Oh, aye?" I'm intrigued, but Reid shakes his head.

"You can ask him if y'all wanna know."

I shake my head quickly. *I'm nosy, aye, but not that nosy!*

Reid smirks. "Anyway, I found girls to be rather bothersome, too much effort. I asked one girl to the prom, Lyndsey Trainer was her name. She moved away a good few years back. Don't think she's even in Texas anymore."

I sit back and let him continue. He has a strange, soft look on his face.

"I asked her to the prom, but I couldn't kiss the girl. She didn't realise I heard her talkin' shit about someone that night, and it didn't sit right that I'd want to kiss the mouth that spat out such vomit." I'm sure my eyebrows are now in my hairline. "Yeah, she got miffed and started making rumours. Then the other girls who were with her tried addin' to it, and others who didn't like them started bitchin' back. Somehow, it was all my fault, but I didn't pay either group a mind."

"Sounds like they were proper wee scroats," I comment, which makes him laugh.

"I ain't quite sure what scroats are, darlin', but…oh, what's the word Abi would use? Bawbags?"

I laugh, spitting out water like a fountain. I forget to turn away and shower him with a mouthful of water.

"Oh, so that's how it is, huh?" He grabs me and tickles me, making me squeal loudly. As we wrestle, what he's taught me comes into play, and I escape out of the hold and run into the woods.

I hear a branch snap, my name being called, so I turn, expecting to see Reid. It's not him. My nightmare just came true.

"Oh, shite," I spit out the curse as I look at that evil incarnate grin. Those eyes; I can't forget those eyes. Not now. I back away then I slam into something: a tree.

"You got clever, doubling back on us."

"Us?" My nightmare is missing a front tooth, but it doesn't look like a recent loss. I wonder if he's heard of bridges. His beady eyes don't leave me and then rake over me. His tongue licking his lips makes my stomach coil. His lips turn upwards into what I'm sure he thinks is a smile. But, it's not.

"Yeah, us, darlin'." He reaches behind him, pulling out a gun. Then he motions for me to move. With the threat of the gun, I do as I'm told. It's about the only time I ever do.

I'm guided back to the cabin, but I can't see Reid. *Did he follow me? Is he hurt?* So many questions run around in my head that I don't realise I'm being spoken to right away.

"I said, hold it right there, missy." I stop and suck in a huge breath as I roll my eyes and grit my teeth. For the first time in my life, I pray that I get through this. "Ah, there y'all are."

I get grabbed and turned before I can stop it and then I'm staring straight into Reid's face. It's emotionless, set. He holds his own gun up and puts it very carefully on the ground. Then he kicks it away from him, but thankfully not towards us.

As he taught me, I see the signal to just wait. So I do. The arm around my throat isn't squeezing, but I have my hands on it so that I can do what Reid taught me. When he tells me to.

"Ain't you a good boy." The ugly excuse of a man behind me is a patronising twat; I can't wait for Reid to give the signal so I can break this guy's leg. I just hope I'm quick enough to do it before he can pull that trigger.

Reid doesn't say a thing. I want him to, then I see his hand. The signals. Two. He's waiting for something; but what?

"Cat got your tongue? Or did the little lady here do that for ya?" I get tugged and fight back, but he's doing nothing more than trying to goad Reid. I can see Reid's jaw twitching, the muscles tense, the veins in his arms. One. His hand moved. One.

"She's a hell cat in bed, ain't she? Bet she's better when she's awake."

"Freeze!" I hear a woman's voice call out that magical word as Reid gives me the signal to drop and roll. So I do what he taught me, leaning back over this ejit's leg so he's off balance, right before I drop my entire weight onto his knee. He can't hold me and hold himself up. The twig snapping in the woods earlier sounded a lot more hollow than the sound he just made as I landed on him. As his arm loosens, I roll and suddenly, there are several people around with guns, all pointing at my nightmare. Voices shout for him to freeze, to not do something, then there's a loud noise, two or three echoes like a car backfiring that make me jump. Birds fly upward, squawking in their hundreds, before silence hits us all.

I begin crawling to Reid, my vision becoming blurry as I do so. I don't want him hurt, not because of me. I can't breathe, praying that he's okay, and for a moment, I feel empty. Then, there are huge arms around me, lifting me. Familiar arms. My teddy bear's arms. He's safe!

"Yer alive!" I cry out, grabbing onto him and burying my face into his chest. He only holds me with one hand, and as my vision clears, I see why. The other is holding a gun; and my nightmare is no more.

I find myself stuck back inside my head as police and Federal Agents clear up the mess. It turns out that two men were stalking us, not just the one from my nightmares, but his accomplice. I dread to think about what they did to me. I'm grateful and angry that I cannot remember.

One is handcuffed, and I note his scruffy dirty hair. The ugly, dark-haired one has a sheet laid over him. I'm glad, as it means I won't have to look at his revolting face again. But I have to be sure. As everyone mills about, checking this, doing that, I sneak away to the corpse outside. Just as I'm about to pull the sheet back, I get stopped. The lady Federal officer is there.

"You don't wanna see that."

"I need to be sure."

"He's dead, sweetheart."

I look at her and stand to face her. I know she's trained, she can probably snap me like a twig, but I need to see. "Then I can look, prove it." I tilt my head slightly. "I. Need. To. See." I punctuate each word. Her stern face softens, and the crow's feet become more pronounced as she genuinely smiles. She's been a stoic son of a gun since she turned up hours ago. No one disobeyed an instruction she gave them.

She lifts the sheet back and lets me look at the face that's haunted me. I want to kick him, injure him now he's dead and see how he likes being abused when he can't stop it. But, he's not "in" that shell anymore. With that random, sobering thought, any thought of anger against him vanishes. But, I'm still annoyed.

"So it's over?" I ask, taking a step back and letting her put the sheet over him once more.

"Still got some loose ends to tie up, but yeah, pretty much."

I nod. "I'm sorry, I dinnae ken who ye are." I extend my hand. "Ye *know* me, Alysia Davidson."

The woman grins at me. "Maggie Forrester, FBI."

It's dark by the time the body is removed and everyone leaves. By the time the Texas Ranger bails, it's dark, and he leaves Reid and me, finally. As I watch the rear lights disappear, I finally feel that I can breathe.

I jump when I hear the bolts of the door snap into place. I can only watch as Reid stomps to the back patio doors and secures them, locking them from the inside.

Then he comes and crouches before me. I can't tell if he's angry at me or because of me.

"I'm sorry, I shouldn't have…" I blurt out, but his rough finger over my lips silences me.

"I started to come after ya, but the one that got handcuffed, he and I tussled, and I shook him off, knocking him out. They were on us as soon as you bolted to the woods."

"I didnae see them."

"Neither did I, darlin'. You," he lifts my face to meet his, his finger under my chin firm but not forceful, "I have never been so scared in all my life."

I can feel my brow furrow. "What?" I ask, right before he kisses me senseless. He pulls me onto his lap and then sits down forcibly on the sofa, so that I now straddle him. We don't stop kissing. My breathing becomes ragged, and I need him as much as I need to breathe. More. His hands cup my head, pushing my hair away from my face and slowly, he pulls back.

"You scared me. I've never been scared like that before."

"I'm sorry. I thought *you* were chasing me."

His hand moves quickly from my head to my arse, and he slaps me once. Hard.

"That's for disobeying what I told ya days ago. Stay near the cabin."

I'm glad I have jeans on; that smack would have stung. "I'm sorry."

His jaw twitches, and he looks like he wants to say something; I'm not sure what. But, nothing comes out. I can see emotions in his eyes that I can't decipher, and it makes my breath hitch. I reach up and brush back some of his hair. It has some length to it and looks good.

"Reid?" My voice is shaky, unsure. That's not hard, we had the living daylights scared out of each other since we got up.

He doesn't verbally answer me; he just puts his forehead against mine and closes his eyes. I wait. His arms are around me, holding me, and I adjust how I'm straddling his lap. I can feel his bulge beneath me, and suddenly, that's what I want. I want him.

I grind into him, which makes him kind of growl. I do it again, and it makes him open his eyes. His mouth falls open, and I take the chance, not just by pressing my lips to his, my tongue reaches for his. I want to know what it feels like to be loved, properly. With someone I choose.

Without a word, his hand traces up the inside of my leg, and he breaks the kiss.

"Alysia, darlin', if you want me to stop, now is the time to tell me. I can live with blue balls…" His voice is croaky, barely there. It takes all I have to fuse my mouth to his once more. Words have left me, but my actions speak louder than anything I've ever said.

I shriek as I'm suddenly lifted into the air, and I wrap my legs around Reid's waist so I don't fall. Not that I think he'd let me. Still kissing, he walks us to the bedroom and slides the door shut. The kissing stops, but only for a moment as he sets me down. My top is removed, and Reid has a devilish smirk on his face.

I begin to reply, but his hot kisses on my neck, the caresses on my arms and back make me forget to do anything useful, other than breathing. My bra comes off, and there's a groan from Reid.

"You're perfect, darlin'," he whispers, right before he licks, nips, sucks one breast while tweaking the other. My breasts are the one thing most people notice about me; they're also the one thing I try to hide, but with Reid, the way he's making me feel, I'm almost pushing them into his face. *And he's liking it!*

He guides me down and grins as he takes off his own top. I've seen him half naked before, when he's been outside or in the shower, even at night when we've slept, but to be this close and personal? I can't help but respond by arching up into him. I love the natural colour of his skin. Mine is still Highland white, but his? It's more noticeable when he takes his jeans and pants off.

"Easy, darlin'," he says as he comes back to me after stripping. *Dear God, is that going to fit inside me?* It's not the length that bothers me. But he's as thick as my wrist. I glance up, and his mouth captures mine, making me forget about the size of him. Reid's hands tease me as they explore. For a huge man, he has a delicate touch, and I can only bite my lip to keep me from moaning. His mouth kisses my stomach as my jean shorts and knickers are removed, making me bare for him. Suddenly, I don't want to be.

"Reid?" I ask, and he stops, crawling back up me.

"Do you want me to stop?" he questions, and I draw in a breath. Without an answer from me, he wraps me up in his arms and pulls me to him. "I ain't gonna force ya, darlin'."

"It's just…"

"First real time, I know." He kisses me before just holding me. This is the first time we've been very naked with each other. Usually, I've worn something. So has he. *Now?* He doesn't get angry at me, but he simply holds me. I run my fingers over his pecs and chest, enjoying the feel of him.

"We'll go as slow as you need, darlin'."

"Cheers. I…got scared." I'm not sure what it was; one moment I wanted him, then the thought of it was like a bucket of ice water over me.

"Why?"

I swallow, not wanting to meet his intense gaze.

"It doesn't matter, darlin'. You can touch anywhere on me. And I wanna make you feel good, if you'll let me."

I nod, wanting that, trying to be brave for a moment. He lifts my head up and kisses me, softly at first, before making me forget to breathe. As he kisses, the caresses start up, his hands softly touch my skin in featherlike motions as his mouth tenderly possesses mine.

I can feel his fingers teasing my entrance, and on instinct alone, I open my legs, giving him easier access. His kisses move from my mouth to my neck, and while he has control, I know he'd stop if I asked him to. But the fire he's stoking, the ripples my body wants to unleash, the aching I now feel, spur me on. The finger becomes two, and the friction builds. I've never experienced this. *I never knew anyone could make me react this way. Why didn't I want to do this with any of the boys I'd kissed before?* When Reid turns his hands and his fingers hit that magical spot, I explode, arching into him with cries of sheer pleasure; every single boy before now is blown away in the aftermath.

Chapter Eleven

♡ Reid ♡

Watching her explode on just my fingers, makes me grin. I capture her mouth as she comes back to earth, distracting her from what my fingers are up to. With kisses hotter than the Texan summer, I can feel myself poke her in the side. I ain't gonna force her, but making her feel good is something I *can* do.

She writhes beneath me yet again as she arches back, her eyes rolling closed.

"God, that's a beautiful sight!"

Her cheeks go pink, but I don't care. She's amazing, and I roll over her, pinning her beneath me. I kiss her, then move down her neck, kissing, nibbling and sucking as I go. Her skin ripples with goosebumps as my mouth leaves traces. Down her ribs, flat stomach, that beautiful, dark copper mound of hair between her legs.

I don't speak; I'm not sure if she wants to hear the dirty words I have on the tip of my tongue, how utterly fucking gorgeous she is. My tongue glides over her folds, and she pulses, pulling away one moment before relaxing and opening for me. She's so damn responsive; she's beyond any teenage wet dream I've ever had.

I don't need to watch her expression. I want to see her writhe and buck, and I lick her, watching, tasting, devouring. I hear her beg, and her hands are in my hair, pulling.

"Oh, God!"

I grin in response and double my efforts, adding in the nibbling and flicking of my tongue over her sensitive little clit and deep within her already wet folds. As she bucks against me, she traps my head between her legs, but not for long. I lick up the honey she's produced, and as her hands go loose in my hair, I take the chance to slide on a condom.

"Alysia, darlin'." I kiss my way back up to her mouth, and she tries to pull back from tasting herself. Well, that's just tough. I kiss her deeply, positioning myself over her, and I check in with her one more time.

"Don't stop," she breathes, pulling me in for a kiss, and for once, I do as I'm told. My tip is already at her entrance, and I slide myself into her deep, warm, wet little pussy. The one that was made just for me.

"Wrap your legs around me darlin'." My command does the trick and hell, she feels amazing as I slowly pull back and thrust home. "Good girl," I growl, which makes her pulse around me.

She likes the praise, huh? Good.

"Such a good girl," I growl into her ear as I pick up my pace. Her breathing is getting more ragged, she's almost panting. She's tiny laying here beneath me, but I find her mouth and kiss her. "You can come," I tell her, not expecting her to do just that, but she does, bucking against me, and her head tips to the side as a groan escapes her mouth. Hell, another one of those and I'm done for. My hips have a mind of their own, and they work her through her orgasm. I thrust deeper and harder, my V hitting her clit every time, and as she cries out again, it triggers my own climax, and together, we both fall off the edge.

I lay on her, being as careful as I can to not squish her, but I am not leaving her. I kiss and nibble her face, jaw, ear and finally, her mouth finds mine. I consume her with the intensity I already feel. I had no idea sex would be this good with someone; until her.

She kisses me back, and I run my hands into her hair.

"That…was…amazing, darlin'!" Our tongues dance, and I can feel the tension just leave her body. I turn us over so she's lying on me. It feels amazing just holding her like this, even if I'm no longer buried in her. It's never something I've enjoyed before, and something I realise, I'm gonna miss for sure.

When we awake, it's dark, but I don't care. We can leave in the morning. She's cuddled into me, and somehow, there's the comforter over us, keeping us snug. I already know that I don't want her to go back to Scotland, but I also know she can't stay. Not yet. I close my eyes and contemplate a lot of things; things I've never before considered.

I must've drifted back off while I was thinking and holding her. When I wake up, she's darting out the door, and I can hear her in the bathroom, which makes me grin. My phone says it's nearly four am, so I wait until she comes back before I copy. When I come back to bed, she's there, huddled up.

"Come here, darlin'." I reach across for her, and she snuggles into me, letting me kiss her a few times on the forehead. "Are you okay? You're not sore?"

"Nuh-uh, naw, I'm good." She yawns then sighs so very softly, and I let her fall asleep on me. I'll bet she hasn't a clue I've fallen hard for her.

It's light when we finally wake up. I'm stunned that it's nearly nine am and that I am alone, in bed. I listen and can hear the shower running. With a smile, I fling on some joggers and head out to make the tea and coffee. She might not be a coffee fan, but tea? Yeah, that girl can drink serious amounts of it.

"Aww, good mornin'!" she coos as I hand her the tea. Strong, a little milk, no sugar. Girl is simple in her wants, and suddenly, I want to make her tea like this every damn day that I can.

"Hey, darlin'." I hold her gaze, and she steps up on her tip-toes to kiss my cheek.

"Cheers," she whispers, before sipping her tea. She's properly dressed in light jeans and a tee with some words on it that I cannot make out.

"Is it drinkin' time?" I ask, which makes her laugh.

"Naw! I'm just saying thank you." She smiles at me between sips and damn, she has dimples! What the hell...if I hadn't already fallen for her before, I might have now. Only now I'm a level deeper.

"Oh, is that what that means?" I grin at her, and I love the wink she gives me back. I sip my coffee and just take her and this time we have remaining in. Maggie hinted there would be some clear-up after yesterday's events, so I know I need to get into town. But, first I need a shower.

◯ ◯ ◯

An hour later, we're back at my apartment at the edge of town. Alysia had stripped the bed and grabbed the towels we'd used at the cabin, but we brought it back here to launder. She thought I had a machine here at the apartment, but I don't.

"So ye use a launderette?" she asks as we take the other bags upstairs.

"Yes, ma'am." My reply makes her go pink, and I know Abi hates anyone calling her that, though she hides her discomfort a lot better these days. Or she just accepts it. Alysia purses her lips, as if to stop herself from making a comment. "I know, y'all ain't the queen. But, it's just—"

"How ye speak. Aye, I ken! Disnae mean I am gonna get used to it."

I stride over to her, more to see if she'll give me any more sass, and she backs away, hits the arm of the sofa and falls over it. I lean over her, trying hard not to laugh at her. What she just did was damn cute—and damn enticing.

"Y'all need to find a way, while you're here, okay?"

"Take me," she says. Then she goes bright red and puts her hands over her face. "Oh God, I dinnae mean to say that! I meant make me."

I laugh, unable to keep it in any longer. "One is just as bad as the other, darlin'." The groan I get makes me laugh harder, and I love how flustered she gets when she's embarrassed; it's so damn cute.

"Come on, let's chill out."

"We need to go and get these washed." She motions to the pile of laundry that she's bought back from the Ranger's cabin.

"We can go do that." I stand up and haul her up with me, intentionally slamming her small body into mine. She lets out an "oomph" as she hits me, and I wrap my hands in her hair and pull her to me, kissing her deeply. It's bliss.

I drop her off at the launderette before I head into the station. Given that the threat to her has been taken care of, I have no issues leaving her side. That is until I catch up with Maggie, who is in Preston's office. I'm told I'm allowed to disturb them; both look mighty pissed off.

"Something I need to know?" I ask quietly, taking the seat where Preston motions for me to sit. He raises his eyes at Maggie and waits.

"One of my colleagues has gone AWOL. There's a warrant out for his arrest."

I turn to her and wonder which dumb-ass has picked to go up against Maggie. My eyebrows are raised as I wait for her to give me a name.

"Grant Esse."

I blink a few times, knowing he was her partner, despite his unfortunate name. "And he's not chasing something down on this?"

Maggie shakes her head. "Nope. He failed to turn up for the capture of those two. One, as you know, was shot. The one we arrested was found dead this morning, in his cell. CCTV has been tampered with."

I sit there, stunned by her revelation. "That means Alysia's still in danger."

"We ain't sure where he is," Maggie begins, nodding in agreement with me. "Not officially. But I have him on CCTV heading out of the country from Austin on a private jet bound for Europe. Looks like he was smuggled out, but they hadn't altered the CCTV."

"So either he wants you to know he's not in the country, or someone else wants you to know."

"Pretty much. The British Consulate in Washington says they'll be here in about five days to talk with Alysia to get her home, after we've dealt with this latest revelation."

I sigh and hope I school my thoughts about her wanting to go home. Preston catches my eye, but I play along. "She'll be glad to get back to family. What about anything personal she had when she got here? And what revelation?"

Maggie shakes her head. "Coming to that. As for her belongings, there's no chance of finding any of it. That includes mobile phone, cards or clothes. They'll likely have been sold on or destroyed."

"Some of the local women have helped her out with clothes."

Maggie smiles kindly at me. "That's good to know. I've unofficially spoken with a contact at Interpol," she looks at Preston, "Which is one of the revelations we were discussing when you arrived." I nod but keep quiet; their faces tell me it ain't good. "He's got Esse down as a person of interest and is going to keep an eye. I've got Internal Affairs going through Esse's files, but he knew we'd come for him. There is one other thing…" Maggie turns to me, and I don't like the heavy tone her voice has taken.

"Oh?"

Maggie looks at Preston again, then back at me. "This was found in Esse's files."

I take the piece of paper and look over it. It shows that Alysia is married; to someone whose name I don't recognise. I blink at it. We knew that though. *What the actual hell?*

"We're pretty sure she was not awake for the ceremony, or if she was, she was too drugged to remember. It might not even have been her that was there, but it's her name. We're not sure, we're checking out CCTV from the venue in Chicago. The Justice of the Peace who is here will annul this. I'm sure you know him, James Arnold Montgomery. I presented the case to him earlier today, and he agrees, it's forged and she didn't consent. We know that's not her signature from the statements you've had her sign."

I nod slightly, but I can feel my jaw is now sore. I'd love to kill the guy right here and now. My anger makes me make a solemn promise to God: *if I can, I will.*

"You have an appointment with him at fifteen-hundred tomorrow, with Alysia to get that annulled."

I nod in understanding, then the meeting concludes a few minutes later, Maggie taking her leave and touching me lightly on the shoulder as she departs.

"You can swear," Preston says, leaning back in his chair. "I was in the middle of a string of words that would make a whore blush when you walked in."

I stand and try to control my breathing, but it ain't working. "FUCK!" The word bursts forth with a force, and I somehow manage to not put my fist through a wall. Preston sits back and lets me spew out far more "fucks" for a good few minutes. With a heavy sigh, I pull in a huge breath.

"The gym's free," he advises. I nod, but I can't focus. "Go and talk to her." My head snaps up, and there's a kind smile on Preston's face. "I can tell ya taken by her, I get that. Enjoy the time together. For the record, with Esse being MIA and under suspicion, she still needs the protection until she returns home, and Maggie's working on after that too. This investigation is still on-going, ya hear?" I nod, understanding. I'm still on duty, but I am more invested now than I ever have been before. I'm just glad Preston understands.

As I leave Preston's office, my phone pings, and a message from Maggie appears.

> **MF:** *I can tell you're invested in keeping her safe. I'm going to need your passport. I'm in the Cozy Bean right now.*
> **Me:** *I'll be a while. Need to talk with Alysia.*
> **MF:** *I'll be around today, staying at the Blissview Inn.*
> **Me:** *Good to know. I'll drop by with it later.*
> **MF:** *Please do. I plan to leave very early tomorrow.*

I pocket the phone and head to the launderette. It has recovered since the machine fire late last year; electrics are a pain in the ass at times, and I'm glad I don't have to deal with them most of the time. I find Alysia sitting in a chair, reading another book. I ain't sure where she found it. It takes her a moment to realise it's me, and the smile she gives me makes my heart leap. Even if she hasn't a clue that I'm about to drop a bomb on her.

"Hey."

She tilts her head, puts her bookmark into the pages and closes the book. I haven't seen anyone use a bookmark so much in a long time.

"What's wrong?" Her voice is soft and her touch electric. I wasn't expecting it, and it makes me jump. And I ain't comfortable that she can read me like a book. "What's happened?" She turns to me, her eyes staring at me intensely. I look around, and apart from the attendant, we're the only ones here. Thank God.

"I had an update from Maggie." Alysia nods. "The one we arrested yesterday has passed away." I watch as her eyes go wide, and her mouth drops open for a second before she covers her mouth. "And Maggie found this."

I hand the marriage certificate over, and Alysia looks at it, then at me, then back at it again, like a game of tennis. "Is this for quacking real?" She looks at me and shakes her head. I love that she won't swear outright, and I wonder what other wonderful words she'll come up with. "Reid, I swear, I didn't consent. I don't recall a darn thing aboot it!" Her voice is rising, and I pull her to me, closing my eyes as I do.

"It's fake, we know. We have an appointment to meet with the Justice of the Peace tomorrow and get that undone, okay?" I try to use my calmest voice with her.

She nods, and I let her go. She jumps up and starts pacing. Then she rounds on me, her nostrils flare and her accent goes very incoherent. "I need to punch something! Anything! That's just cow's dung."

"We can head to the station and let you rip into a punch bag."

She nods. "Aye, please, afore I make a hole in the wa'." I understand her perfectly, but I know that these walls are brick, so that would not be fun to watch.

"Daisy, can you keep an eye on our stuff, please?" I look towards the launderette attendant, an older lady about my momma's age. Daisy just nods and smiles, then waves us off. Grabbing Alysia's hand, I walk her to the park, and finding a quiet corner, I tell her to let it out, to scream. She does, and that attracts someone that I didn't know was around. Buster. Wherever that dog is, either of its keepers are around.

"Oh, it's yerselves! What's happened?" Abi hugs Alysia as she bursts into tears. I grab the document from her hand before she scrunches it up any more and hand it to Nick.

"That's a load of baloney!" He hands it to Abi, and as Alysia pulls away from Abi, I pull her to me. Her arms wrap around me, hard.

"Well, that's a pile of utter fucking shite! How the hell can we get that undone?"

Abi hands me the document back, and I huff. Abi's ready to do whatever it takes for her new friend. Just as well I'm a step or two ahead.

"Alysia has a meeting with a Justice of the Peace tomorrow afternoon. Feds have already given him the case files."

"Well, if it's in hand, that's good." Abi smiles softly at Alysia, who smiles back. "It'll get sorted." Buster whines, and Abi fusses his ears, looking at her dog. "Aye, okay, pal!" Then she turns to us, offering a gentle smile for Alysia. "Listen, yer both welcome to come by tonight, catch up, get grounded, have some beers, aye?"

Alysia looks up at me and nods very discreetly. Okay, she'd like to have more than my company, which I think I can understand. In agreement, we arrange for later in the evening, then Abi and Nick head off, taking Buster with them.

Once they're out of sight, Alysia sighs heavily and sits on the bench. Then she leans forward and puts her head into her hands.

"We don't have to go tonight," I tell her, but she turns and smiles.

"That's no why I'm feeling like this. What the bleedin' hell do I tell my mam and da?"

I shrug and sit next to her, pulling her to me. "The truth? You found a document that's likely forged, saying you were married to someone you don't even know, can't recall and couldn't pick up out of a line-up. We knew that you were *'married,'* just not to who or when."

Her lips go thin and her eyes widen. I think she's finally caught up to where my thoughts have been since I saw it.

"Reid, what if he's still out there?" *Yep, she's on the same page. Fuck.*

"We'll deal with him or them, if they show their face. I promise ya, darlin', I ain't gonna let them get you again." That statement makes her throw herself at me and hug me tightly. I enjoy the few moments we have, just holding each other. "I need to get us back. Are you good?"

She nods, but her shoulders are slumped. She's anything but good right now. "Aye, for now."

"Let's get going." I hold my hand out for her, wanting her to take it. And she does. But her lack of grip tells me she wants to run.

Chapter Twelve

♡ Alysia ♡

Reid showing me the proof of my *'marriage'* makes me so angry. Usually, I'm as placid as anything; another "aspect" my family like to badger me about. However, this? It's making me see red. After calming down in the park, we head back to the launderette, and the kind lady has everything folded for us. I thank her, and she tells Reid I'm a nice girl with a wink. He nods, says he knows then we leave.

When we're back, it feels surreal, slightly weird. Reid still seems on edge, and I don't know why, but I feel as if he's keeping quiet because of it.

"Okay, what else has happened that ye've not told me?" I ask as I put the fresh laundry down on the table so I can pack it. I know I didn't cause this mood in him, but this tension, or whatever it is, is radiating off him, and I can't ignore it. *I have nowhere else to go to ignore it.*

Reid sighs. "Can I tell y'all tomorrow?"

I shake my head. "Naw, I need to know, please. I've decided I dinnae like being kept in the dark." I stand with my back straight, unflinching. I was tempted when we were at the park to run into the trees and just vanish again. But, my life can't be lived when I'm hiding, I realise that now. If they want to find me, they'll find me, the cabin has taught me that. But I'm not going down without a fight. Reid's taught me that.

"One of the Federal officers who was on the case has vanished."

I wait for the rest of it. "Oh," is all I can say a few moments later when he hasn't added to it. "Vanished in a bad way?" *I'm not sure if I need to be worried or not.*

"We don't know. He *was* Maggie's partner. Interpol are on the lookout too." He shrugs, but it's not a casual shrug, and though I think he might be trying to not be bothered by it, I can feel the tension.

I pull in a breath and decide that there's nothing I can do about it, so I might as well focus on that stupid piece of paper. "Okay. So when did ye say we're going to get this sorted?" I ask, nodding at it. Reid smirks at me and I wonder if he's appreciated the change of conversation.

"Tomorrow, our appointment with the Justice is at three. Sound good?" I nod, and he taps the chair restlessly. "Okay, well, we're invited over to Abi and Nick's, so why don't you grab a shower?"

We'd showered this morning, but the day is warm and I do want to freshen up. I can tell Reid might want to as well, given his instruction. We have about an hour before we agreed to be over at our friends'. "Shall we take some food with us? Or drink?" I ask, and he smiles.

"We'll get some beer on the way. Do you want to walk or drive over?"

I think about it for a minute. "Will we be okay walking over, but driving back? Do ye have cabs in this wee small town?"

Reid chuckles and shakes his head. "We do. We'll get an Uber back." He seems to think it's funny that I called this town "wee". Well, it is small!

Before we get to Abi and Nick's, Reid says he has to drop something off for the Federal agent who is staying at Blissview Inn. I wait on the porch as Reid takes it to her; he's inside for hardly any time, then we head off to Abi's.

We're greeted warmly with hugs, and Buster almost pushes me over, he's so happy to see me. Abi gets to him first and orders him to go to his crate, and he does so, with a sulk. She just shakes her head. I watch as he tries to creep out of the crate, but she's stern and orders him back into it, without looking at him or the crate.

"Now, stay there until I tell ye otherwise!" she commands. The dog huffs and puts his head on his paws, then Abi turns and carries on doing what she was doing. She glances up at me, trying to hide her smirk.

"When did ye say ye were meeting with the Justice?" she asks as she throws more items into a salad.

"Tomorrow," Reid replies as he accepts a beer from Nick. "But, not until the afternoon."

"We're off up to Waco for the day." She smiles. "It's been a wee while since we visited," she says, glancing at Nick. He chuckles and shakes his head.

"You weren't bein' subtle about wanting to go, darlin'," he laughs, pulling her into a hug.

"You'd think something was wrong with me if I were," she replies, lifting her chin up. I glance at Reid who is trying to hide his smirk too; it's not working.

"Yeah, there is that," Nick confirms and slaps her arse as he walks past, which makes her giggle, but the grin is infectious; my cheeks now hurt! Their whole interaction makes me smile, and I crave that kind of understanding. Then we're sitting down to steak and salad, and when Buster creeps quietly towards the table, Abi has to tell him again to go back to his crate.

We get an Uber back to Reid's and crawl into bed well past midnight. I'll unpack the package Abi had delivered for me tomorrow, knowing what it is. We played a card game, *'Cards Against Humanity.'* I'd never played it before and some of the results were…interesting, causing belly-busting laughter, which I needed. Especially as Abi and I had the same answers to some of the questions. I think we all needed that. Content, full of food and being wrapped up in Reid's warm arms, I drift off to sleep.

The following morning, I wake to find Reid's not in bed, but I can hear live music. I'm puzzled, but loving the tune that's being played, which I think is 'Cheap Thrills' by Sia. I creep towards the bedroom door, though I doubt Reid can hear me. But if he's playing an instrument, I don't want to disturb him.

I peek my head out of the doorway and yes, he's there with a cello between his massive legs and it *is* him playing. He's only dressed in shorts, his back is to me, and he's swaying with the music. He's got muscles on his back, and I lick my lips. I see he's got headphones in, so that's why he's playing that tune; he must be listening to it and playing along. I lean against the frame and smile as his fingers slide up and down the neck of the instrument, his bow dancing across the same strings. The man has too many talents to be true, but here I am, listening to him. The song stops, and I hold my breath, then he picks up another tune; this one I don't recognise, but it sounds sad. The tune goes low, then high, and it makes me think of flowers in the spring, swaying in the wind.

Then, a song my older siblings either love or hate because it's my dad's favourite. The 'Sound of Silence.' I haven't moved and hardly breathe hard as Reid begins, the tune beginning low and slow. I can't see what his hands are doing, but I can tell his left arm is shaking a little as his right moves the bow the speed he needs to.

Without thinking, I start to sing along. I can't sing the high notes, the altos and everything. I sing when I want to, when I'm moved to, and I'm moved to do so right now.

Reid stops and removes an ear bud, but I carry on singing and come around to face him. I motion for him to keep going and with a grin, he does. By the end of the song, I'm close to tears. I've never sang with someone like this.

"Morning, kitten," he murmurs, his voice low and raspy. His nostrils flare and his Adam's apple bobs. It makes me ache in places I've never ached before.

"Good morning." I notice that my voice is barely there.

"How long had you been listening?"

"Since 'Cheap Thrills,'" I admit. "You play beautifully."

He chuffs, like I think a dragon would, if any existed. "My father thinks I should have taken up playing classical music. I prefer this."

"You do you. I love that you play, and that you trust me enough to play when I'm aboot. You make the tunes more beautiful when you play them."

He throws me a smile that makes me realise, I'm in love with him. *When did I fall for him?* I want to wake up this way often, to have him there, around me, to come home to him. To sing with him. *Oh boy!*

"You're looking at me funny, kitten." Reid begins to pack the beautiful cello away, but I can only smirk at him.

"Am I?" I try to keep my voice upbeat; I don't think I can admit to him that I have fallen for him—not yet. *Maybe not ever.* It's a secret I'll have to take away with me. "You entranced me with your skills. Is there nothing that ye cannae do?" I inquire, which makes him chuckle.

"There are lots of things I can't do. I can't fight fires, they're too hot." It's my turn to chuckle at that. I notice the sigh he takes before he carries on. "I haven't played in months. I haven't wanted to; until today. I woke up and just wanted to." He turns to me after putting the instrument back in its place.

"I'm glad ye did. I haven't sung for months either; until today. Your music, it made me want to join in." I look up into his eyes, seeing for the first time what he sees. *Me.*

"Let's eat, then we can take this laundry back to Brad and spend the day in town." His smile makes me smile, and I find myself entranced by this big, burly, protective man. *The one I've secretly fallen for.*

The drive to meet Brad is quick, and it turns out, he's at Station 28. He gives me a funny look when I hand him back the laundry pile.

"Ya'll did the sheets and things?" he asks, and I nod.

"Aye," I smile. "You let me hide there for a wee bit. It was the least I could do."

Brad shakes himself out of whatever was going through his mind as he takes the clean laundry from me. "Well, to be honest, we have never had anyone do that. It's appreciated, thank you, ma'am." I refrain from telling him I'm not the Queen; something with the way his eyes widen tells me he's heard it all before.

We head out and begin to do what I call 'mooch about.' I take in the stores, allowing myself time to look around. In one of the shops, Fred's Outfitters, I see a cute little leather bag that's for sale. What they call a purse, I call a bag. It's small, perfect for me to carry my purse. I'm admiring the blanket design, the feel of it, then Reid shows me a coin purse in the same idea, and I fall in love. I check how much everything is and go to pay.

"Would you like to start using it now?" the old man asks me as he drops a silver coin into the coin purse.

"Aye, I would. How did ye ken about the silver coin?" I ask, unaware that anyone outside of Scotland would do that with a new purse. It's something my Nana always said to do, to ward off bad money going to a new recipient of the purse.

"My gran, when she was alive." He winks at me as he cuts off the price tags.

"Well, thank you," I reply and spy the tip jar. Before he can stop me, I find a note and stuff it into the jar. With a smile to the old man and a wave, Reid guides me to the Cozy Bean.

"Our meeting with the Justice ain't until three, so we've got time." He holds the door open for me, and I slide in, finding a booth seat so I can sit and work out my new purse and bag. The sounds are louder, the smell of coffee and food is intense. *Why is it all so much more vibrant today?*

While we wait after our lunch, I sort out my new purse and bag, adjusting the strap to be the length I want it to be, the coins how I want them. All I need now are any new cards.

"Oh, I forgot to tell ya, the British Consulate will be here in about four days. They're going to help you replace your passport and other things."

I smile at him, but my stomach sinks. A passport means I will have to travel back to Scotland. "We have time to enjoy the eateries here at Piper Falls though," he winks, "as well as explore why the town is named as it is."

"Oh, aye?" I tease, wondering what he's planning. I'd love to see the falls though.

"I plan to take you out. And I'm not sure if the Justice of the Peace can do what we want him to in a few hours. It might take at least an overnight thing."

"Oh!" I can feel my neck and cheeks going very warm.

"I love that you trust me," he says, smiling at me.

"I think that's my problem," I reply, without thinking, and I see his face fall. "Oh, not trusting you…oh, shite! That's not what I meant." I suck in a breath as my brain scrambles to explain what I actually meant. Which means, finding words and saying them out loud. "I meant, I trust far too easily, in general. But you? You're easy to trust, you've proven you have my back. But I take people at face value and don't always *'see'* their body language, or pick up on what they say for cues as to their true motives. I don't question folk as I maybe ought to. I might not *be* here if I didn't trust so easily."

Reid grabs me and pulls me into a bear-hug. "You carry on trusting, darlin'. It's good to question things when the alarm starts beeping, but bear in mind, not everyone shows you who they are right from the start. Sometimes, you have to give them time."

I close my eyes and snuggle into him. He's warm, hard, dependable, and I love how he rests his chin on my head. I want to utter those words to him, but I don't want to be the first one to do it. I squeeze him as I hug him before I break away.

"But always trust in people. That's a part of your charm." He squeezes me after I do it to him. "Come on, darlin', let's go meet this Justice."

He helps me put my new bag over my head and shoulder so it tucks in how I like it, then we're off, and he keeps me on the inside of him, away from the traffic.

♡ ♡ ♡

The Court House is impressive, to say the least. It's a stone building that has Roman columns on the front, supporting the building above the flight of stairs. It has huge flowerbeds lining the path before it, and you walk past a beautiful fountain before you climb those stairs. The Court House and Town Hall are next to each other, making for an impressive display of authority and power. For a small town, these structures are huge. I stop to gape at the building that's going to help me gain my freedom, making Reid stop with me.

With a gentle smile, Reid extends his hand and marches us up the stairs to the entrance so that I'm only next to the large fountain for a moment. I let him talk to the lady on reception as he identifies us and who we're here to see. The inside also takes my breath away. You could hold a marriage ceremony here, the interior is lavish enough to do so. Parts of it remind me of the Castles back in Scotland, showing off their heritage and history. Images from when the building was being built are in ornate picture frames.

"If you would like to head up to the second floor, there's a waiting area in the Justice's corner. You can take that staircase." I see her pointing to a corner, and Reid is paying attention. I get distracted by all the items on display in this little mini museum.

"Thank you, ma'am." I hear Reid's voice, and it pulls me back to the moment.

"Oh, sorry! Thank you," I add with a huge smile before he guides me up that staircase, around a corner, down a corridor and through another door.

"I'm glad you were listening," I tease, which makes him chuckle.

"I knew where to go anyways; I was just being polite and lettin' her do her job. But I am glad you noticed that I was payin' attention."

"This building is amazing!" For some reason, that just makes Reid grin.

When we get to the next waiting area, Reid checks his watch, then he takes a seat. "I figure we're going to be kept a little while," he remarks as he stretches his legs out, crossing them at the ankles.

"Oh! I'm going to look at all the artifacts." I grin as I look around. *Where do I start?!*

It takes about half an hour before we're called through, and I've examined every historical artifact I can in that short time. Swallowing my nerves, I allow Reid to take us through to the Justice's office, surprised that my legs don't give way as I walk.

Justice James Arnold Montgomery is a much older man somewhere in his sixties. His head of white and pepper hair reminds me of Steve Martin when he was younger. He motions for us to sit, and we do so as he shuffles around his huge desk to sit back in his posh leather seat. There's a breeze coming in from the window, making me feel warm.

"Now, Special Agent Forrester told me why you folks needed to see me today. But, I want to hear from you," he nods to me, "Tell me your side of the story, young lady."

I look at Reid and he nods. So I suck in a breath and give this Justice of the Peace an abridged version of what happened to me, from my time in Chicago to when I woke up in Piper Falls General. By the time I've finished going over what I do remember, thanks in part to the statement Reid obtained from me, I'm more than confident about this certificate being a huge, fat lie.

"Could you sign this for me, please?" the Justice asks, and I sign my name on the paper he hands me with the pen. When I do, I tilt my head and voice my thoughts as he picks up the items.

"I'm sorry, but why did ye ask me to do that?"

The old man smiles. "I haven't met you until today. I wanted to see what version of signature you produced." And he goes through the files, copies of my statements that Reid had me sign. Then he compares it to the certificate of my 'marriage.'

"I'm quite satisfied, Ms Davidson, that you did not sign this certificate, nor were you present at the time it was signed. I'll have the paperwork drawn up to annul this, but it will likely be at the end of next week before it's ready. Will that be satisfactory?" he questions, his warm smile lighting up his face.

"That, sir, would be fabulous, thank you," Reid speaks and stands to shake the Justice's hand. When he comes to shake mine, he holds on a moment longer, his eyes searching mine.

"I'd like to hear it from you, young lady."

I pull in a breath. "Now wouldn't be too soon, and I understand ye'll get it done as quickly as ye can. For that, thank you." I remember I need to be formal, so I stand and perhaps a wee bit too late, I think to treat this as an interview. The rule I was taught of never shaking someone's hand while sitting repeats in my head. I shake his hand with more confidence than I feel, making him smile.

"I believe you'll be just fine, Ms Davidson."

"You have a good day, sir." Reid is behind me and motions for me to leave. I smile at the Justice of the Peace and let Reid lead the way back to the entrance, outside to the fountain. Without thinking or waiting, I find a bench and sit on it, glad to be out in the sunshine, to hear nature, the bubbling of the water.

Reid doesn't say anything, though I know he's sitting next to me. I close my eyes and focus on my breathing. Until I was taken, I never had issues like this, and I begin to wonder if I will ever get over them.

I feel an arm wrap around me, but Reid still doesn't say anything. He just lends me his warmth, support and strength. He squeezes me a few times, and it makes me open my eyes. When I look at him, I smile.

"Thank you," I whisper, my voice barely remembering to work.

He just nods and stands, holding his hand out. "Let's go see if the Blue Bonnet is still open." There's a smile in his eye and a smirk on his lips, and I wonder what he's planning.

At the Blue Bonnet, Harper is clearing up as we get to the door, which is locked. Reid raps on the glass, and I can see Harper jump at the noise, then she's smiling and coming over to the door, unlocking it. From the back, a blond-haired man appears, smiling, and Harper vanishes into the back. I wasn't expecting him to just appear, and I step closer to Reid.

"Hey, Keelan, how's it going?"

The blond man nods and smiles. "Hey, Reid. It's going well, thanks! Are you two doing okay?" The men grin at each other, and I wait, not knowing who this man is, other than his name. Harper reaches up and kisses Keelan softly on the cheek as she reappears from the back carrying a box. With that simple motion, I let go of the breath I was holding.

"I saved y'all one, just as you asked."

"Thanks, Harper, you're a star. We'll leave y'all to it." I try to look in the box, but Harper's not used a clear box this time, so I can't see what goodies are in it. I give Reid a weird look, and it just makes Harper chuckle.

"You'll see when you're home, now, go and enjoy! Go on, shoo, let us clean up in here so we can get home."

Reid salutes her and leaves some money on the counter before he nods to Keelan as we leave.

♡ ♡ ♡

"What was that about?" I ask as we begin to walk back to the loft.

"The pie box? Dessert. You'll see!"

"Huh uh…Who was that guy?"

"Keelan? He's a firefighter, and he's been dating Harper since she ran to Piper Falls to get away from a crazy guy who was killing girls that looked like her, but weren't her. She's also Preston's cousin. He's my Captain."

I nod in understanding. "So he works with Abi and Nick?"

Reid nods. "Yeah, he does. He's on a different shift from them though, so he's not often out on calls with them, unless things get messy."

"Oh."

Reid stops for a moment and steps into the shade, taking me with him. "I didn't introduce you both, and that's on me. I'm sorry, sweetheart, I should have."

I smile at him. "I need to not be cautious of everyone."

Reid purses his lips, and it takes him a wee moment before he speaks. When he does, his voice is low and slightly forced in an even tone. "Do you know why you were scared of him, kitten?" I blink and lower my eyes. "Does he remind you of someone?" *How did he work it out?*

"Yes," I whisper, making him put his finger under my chin to raise my head.

"I need to know who, darlin', so we can start looking for him."

My answer is quick and unbidden. I don't need to think about it. "He won't be hiding. The boss of the marketing company back in Stirling, that's who. Keelan reminds me of him. Same colour hair and style. Only,

Keelan didn't set me on edge as much as Trent does, he just looks like Trent."

Reid just nods and smiles. "He's a few thousand miles away, darlin'," he says as he pulls me into a hug. I can't tell him that in about two weeks, I have the feeling I'll be much closer to Trent than I am to Reid.

Chapter Thirteen

♡ Reid ♡

Seeing Alysia reacting to Keelan makes me kick myself. I know she's still in danger, so does she, and it was sheer dumbness on my part that I didn't introduce them. When we get back to the loft, I let her go take a shower while I order dinner and then carefully put the pie Harper made into the oven to warm.

Before I order the pizza, I send a secure message to Maggie, asking her to look at the CEO of Alysia's employer, that she reacted in a way that makes me think there's something else happening at her work that she's maybe not aware of. You don't react in fear to a total stranger that looks like your boss, unless your boss makes you uneasy. Well, beyond the scary management role that they hold.

Maggie acknowledges me, and then I get on with ordering the biggest pizza I can. Satisfied that it'll be here in about seventeen minutes, I wait for Alysia to finish. After meeting the Justice and browsing the stores, I'm pretty sure she's had enough of being around people. I set out a few choices for home movies, not quite sure what she likes to watch when she wants to relax. I need to use this time to find out about her, what makes her tick.

By the time she emerges from the bathroom, the pizza is being delivered, the drinks are poured, the popcorn is made and all I need is for her to pick a movie.

"Oh! What's a' this?" she asks as she emerges from the bedroom in some shorts and the thinnest of t-shirts. Her hair is damp, and she runs her fingers through the strands, making it curl. I catch myself holding my breath as I look at her. "Reid, are you alright?"

I smirk at her question and simply nod. "Yeah, I'm more than alright. I decided to let you pick the movie." I motion to the small selection I've left out, distracting her from my reaction to her. I watch as she goes through the small pile, reading the back of each. *Groundhog Day*, *Meg*, *Meg 2*, *Night at the Museum*, *Terminator* and the first *Fast and Furious*. After a moment, she smiles and hands me the *Meg* disc, and I grin.

"You like your cheesy action movies, huh?"

She shrugs. "When I get a chance to watch them, aye!" She grins and helps herself to a handful of popcorn; I open the pizza box from Papi's, and as the trailers begin, we tuck in.

It's late and dark when the movie ends. For most of the time, Alysia was tucked in next to me. We paused it when we needed to replenish drinks or visit the bathroom. Otherwise, we were just there, present, in each other's company. It was refreshing that I didn't feel uncomfortable around her, or mind when she burped from the cola. We both laughed at it, then snuggled back into each other to watch the movie.

"Thank you," she whispers to me in the dark as we snuggle down.

"You're welcome," I tell her as she yawns. "Sleep well, kitten." I grin when I only receive a soft snuffle in response.

The following morning, I find she's on the floor, fast asleep, and I wake only because I reached across and felt she wasn't there. Why she's on the floor boggles me, and I go around and check she's okay.

"Alysia, kitten, I need you to wake up." I try to hide the alarm and concern in my voice, but I think that is what disturbs her.

She stirs and moans loudly. "Oww! Why am I on the floor?"

I snort. "I was wondering that. Did you have another nightmare I didn't hear?"

"I dinnae think so," she answers as she slowly stretches her legs, then winces again as she does.

"Can you get up?" I ask, and she nods, slowly righting herself up off the floor, and with my help, she sits on the bed. "Now, let's check you over." She grins at me, but pulls a face as she stretches herself.

"I think I fell outta bed," she grins. "I've no done that since I was wee." I laugh at her use of the word *"wee."* My mind has a very different take on that word. She pushes against me. "By wee, I mean small, ye ninny."

I raise my eyebrow at her, noting her smirk and bright eyes. "You're getting cocky, young lady," I chastise, but she just shrugs. It takes me a few moments to work out she's just bruised from falling out of bed. Thankfully I had a rug on that side of the bed, so she wasn't too badly hurt. As I check her over again, her breath hitches and then she giggles. I've found the most dangerous, ticklish spot on her: the soles of her feet.

"Reid, dinnae do that!" she squeals and pulls back, but not quite quickly enough, and I land above her, not quite squishing her, but she sure ain't gonna be able to move. It takes her a moment to work out she's pinned beneath me, and it takes her less time than that to reach up and try to kiss me. I pull back and she gives me the most confused look, which is when I crash my mouth into hers.

In seconds, she's melting into me and wrapping her arms around me as best she can. It feels good to kiss her first thing, natural. Her moans make me stop and pull back; I couldn't have hurt her, could I?

"I can get used to waking up to that." She beams at me.

"So could I." I duck down and kiss her thoroughly once more before I release her and get up. "But, let's try and avoid you being on the floor next time, huh?"

She giggles, and I rub my nose against hers, craving the connection. Then I grin, knowing what we can go and do today.

"How about we get up and go for a hike?"

She nods with a matching grin. "I'd love that! Where would we go?"

"Let me show you where Piper Falls gets its name from." I could live on the smile she gives me just from that suggestion.

"Careful," I call out as we clamber over another rock formation, turning to help her over it. Despite moving with what I thought was haste, it still took us an hour to breakfast, clear down, get dressed and hike out from the Loft. I texted Preston, so he'd know where we were. Preston's reply was cautious, asking me if it was wise, but grateful I'd kept him in the loop. Even though this is my home state, I was armed, still technically being on duty.

Alysia had questioned why I was wearing it, and I did suggest it was purely for wildlife protection. The look she gave me suggested she didn't quite believe me, but she didn't push me on it.

She gives me a huge smile, and we carry on up the trail, heading towards the falls and the reason Piper Falls is called as it is. In heavy rain, the little waterfall can gush down the dual rock formation; in the hot dry summer, it'll just trickle and drip like a pipe down one side. Not that you can tell that right now; it's barely moving. It must have been like that when the original settlers arrived. When it rains further up the river, the pipe (as the river neck was called) expands, allowing gallons of water to cascade over the Falls.

Until now, I hadn't given a hoot about recording it or showing it to someone. How quickly the times, and my thoughts, are changing.

From the side of the river, we can look back towards the town, though the clock tower is lost behind the tree line. Tangled Knotts might be half an hour down the trail from where we are, but I know it's there. Grinning, I find a decent rock and unpack the blanket; it offers at least a little bit of padding for both our butts. Then I pull out the bottled water and snacks, smiling at her.

She joins me and sits close to me, never saying a word. The beauty of this place means that we don't need to. I take the chance to look at her as we take a break. I don't understand why her skin is so white, and I offer her some sunscreen.

"Aye, always wear sunscreen," she confirms with a grin.

"Yeah, you always should. I love that song, though he hardly sings in it."

"Life lessons are best said. If it were sung, it would be more Johnny Cash style, I think." She grins at me. She makes it so easy to forget that she's nearly a decade younger, or that she doesn't belong here. Not yet. "Are ye okay?" she asks, and I can only nod. The time is fast coming for her to go home; and I ain't liking it.

We're out on the trail until late afternoon, exploring, walking and barely talking, just content to be together. As we walk past Tangled Knotts heading home, an idea occurs to me, and I feign the need to use the facilities they have for hikers that go past. As Alysia heads into the ladies, I take the chance to book us a table on the booking app that the restaurant has and see that they have a reservation available at eight pm. At least if she's going to go, I can make sure she's going to go with good memories of my country, of this town. Of me.

I have my phone tucked away again before she comes out of the ladies, and with a smile, I hold her hand as we head back to the loft.

"How about we go out tonight?" I ask, and she turns on that huge beam of a smile at me. *Damn.* "I'll take that grin as a yes, darlin'?"

She chuckles and nods. "Aye, ye can for that's what I meant. Where are we gonna go?"

I think about telling her for a moment. "Somewhere where jeans ain't gonna be the dress code." I wink.

She tilts her head to the side and thinks about asking me something, likely where, but I school my expression and give her a look that I hope says, *'Don't spoil this.'*

"Aye, okay. I'll need to look and see what I have in my collection. I need to find a suitcase too, at some point." Her voice has that heavy hint in it just now, and I can't help but feel that I've been cheated somehow.

When we're back, I let her shower first, taking my clothes out of the closet and placing them on the couch while she's in there. I want her to choose something she's going to be comfortable in, though I'm sure whatever she picks, it's going to look spectacular on her.

I grin at her as she emerges from the bathroom, the steam from the shower following her as it billows in the cooler air of the living room. She's using the large bath sheet and that just about covers her. When she's in the bedroom, I dive into the bathroom, quickly washing so I don't miss her coming out of the bedroom in her chosen outfit. Seven minutes later, I'm dressed and quickly tidying the loft when I hear the bedroom door open.

Standing there, in a knee-length brown leather skirt and an ivory lace top, is Alysia.

"Darlin', you're gonna cause car crashes."

"Ye like it?" she asks, twirling around. The shoes aren't high-heeled, they're tiny little things, but they make her legs look fantastic.

"Like's a *little* bit of an understatement, kitten," I tell her, which makes her giggle. I quickly book our Uber and hold out my hand. "Shall we?" I ask as she grabs a light buttoned-sweater. She purses her lips together, then nods as she takes my hand.

She seems a little surprised I called the Uber, even more surprised as I open the door for her to get in, before getting in myself.

"Don't frown, kitten, you'll get worry lines." I'm kinda teasing her, but I can't bear the thought that she would wrinkle that perfect, pale, freckled skin by worrying. The sun has added to her freckles; I'm sure she has a few thousand more than earlier today, not that it bothers me none. They add to her beauty, and when she blushes, I can't help but forget to breathe.

It takes her a moment or two to recognise which direction we're going in.

"We're going back to the trail?" she asks, and I shake my head slowly.

"Not quite, no. Do you remember what was there?" I question as the cab turns a corner.

"Tangled Knotts," she breathes, and I smile, nodding to her slightly just once.

"Tangled Knotts," I repeat as the Uber slows down, then stops. "Let me come and open the door for ya, darlin'." I'm surprised when she does as I ask her; she's usually so headstrong and stubborn, but tonight, she's not being her usual self. As the Uber pulls away, I keep a hold of her hand and stand at the top of the walkway for a moment.

"Kitten, are you okay?"

She nods, her eyes bright and expressive. "I've just never been out on a date to anywhere that was as nice as this place looks."

That makes me raise my eyebrows, and I pull my shoulders back a little more, before offering her my arm.

"I'm glad I'm gonna be the first to take ya out like this, darlin'," I admit. I am proud to have her on my arm, to have her out with me. And I feel sorry for her, having to suffer the attention of boys, until now. And my mind gets made up: I do not want this to be the last time.

We're greeted and seated at a small booth set for two. The candles on the table add to the atmosphere while the soft light from the industrial bulbs above create a soft, warm glow over us and the room in question. Tangled Knotts has a floating deck out over the river with its speciality being locally caught fish and seafood. The place has a light, airy theme running through it.

"Reid, this is too nice." Her voice is low, whispering almost, just loud enough to know I've about rendered her speechless. The leather booths, wooden plank floors and polished wood tables make it feel like we're inside an old ship.

"It's one of the nicest establishments in town, and they specialise in seafood. The other is Aurora Heights, but we'll venture there another evenin'."

"Oh, aye?" She raises her eyebrows at me as the starters are bought out to us. Once we're alone again, we continue to talk.

"Oh, for sure." I wink at her as she pops a breaded shrimp into her little mouth. "Have you added to that journal since we left the Ranger's cabin?" I inquire, and she shakes her head before biting that bottom lip.

"Naw. I was hoping ye wouldn't ask aboot it." Her honesty makes me chuckle.

"Not a chance, kitten. I'd like for you to pay attention to that for me though, okay?" I see her sigh, and her shoulders drop. She really doesn't want to do this, but I need her to go on from this, excel at whatever it is she decides to do. Without me.

She looks at me with such intensity, I can't help but feel hard done by. "Because ye ask, I will." I have a feeling if I asked her to hang the moon, she would.

Alysia watches the grill intently as the mains are cooked, then brought out to us. That is one thing I love about Tangled Knotts—their open grill and kitchen, you can see everything that happens as you watch your food being cooked. Alysia went with the wild salmon and green bean salad while I picked the sea bass and spicy rice. I'm not usually one for fries, but when Alysia asked for them, they delivered.

"I have tae admit," she says as she bites down on a chunky fry, "these are braw. Ye need to try one." She offers me the silver goblet with them in, and I partake. Triple fried chunky fries are rather good. Certainly worth sharing, a whole pot like this would spoil the rice and the taste of my fish. Grabbing one more chunky fry before she eats them all, I add it to my plate and watch as she devours the salmon, salad and fries.

"I just hope you have room left for dessert," I tease, and she nods.

"I sure do!" She grins at me and licks her lips. For the first time, I wish I was a slice of the German chocolate cake she ordered at the start. There's clearly something going through her mind as she gives me looks and slowly licks her fork clean with each bite she takes; she must have a thing for coconut pecan frosting. I don't try to fight the images she's creating in my head. I lean across to her, trying to be careful that I don't dip my shirt in my peach cobbler.

"Kitten, y'all have to save those looks for later, okay?"

She purses her lips and smirks, and her cheeks pink, but she changes from being provocative with her food to just eating and enjoying it, meaning I can enjoy my food while I watch her.

We're offered coffee, which we accept, and I ask if we can take it out on deck. Usually, it's open for evening viewing, but not tonight, it seems.

The waitress checks and gives me a nod then, unlocking the doors. I can see why they've been locked and the tables stacked; the wind is coming in fast, as if we're in line for a twister or some bad weather. Alysia though, doesn't seem fazed by the wind.

"It's so beautiful here, and I love the warmth."

I chuckle. "You fall asleep when it's only slightly humid."

Alysia shrugs. "Aye, well, I'm no used to the heat. Goodness knows what you'd do in the cold of Scotland." She toys with the mug in her hands.

"I'd like to find out."

"Would ye?" She turns to me, her expression telling me she wasn't expecting that to come out of my mouth, and I nod. I'm not always sure what I'm going to say either.

"I would. I've got some leave that Preston's going to pressure me into taking before the year is out. I don't mind working the holidays; most of the officers have kids or partners, they've got family."

"So you'd work around them?"

I nod. "When I was in uniform, yeah, I took the holiday shifts so they could spend Thanksgiving or Christmas with theirs. I would often get New Year off and go to visit my brother in New Mexico and spend time there; we'd do Christmas at that point. It helps that Piper Falls mainly behaves during the holidays."

"Does the town like to paint itself red?" she asks, trying not to laugh. It makes me smirk.

"If it could, it would! But the residents don't always like it. They sure are fond of partying but within limits, thankfully."

"Unless yer Abi's sister." She tries to keep a straight face as she teases me, but her face is saying what her mouth won't. I can't help but chuckle in response.

"Yeah, unless you're Vicky, that's true. But, to be fair, she didn't know. The stripper uniforms were a little *too* genuine looking. I believe they've changed them now; Preston had a word."

That makes her chuckle more. "I'll bet it was more than a word."

"Y'all probably right." I finish my coffee just as she does, and in moments, I've paid and I'm walking us home.

"I'm sorry, I didn't think about paying for half."

I stop and pull her to me. "That's not how this is gonna work, darlin'. When I take you out, it's on me. Now, if you were to take me out, I'd still be payin' for it."

"That's no fair," she quips.

"Life ain't, but no girl goin' out with me is going to pay." Alysia stills for a moment, her eyes going wide as she absorbs the truth that I've just uttered. "You've been with too many boys, darlin', if you're going Dutch on a date." We carry on walking; her tucked under my arm as she is, is damn perfect.

We get back to the loft and just as we enter the garage part, lightning lights up the dark, the thunder rolls just overhead, making Alysia jump and squeal.

"I wasnae expecting that!" she declares as she climbs the stairs. I can hear her taking in big deep breaths.

"I felt it when we were at Tangled Knotts," I reply.

"Is there somewhere I can sit and watch nature have a tantrum?"

"You wanna sit and watch the storm?" I ask, and she nods at me with an expectant, pleading look on her face.

"Aye. I have a wee Juliette balcony back home. When it's like this, I throw down a towel, open the doors and just sit and watch. Nature is brutal, but beautiful at the same time."

"I ain't got one of those, but I do know where we can watch it from, come on."

She follows me in a heartbeat back down the stairs to the far side of the garage. I open the side door which has an overhang to keep you dry if you want to walk around to grab wood from the store.

As she stands under the overhang, I grab a few chairs that have seen better days and place them underneath. Just as I do, another sheet of lightning lights up the night.

"Ye can see for a good distance!" The way she looks at me, it's like I planned a thunderstorm to hit right after our date.

"That you can, it's about a mile to the tree line in this direction."

The thunder rolls, and then we hear something that sounds like a herd of horses thundering across the plains.

"Here comes the rain." Her voice is soft and the rain is anything but. In moments, it's pounding on the dry ground, the roof and all I can hear is it hammering on everything. Pretty soon, I can hear the gutters gurgling as it does its job to the best of its ability; but it wasn't designed for a lake's worth of water to be dumped on the town this quickly.

I glance at Alysia when another bolt of lightning lights up the sky, and she's grinning like a child in a candy store.

The rain eases off, but it's still pouring when I see her take off her shoes and walk out onto the wet grass.

"What are ya doin', kitten?"

She turns to me, and I can see her absolutely beaming. She flings her arms out and looks up as the rain cascades down over her, then she spins slowly. "I love the rain!" she shouts to me as she turns. I shake my head and stay under the eave as she spins around several times, then stalks towards me. "It reminds me of home. It rains a lot in Scotland, but as every true Scot knows, there's no such thing as a bad weather day. Just poor clothing choices to match it."

I grin at her comment, but she likely ain't far wrong. Her face goes serious for a moment, and she's already soaked through; I can see every dip, curve and pebbled piece of skin her clothing was hiding.

"There was a time, I thought I'd never get to see or feel the rain again." She stands just out of my reach, if I were to move my arms. Her eyes have that disengaged look, recalling something, and I know, I have to let her get it out. "I knew if I ever did, I'd dance in it, rejoice. Being drenched by the rain was better than being in that smelly container."

I hold a hand out, and she takes it, looking me in the eye as I step out to her. I don't care that the grass is now muddy or under inches of rain. I pull her to me, and as the rain pours down over us both, we dance slowly.

♡ ♡ ♡

The following morning, when we awake, she's still in bed. We'd showered to wash the mud off when we got inside last night, as well as warm up a little. In her case, a lot. Then, we slept. After our date, something changed in both of us when we'd danced in the rain. I'm aware that I'm in love with her; no one is going to compare to her or even come close. She got quiet and withdrawn, and I'm putting that down to her realising the horrors she's faced ain't just going to go away.

I smile as she snuggles into me a little more. "Teddy bear," she mutters, and I can't help but grin. My arm is already draped over her and I pull her to me.

"That's me! Good morning, darlin'!" I'm quite happy to once again be waking up with her by my side. There's a contented sigh from us both at the same time as I breathe her in. My mind catches up with what it wants; and I need to find a way to make it happen.

My phone rings, and I frown as I answer.

"Detective Flanagan."

"This is the British Passport Office from the British Embassy in Washington DC. We're looking to speak with Alysia Davidson, please, sir?"

"I'm here," Alysia pipes up before I can stop her.

"Ah, good morning, ma'am! This is to advise you we'll be in Piper Falls this evening."

"Oh? Why for?" Alysia's baby-blue eyes widen as I feel my face fall.

"To issue you with your new passport, ma'am. You were expecting us, were you not?" I can't help but think that they're being more than stuck up, beyond formal.

"Well, aye, but I was kinda hoping ye'd take yer sweet time," Alysia replies. I try not to laugh at her brutal honesty. Just like Abi and her sister, you know where you stand with these Scotswomen.

"Ah, we're sorry about that. We're about to catch a flight from DC down to Austin."

"You'll need to hire a car at the airport and take the i35 to Piper Falls. I'm going to assume you're booked in at Blissview Inn?" I put my finger to my mouth, and Alysia nods.

"Yes, sir, we are. Looking at the flight and drive time, we can meet tomorrow morning if that's convenient? That should give us time to get to Piper Falls and set up."

"I'll book a conference room at the Police Station on Main Street, say 10 am?"

"Thank you, Detective, that would be great." Their New York accent is unmistakable.

"We'll see you tomorrow morning. Who should I write down as attending? You said 'we' a few times."

"My colleague and I. Maria Calvin and Kingston Brown. We'll be making Ms Davidson's passport on site, so we'd appreciate a room with a table, a blank wall and some sockets, please. We should have it done in a few hours."

Standard office equipment, but I know which room I want. "I'll have that organised," I confirm, and they quickly thank me, then ring off as their flight gets called.

I sigh, noticing Alysia's face. "I was also hoping they'd take their sweet time."

I quickly send an email to Henry Charmichael's secretary, letting her know about those bureaucrats visiting and of our need for an office for half a day.

Alysia nods, and I can't help but see that she ain't happy. She ain't the only one. "Well, they'll be here tomorrow. We can deal with them then. What's on your agenda for today?"

I shrug. "Nothing set in stone, but I could do with checking in with Cody and Caden, see what's going on."

"And I'm to be yer wee shadow?" Alysia asks, her chin lifting. Sassy woman.

"Ya are, darling."

"Well, we'd best get dressed then! I saw that the cafe has breakfast wraps? I'd like to try one." Since she's likely heading home pretty soon, I oblige and agree.

♡ ♡ ♡

It takes us twenty minutes to get to the Cozy Bean and for us to order two breakfast wraps and coffee to go. Nick is there, sat outside, enjoying the same, and I can't help but notice he looks darn tired. Buster is at his feet, and he huffs before wagging his tail as Alysia fusses him a little.

"You alright?" Alysia asks, and Nick nods. There's a coy smile on his face as Alysia asks.

"Yeah, long-assed shift. I just need some sleep and could not be bothered to cook."

"You sure that's all it is?" I check, and Nick nods again.

"Sure is. Abi's on shift and…" We turn and watch as the engine roars past, the horn blasting at the junction. I can't see who is driving, but Nick grins. "Essie might regret asking Abi to drive today."

I chuckle and shake my head. "We'll catch up with you another time." Nick waves us on, but not before we give Buster a quick fuss and head on to the station.

♡ ♡ ♡

"Detective Flanagan!" I turn as Samantha Burton's voice rises above the usual hum-drum of the station. Other officers bustle past as Alysia and I stop in our tracks.

"Samantha." I pull my shoulders back and acknowledge the busy secretary of the man who pays my checks each month. She's much older than I am, but I wouldn't like to annoy her; I have seen her make grown officers cry.

"I got your email, Henry's aware, and I've booked conference room two for you. I thought you'd want to know." The middle-aged lady gives me a smile, and when I thank her, she hustles away. Samantha's always doing something; I don't know how she gets it all done in a day.

She might be Henry's secretary, but she's a very down-to-earth, muck-in kinda lady.

"It's really happening," Alysia breathes, and I nod.

"It sure is, darlin'," I agree. And I don't like it.

Chapter Fourteen

♡ Alysia ♡

I watch as the formidable lady bustles away after telling Reid what office is allocated to these bureaucrats from Washington tomorrow. The stark realisation that I'll be going home, without him, far too soon takes away any happy mood I had at the café and last night's dinner date and rain dance. Reid guides me through the corridors to his office, and I'm aware of his warm hand on my lower back. *Why do I never want this to end? The truth is, I already know, but I don't want to be the first one to say it.*

It feels like forever since I was here last; nothing seems to have been touched or moved, not even a pen. I did bring a book with me, but I have a feeling I'll have read most or all of it before Reid has finished with his day, even one as thick as this book is.

I watch as Reid fiddles with the air-con controls and then he motions to the rather square-looking sofa. "Make yourself at home, darlin'."

"No chance of catching flies in here."

"Why would… Oh, you mean you won't be able to nap."

I nod and smile, letting his smile bring out my own. *Again, I notice every little thing about him. Is it magic?* "It's okay, I'll find something to do." And I tap my book firmly. I'm not ashamed to read smutty books, but

148

I am glad it's got a discreet cover, so it's not obvious that the inside is full of scenes that can make me blush. Or give me ideas.

I settle down and get comfy, as able as I am on this rigid-looking sofa. It's designed, I think, for a quick sit, a brief meeting. Certainly not something you'd want to spend all day lounging on. Getting as comfortable as I can, I smile at Reid before opening my book to the page I was on, and then I settle in to read. I ignore Reid as he moves about, clearly on the job. I try not to think about mine or the life I'll be going back to far too soon.

◡ ◡ ◡

It takes about half an hour before I decide that I can't sit on this sofa any longer. It truly is as unforgiving and rigid as I remembered it being.

"Sorry, it ain't that comfortable for readin' on, is it?" Reid asks, and I shake my head.

"Naw, but it's okay. It is what it is." That makes Reid raise his eyebrows then wink at me. As I'm shuffling about, someone walks in with a huge bean-bag shape thing that I recognise from Reid's flat. I turn to Reid, and I can feel that my face is scrunched up.

"What's this?" I inquire. I've seen it tucked away in his bedroom, but I've never sat on it.

"I reckoned this would be much more comfortable." He smiles. "Thanks, Ethan." The uniformed officer grins at Reid, hands over a key, salutes me with a smirk and heads on out. Reid sets it out on the floor, and I am still puzzled by it, even more so with the foot stool. "It's my gaming bean-bag. I use it when my nephews are over. They mostly jump around on it when we're playing our games; the eldest is six, and he can't sit still if he's gaming." He places it in the corner and pushes the sofa up a little, so it can sit nearer his desk.

"Oh!" Knowing that he'd use it with his nephews is a good thing, and I settle into it. It touches me that he thought to send someone to fetch it.

"This is braw!" I look up and throw him a huge smile, feeling much more comfortable. Then he settles back at his desk, leaving me to carry on reading my book.

I know when Reid leaves his desk, and I pause reading when others pop on by. He tells me where he's going, and I have no idea what a "bullpen" is, but he visits there a few times. Eventually, the need for food makes it so I have to get up and find him. Marking my place in my book, because heaven forbid I dog-ear a page (something my Granny would tell me off for), I set it on the foot-poof and let my curiosity out. The station has many doors, and I still don't feel I can find my way around this place, even though I've been here a few times now. But I'd like to get a drink, find Reid.

The voices are so familiar, but while I can hear them, I can't focus on what they're saying—and suddenly, everything swims before me. The noises are louder, the world feels off and somehow, I find my way to the front desk. As I stumble past a door, the sensation of being unable to breathe passes, and I see bubbles in the air.

"Oh, hi! Ya look a little lost. How can I help ya?" The blonde lady is about the same age I am, somewhere in her early twenties. I try to speak, but nothing works; there's a cold fog stifling my ability to move or communicate. "Oh, you came in with Reid, didn't ya? Hey, you okay?" she asks, but all I can do is let my legs buckle and allow the darkness swallow me.

"Alysia, darlin', can ya hear me?" I try to speak, but I can't even manage that. A grunt escapes me and it's hardly dignified. "There ya are!" I can hear and feel someone moving very close to me. "Hey, open your eyes, darlin'." I do and look straight into Reid's whisky-coloured, wide eyes. "Well, hello, kitten." He doesn't berate me, just smiles and softly moves some hair out of the way. "What happened?" His voice is low and soft.

"Couldn't find you," I mutter, my voice shaky and just audible. "It got too much, and I couldn't breathe."

He sighs and smiles softly at me. "I think you had another panic attack, kitten."

I huff and sigh, closing my eyes. I can feel his hand squeezing mine.

"Do you think you can maybe sit up? You scared poor Caroline."

I grunt and close my eyes again. "So embarrassed!" I mumble, really not impressed with myself. I'd also quite happily just stay right here and not move. The chances of the ground opening up and swallowing me aren't likely to happen though, despite that wish being ultra strong.

I crack open an eye when Reid doesn't respond. No one else seems to be in this room right now. It's just him and me, which means I can breathe.

"You're not telling me off."

"Should I? You couldn't prevent it, it's just one of those things. I would like to get you up and out of here though. This floor just ain't comfortable."

"It's better than your office sofa," I quip without thinking, which makes him chuckle.

"Yeah, but that gaming bean-bag chair needs you. And I feel some fresh air and some food might also help. Shall we get you up?"

I roll my eyes but nod, and slowly, I push myself up to sitting and with Reid's strength, I'm on my feet seconds later. "There's my girl," he says. My breath hitches as his words sink into my head as he wraps his arms around me to support me. If only the words could be true.

Half an hour later, we're sitting in his squad car, which is some big black, nondescript thing that looks and feels like a tank. We're in the station car park, secured and safe. There are so many controls on it, it feels like an aeroplane cockpit. The windows are down, and Reid's not complaining about the lack of air-con. At my feet, the empty food bag from our burrito wraps holds the evidence of our food intake. Well, Reid's. Mine is wrapped back up as I could only manage half of it. However, some fizzy drink and the sunshine have helped.

"Are you feeling better?" he asks as he reaches the end of his drink cup. The size of the soft drinks in the States astounds me. You can't get a drink that size at a take-out in the UK, and their medium is our large. I still haven't finished that.

"I am, thank ye. A lot better."

He nods and pops the empty drink cup into the bag at my feet. "What do you think happened?"

I shrug, not wishing to go into it, but I know he won't let me avoid this. "I got hungry and came to find you, but I think I got overwhelmed, then maybe I panicked? I'm not sure." I shrug and take a long sip of my fizzy drink. I'm not sure what flavour Reid picked for me, but it's terribly sweet, and I take my time drinking it.

He just smiles. "I think you probably ain't far wrong, kitten. It's something to note in your journal and take stock of. How would you access counselling services back home?"

I shrug. "I have nae idea. Why would I wanna talk wi' a heid-shrinker for?" I look at him over the huge drinking cup. I know I'm being sassy, but I also don't want to go to a shrink, given that one of my brothers works in that field. Asking him to find anyone to talk with in that field, it sends shivers down me.

Reid chuckles. "They can help you sort out your thoughts and give you positive stuff to focus on."

I huff, but I also know he's likely right, so I can only sigh in response. "One of my brothers works in the mental health field. But, I'm no sharing my darkest thoughts wi' him." I take a slurp of my drink so I don't have to speak.

"But he'll know people you can talk with, and he won't be able to find out. Well, he shouldn't be able to find out details."

I shrug, but sigh. "I'll have to ask him when I'm home." I haven't the energy to argue with Reid, and I don't want to.

"I'd like you to, kitten. Promise me you will?" He's looking at me so intently as his voice pleads with me, I think I'd do anything he told me to right now. So, I do what I can; I make him a promise. With a smile, we head back inside the station; Reid makes sure I bring my drink and the remainder of my food. I smile at Caroline from the reception desk as she walks past us. The lass just gives me a wink, which makes me smile.

Back in Reid's office, I find the gaming chair and make myself comfortable in it. But I don't want to read. Moments later, Reid's handing me a pen with a new yellow notepad. "Get your thoughts outta your head, kitten."

I sigh and take the instruments of mind-torture from him. He doesn't stand over me, expecting me to do it **now**. As I hear his fingers dance over his keyboard and his voice talk on the phone, I focus on the paper, which remains strangely blank for ages. As Reid talks, I begin to think about what is in my notebook back at his flat, and my hand begins to write. I don't think about what I'm writing, I just write.

I'm not sure what the time is when Reid looks over my shoulder, but when he does, I sigh in contentment. There are mind bubbles everywhere, lines between them all, notes and lots of things on new pages that stem from others.

"Nice mind map," he tells me as he turns the pages. I love how he doesn't criticise or judge.

"Is that what this is?" I ask, looking back over every scribble and bubble I've drawn. I do feel lighter having gotten all that out of my head. "I'm not sure what to do with it all now." Admitting that, even to Reid, is scary.

"Show it to whichever mental health professional gets to work with you. They'll know what to do. But, it's okay to take things slowly, to not know the way out of this." He kneels and his trousers pull tight, showing me his thick thighs and muscley forearms. I nearly forget to breathe; again.

"Let's head back home," he suggests, slowly standing and my eyes follow his. Without thinking, I take his outstretched hand and let him guide me up. I forget, briefly, that we're at his work. It's when he takes a step back, and I have the air about me to breathe, do I remember where we are.

"Reid, oh! You *are* still here, fabulous. Henry would like a word—with you both." I turn to see the lady from this morning standing in Reid's doorway.

"Sure thing, Miss Burton."

She raises her eyebrows and has a coy smile on her older face. "Reid, what have I told you about calling me Miss Burton?"

"Sorry, Samantha." He grins at her and she chuckles. I guess they like teasing each other about formalities. Samantha turns her gaze to me.

"Don't mind us. Miss Burton was my sister. Something Reid knows very well."

She looks at Reid; if she were a schoolteacher, I'd be scared.

Reid holds his hands up. "I ain't gonna argue with you. Your sister was formidable as a teacher." I try not to smirk as my thoughts semi-tie-in with the facts. "It was a tragedy what happened to her." I hide my surprise as best I can, deciding that finding out more about Samantha's sister can wait until later on.

Reid motions for me to follow Samantha, and I do, but I can feel him close by, almost touching but out of reach, keeping things between us professional.

"Richard, it's fairly simple. The site is about two years out of date in places. Some of the businesses listed have closed, units have been renovated, rented out again; it's simply out of date."

There's a rumble from the other end of the phone as Samantha guides us into Henry's office. As he listens, he motions for us to sit, and I do as I'm told. As Henry talks, I take in his brown eyes and messy hair. He has a lean build and a bit of scruff on his face. It's not untidy, but groomed.

"Well, it is your department, not mine. Surely you can get an intern…" The voice coming back doesn't sound pleased with that suggestion. "I'm telling you, it's out of date and is reflecting badly on the town. I'll let you sort it, somehow. I have a late meeting I need to go into. We can catch up later." Henry hangs up and sighs.

He turns his gaze upon us. "Sorry about that. The town website is out of date, and Richard doesn't want to pay someone to update it. Anyway, that isn't why I asked you both to drop by at the end of the day."

"Oh?" My mouth reacts before my brain can tell it not to say anything. *Reid doesn't look across to me, so is he thinking the same as I am?*

"How are you after earlier, Miss Davidson?"

I smile, touched that a man as senior as him would care enough to ask.

"I'm better, thank you. We think it was down to a few factors working together, and at the moment, I just can't cope with too much at once."

"I'm sorry to hear that. Is there anything that can be done, medically?"

I shrug and look at Reid, who softly shakes his head. Henry just nods and smiles softly, but his smile looks sad.

"I understand that some bureaucrats from the UK Passport Office will be here tomorrow. What do I need to know?" His tone is a little more upbeat.

I sigh, again. "My passport and documents were taken from me when I was kidnapped. To go home, I need that document. I was hoping they'd drag their feet a bit…" I shrug.

Henry smiles. "There is a lot of public interest about you, and the other missing women, and that container fire. Capitol Hill is under a lot of pressure from foreign governments to return their citizens and share case files."

"I was aware the container made the news, I saw that at the petrol station, but not the rest of it. To be honest, I just want to hide away." Henry smiles softly at me, the way my dad would.

"Hiding ain't something that's gonna help here, Miss Davidson; I'm sorry. Have you had contact with these bureaucrats before?"

I shake my head, but Reid speaks up. "They check out, sir. I ran their backgrounds and had Maggie confirm their identities. I have their images, as do Caroline and the others. We'll verify them tomorrow when they're here."

Henry smiles. "Good work, Reid. Is there anything else we can do for you, Miss Davidson?" Henry turns to ask me, but I just gulp at the question.

"I'm no sure…" I respond, unable to think of anything other than getting out of here, as well as his conversation when we entered. "But, there *might* be something I can do for you?"

Henry sits back, the look of surprise on his face is obvious, and he doesn't try to hide it. Instantly, it puts me at ease because he's not putting on a front or hiding.

"And what would that be?"

"I'm…my background is marketing. I'm at a loose end, twiddling my thumbs. Let me update the town's website. I can word it as a new person exploring the town."

Henry's eyes go wide.

"Alysia, are you sure?" I turn to Reid and nod.

"Aye, I am. I just need access to the HTML, or I can rewrite it in a document and send it to whoever has access. It'll help keep my mind occupied. The Justice of the Peace is annulling my *marriage*, and while I wait for my passport, it'll be down to Maggie and Reid as to when it's safe for me to return home. Until then, it'll help keep my mind working." Henry's eyes go wide as I take the chance to plead my case. "Please, honestly, it'll give me something useful to do that's not focusing on me."

Henry looks at Reid who gives him a brief nod. "Okay, thank you, Miss Davidson. I'll find a way for you to see it and update it." Reid stands, and I copy, shaking Henry's hand with a smile before I let Reid guide me to his squad car and back to his flat.

"I didn't expect that," he says as we slowly drive home. The speed limit in town is low, twenty-five miles or something. It's never that low back home.

"Naw, neither did I. Did ye honestly check out the passport people?" I ask, and Reid nods. As he does, I can feel myself drooling.

"I sure did."

"Why for?"

He turns to look at me, briefly. "Why for?" He scrunches up his face, clearly he's not heard that phrase before.

"Aye, why did ye?"

He chuckles, shaking his head. "I'd be a poor investigator if I just trusted someone without a reference or checking them out, wouldn't I? My mission from Maggie was to find ya and keep you alive."

I smile at that. "You have."

Reid shakes his head. "Until you're on the plane going home darlin', I ain't finished my duty to ya." Somehow, that makes me smile with pride. "Now, I'm gonna guess you're people'd out, right?"

I nod. "Aye, very much. I'm sorry about earlier; I have no idea what on earth happened."

"I think I do. I reckon it was a combination of lack of food and drink, along with the stress that overwhelmed you. I'll try not to leave you alone too long, or leave you without a way to make a drink in future."

I smile. "I could hear voices, but I couldn't at the same time, if that makes sense?"

Reid nods and gives me a faint smile. "It does. Too many things stimulating ya, it made your mind and body say no, enough, so it shut down. It's okay."

"Is it? I felt like a right ejit."

Reid laughs. "How ya felt is very different to what Caroline felt. Did you know she caught you as you collapsed?"

I shake my head. "Naw…she's sweet. I like her."

Reid grins. "She's the Mayor's niece and if I recall, Henry's God-daughter."

"Ah!" I wiggle back into the seat and glance across at him. "Tell me, what was going on with Miss Burton?"

"That…" Reid pulls onto his road and sighs. "I'll tell ya over dinner." He shuts the engine down, and by the time I move to open the door, he's there, helping me down.

When we get into the loft, he lets me just chill out. I feel somewhere resembling a normal human being by the time he has prepared the food.

"I'm sorry, I should have helped you more," I apologise again as I help lay the table.

"It's okay," he assures, making me sit. Minutes later, we're sitting down to pasta carbonara, cheesy garlic bread and some light, fruity drink that Reid says comes from Ericksons via the local farmers' market. A place we can visit on Saturday.

"I'm dreading meeting the passport people tomorrow," I share as I bite into a slice of garlic bread.

"I've checked them out, they're legit. But, why are you not looking forward to it?"

I sigh and then look straight into his eyes. "Because it means I'm a step closer to going home." He reaches across and grasps my hand. His hand is warm as it covers mine.

"It does. But, we still have the annulment from the Justice of the Peace, which could take as long as the passport to come through. And I doubt the passport will be ready tomorrow."

I shake my head. "I'm anticipating it'll take three weeks, that's how long it would take back home. I can get an Emergency Travel Document, but I'd rather they take their time."

Reid smirks. "I'd like that too, kitten. Because it means we can enjoy each other's company for longer." I smile at him, and I'm quite content to help him clear dinner away so we can have dessert.

"I never was one for dessert." He smiles, patting his stomach and that makes me grin. There's no fat on the man, at all.

"And you are now?" I question as he serves up apple pie with a huge helping of creamy vanilla ice cream.

"Only because you're here. I'm going to have to work it off in the gym tomorrow."

"I'd like to find a yoga class." He nods at me.

"There's a yoga class at the sports centre in town. Can't recall who runs it, or when it happens, but we hardly get issues with anything there." I smile at him.

"You'd let me go to the centre?" I ask, and he laughs.

"Kitten, I ain't letting you do anything! You don't need my permission, do you understand? If you wanna go, I'll make sure you get there safely and get back to the station." I beam at him, understanding one thing. He's not dictating my life to me the way my family does, and it makes the thought of leaving him unnerve me even more.

"Thank you," is all I can whisper moments later.

"Let's tidy up, then we can take a walk if you'd like?"

I nod, smiling again. I would love to take a walk with him. Anywhere.

Wearing a light jacket and a pair of what Reid called sneakers, we head away from his flat towards town. Abi mentioned the other night that the town is small enough to walk around in less than an hour, so I hope we won't be out for long. The sun is just starting to set, and the clouds in the sky form in cirrus waves, more than I've seen in a long time. Then I wonder, when was the last time I looked up at the sky properly? It's been a while, not counting the rain the other night, or the bright sunshine that made it impossible to look directly up.

"You're lost in your head again, kitten." Reid's hand finds mine, and our fingers interlace. I breathe in the air, the scent of him. "What ya thinkin'?"

"I was just wondering when I last *really* looked at the sky, or looked up from the situation I'm in. It feels like it's been forever."

"Sometimes it is good to look up and see the stars sparkling down at us, or the sun setting in the sky. It reminds us just how small but powerful we are."

"Is that what you see, when you look up?"

Reid grins. "My mama always said, 'You shine on as you are. When the darkness is just right, people will see your brightness, your light. If they gravitate towards you, be honest and above all, be kind.'"

"Your mum sounds wise."

Reid chuckles. "She always had these sayings when we were growing up, but I realise now that she was ahead of the times; all her stuff is what we class as memes these days. You could put them on a fridge magnet and look at them every day."

"Words to live by," I admit, and he nods, though he has a soft look in his eyes. I can tell, he loves his family very much. "Does she sell them as memes?" I ask, and he shakes his head, chuckling at my suggestion.

"No, ma'am, she does not." I chuckle at his use of 'ma'am,' as if I'm the Queen or something. He must see my look as he rolls his eyes and grins. "It's a term of respect, okay? Ya'll just gonna have to let me have that."

I smirk and raise my chin. "Aye, alright then." It makes him chuckle in return.

Reid makes us cross the road at a bank that has a cash machine just inside. I swear he looks around for danger more than he has at any other point, and his grip is like a vice. By the time we turn the corner and get to Pig Tails, his tension goes. He hasn't displayed this behaviour before, so I wonder what's caused it.

"And here ye are, worrying about me."

"We do."

I nudge him. "And who worries about you?"

"Oh, plenty of people do that, kitten, trust me."

"And do you tell them when you're low? Who do you reach out to?"

There's a woman across the street with brown hair, dressed casually in jeans, with three children; two of them wave to Reid, and he waves back just outside the Dance Studio. The smallest is wearing a dance leotard, and the oldest glances away, focusing on something that isn't us. The wee boy with red hair waves. His smile lights up his face, making me turn away and swallow hard; he's been with me, but what if she's an ex? *An ex with kids that might be his?*

"That was Mallory. Her husband and I were best friends. He died...well, his story is a part of Miss Burton's story. Let's head back, and I'll tell you about her, Noah and what happened that night."

One mug of tea in hand, Reid's finally settled on the sofa. There's a tin of cookies on the coffee table that he is staring at intently. "Just over two years ago now, Miss Courtney Burton and Officer Noah Dolan were killed. Noah was on patrol and radioed in to say he was dealing with a speeding vehicle, but then didn't answer his radio when dispatch asked for him to check in. I got dispatched to find him, and when I did, he had already passed from being shot. From what we gathered days later, Noah pulled over then approached the now stationary van, and the driver opened fire on him, shot him and then went to find an ATM. That is where Miss Courtney was. She was my fourth grade teacher and was the one who gave me a love for the cello." His voice drops, and he licks his lips. I hold my breath, wondering what he's going to say, and I doubt it's going to be good.

He pauses, briefly, before he ploughs on. "She must've been at the ATM, just doing her business and taking cash out for the week. He mugged her when she came out of the vestibule and then shot her, killed her outright. By the time I'd gotten to Noah, her call had come in and the PD were on the hunt for a double homicide murderer."

"You found him?" I ask, and Reid shakes his head.

"Not that night. We had a BOLO out thanks to cameras in the vestibule and Noah giving dispatch the licence plate. Caden saw him trying to leave town via a backroad. We chased him, laid strips down. We pitted him and surrounded him at gunpoint. Caden made the arrest. We'd learned during the day that he was wanted for murder in Tombstone Pass, which is up near Waco. Damien, the murderer, had gotten into a fight with his girlfriend, killed her. He fled down here, stealing a van from work so he wasn't as easily traced.

"I was one of the officers to go and tell Mallory, his now widow. I waited for the Coroner before Officer Matt Bradley and I went to tell her. She got a neighbour to sit with the kids and I... Matt and I were with her when she told their kids that their daddy was never going to come home or hug them again."

Reid disappears behind a glassy, bubbly fog, and I find that my eyes are leaking. "That's who those kids the other day were. Tiegan, Ollie and Mia. Mia was only three at the time, so she didn't understand. Little Mia takes after her momma in looks. Tiegan and Ollie, they take after their daddy, and they got it. They knew he wasn't going to come home to them.

"It's been a long road for them. And for Samantha. Miss Courtney would teach me cello once a week after school. She'd show me how to do the chords, then let me play along with music that had a cello in it. Sometimes it was pop music, and I'd add to it, or play it. She never judged me when I said I didn't want to play professionally, only for the enjoyment of it.

"She stood up to my dad who wanted me to train classically. She said that the love of music should outweigh the need to be professional, and that whatever my path was, music was never my main reason for a career."

He lifts his head and looks at me, then taps the tin. "I check on Mallory regularly. Sometimes I'll drop in, sometimes I'll just text or call. I always try and speak to the kids, though I'm sure Tiegan doesn't like me because I didn't save her daddy."

His Adam's apple bobs, and he swallows a lot. It is quite clear he still carries around blame about that night. All I can do is go to him. I don't climb on his lap the way I want to, but I do go and hug him, letting him just sit there and hold me.

Later as we get ready for bed, I quickly brush my teeth and hair, then I add a little bit of perfume to my oversized t-shirt before I climb into bed. Since our stint at the Rangers' cabin, we have slept in the same bed numerous times. It's been a while since we did more than just sleep or cuddle. He's an itch I need to scratch, and the times to scratch that itch are reducing every hour. I know he's been letting me set the pace, but I need to take charge. I just hope he lets me for tonight.

By the time he comes to bed, I'm almost half asleep.

"Did I upset you?" I ask and hear a huge sigh from Reid.

"Naw, darlin', you didn't. Just, telling you about Noah and Miss Courtney stirred up a lot of things I thought I'd put to bed."

"Do we ever really put things like that to bed?" I inquire as he climbs in and pulls me to him. It's a few long moments before he speaks. I can hear him breathing, feel his chest rise and fall, the solidness of him.

"I guess not," is his delayed reply. I sense more than see him turn to look at me, and I reach up to touch his face. His stubble scratches lightly against my hand, and I love the feel of it, so I stretch my palm out a little more, making him turn and kiss it. It takes me a moment, but when he stops, I turn his head and find his lips gently with my own, hoping to ease both of our discomforts and slay the demons, at least for tonight.

The arm that's around me, pulls me closer to him as the other reaches up behind my head, angling me. The kisses are sensual to start with, before becoming more intense. With a grunt, he pulls me on top of him, and both hands grab my arse.

It's only then does he realise I have no knickers on. "Alysia, darlin', you're a whole load of trouble." I grin in the darkness and as I'm now sitting on him, I grind slowly into him, chasing something within me I've not felt with anyone else. The need to explode, a need for him, it's new. I've only ever felt like this with Reid. His hands move to grip my hips, and he lifts me up, right as I grab him and place him at my entrance, then I slide down onto him, letting him stretch and fill me.

"Damn, darlin'!" Even in the pale light, I can see him arch up, and I whip off my top, throwing it somewhere; I don't care where. Slowly, I begin to move, and his hands guide me, telling me how he likes it. I grin when I have my rhythm set as his hands come and play with my breasts—feeling, touching, tweaking, grabbing. Neither hand can decide what to do, and I love it. I toss my hair back.

"Fuck, kitten," he groans as he sits up, making me stop. He stops me from falling and grabs me, helping me to move so I'm sat over his lap, my legs around his wonderfully strong hips. Then he helps me begin moving again as his tongue feasts on a breast, his hands tangle in my hair and he pulls my head back to lick and kiss my neck.

"I want to have you in so many positions, kitten," he growls. "So many." I groan as I feel my body climbing the mountain of ecstasy.

"Yes," I breathe out, wanting him to do it all to me. *Tonight. Now. Forever. Always.*

He pulls on my hair a little more, and I can only hang on as he thrusts into me, licking parts of me that have never been licked. He moves positions again, making me lie beneath him for what feels like too long to be without him. As he thrusts and rearranges my insides, he clasps my hands in his, and his kisses absorb my first cries. He doesn't stop, I thought he would, and moments later I'm crying out again, twisting my head so I can cry out.

"That's it, darlin', let me hear ya. It's all mine." He kisses my jaw. "You're mine," he says, and moments later, I'm again vibrating at his command, clamping down on him as hard as I can, but it doesn't stop him. If anything, it encourages him, and soon, I can feel the moisture dripping between us and then he stills within me.

Our breathing is laboured, the sweat from us is delicious as I'm sharing it with him and because of him. No matter where I go, I will be back. I will find him and follow him anywhere.

Chapter Fifteen

♡ Reid ♡

Alysia may well have been people'd out, and I'd never seen Linda look so pale as when she'd come to fetch me. Caroline, like most people at the station, knew First Aid and quickly dealt with Alysia just fainting on her. I was half tempted to take Alysia to the hospital, but she seemed better after food, drink and dumping all those worries out of her pretty little head. The mind map was amazing.

Alysia's offer to Henry about the town's website was also something of a surprise; I knew her background was in marketing, her resume told me that, but I had discounted it as an avenue to keep her mind busy, not thinking that she'd want to 'work' while recovering. Half the problem today, I feel, was that she was able to think, and it just got to be too darned much.

After chatting with her about Miss Courtney Burton, I was drained. I thought I'd put all that to bed, but I guess it got loose, like weeds in a garden, spread out. I didn't want to talk with Alysia about it, but I saw her face when Mallory and the kids waved to me. It let her know she's not the only one fighting battles; that she's human after all. And man, is she aware of it.

I thought she'd gone to sleep, waiting for me, which was a good thing. Her thinking I was upset with her, rather than like her, I did not want to deal with what we'd discussed on the return from our walk. Little minx was waiting for me though, half dressed, or more undressed. It didn't take me too long to fill her, but I doubt she's going to want me to man-handle her the way I want to. I have no idea if that's going to trigger her.

With such a short time between us left, I need to take my fill of her now in all the ways that are possible. Having her curled up against me is bliss, and I manage to extricate myself to visit the bathroom in the small hours. When I come back to bed, I'm already at half-mast, and the way her ass is positioned in the air, the sheet draped over her legs, is tempting.

She's so fucking gorgeous and has absolutely no idea.

Laying over her, I cover her small, soft body with my own and begin kissing her neck, moving her hair so I can get to her ears, her jaw. My dick is already wanting to bury itself deep within her, and I grab a condom, wrapping up. It's then I realise we didn't earlier, but we'll deal with any consequences later.

"Kitten, I need you to wake up."

"Hmm?" Her voice is small.

"I need you," I whisper. "Let me love ya, right here, now, as you are."

"Reid…" she breathes out, and her fingers grip mine. "Yes."

I pull back, lift her hips and slowly bury myself back into her, glad she's still slick from earlier. She tenses up for a moment, before relaxing and turning her head. "I'm good." She nods, letting me know she's okay.

Slowly, I pull back before pushing home, burying myself deep in her. It's easy, loving her like this, and it doesn't take long before she's begging me, though for what, I do not care.

"Oh, gawd, Reid." A few more thrusts and she's pushing back against me, making me grab her hips as I slam into her again and again, making her groan. It's not enough, I'll never have enough of her. When she pushes up, I grab her throat and pull her against me, making her back hit my chest with a thud.

"Scream for me, darlin', let me hear ya holler." I tweak a nipple on the other breast as I hold her to me. Her hands grab my arms, but she's not pulling them away from her, or even trying to.

She comes, like a good girl, and her cries fuel my own drive, making me fill the condom. I hold her to me as she vibrates, and I grin as my hand reaches her sensitive nub. A few rubs and tweaks, and she's bucking against me, coming for me again.

"Such a good girl for me," I tell her, turning her head and kissing her. She is. No one has ever come for me like that; no one has made me come as I just did, not this often. Her arms clasp mine around her torso, and when I find that the condom has split, I surprisingly find that I don't care.

Waking up with Alysia curled into me, with her back into me, is bliss. I've already fallen for this beauty, despite the age gap. I pull her to me and hug her tight as I think of Noah. How I'd love to talk with him about this girl and the plans going through my head. Then I realise, I can also ask Nick and Abi; they've done this, though that would mean Alysia somehow moving to Piper Falls. *Could I do it the other way?*

Alysia moans softly, still sleeping in my arms, and I snuggle into her hair, smelling her perfume and the scent from us from last night. I haven't told her about the condom being split when I took it off, nor have I reminded her that I was bare the time before that. And the want of my own family, with this woman, settles deep within me. Somehow, I'm going to make it happen.

We get into work about half an hour before the bureaucrats are due to arrive. We ate at home, enjoying simple cereal and toast together with tea and coffee. I make sure Alysia has a bottle of water with some skinny syrup in it so that she drinks it.

As we wait, I hear the Firehouse sirens cry out, and it makes Alysia smile. "Do ye think Abi is on duty today?"

I shrug and shake my head. "I think Nick might be. Ain't too sure on their shifts, to be truthful."

Alysia grins. "Aye, I don't get their working patterns either." I watch as she takes the pad from yesterday and tears the pages off carefully, before putting it into the book she's begun for her journal. "Do you have any glue sticks I can use, please?" she requests.

"I do not, but I do know where to get one. Come on." Stationery like that ain't something I'd use, but I know Caroline and Linda would, so I take Alysia there. Signing in are the two bureaucrats I've already run background checks on. We smile at them, and I guide Alysia back to my office before Linda comes and gets me. It's showtime.

♡ ♡ ♡

We head to conference room two, and both of them turn to us as we walk in.

"Detective Flanagan…" The man holds out his hand, and we shake. It's a wimpish handshake, no authority or strength there at all. He comes up to my shoulders, and he's skinny. If I were picking someone for a track team, he'd be on it. "I'm Theo Squire, sir." He's got a British twang to his voice, but he's certainly a New Yorker.

"And you would be…" I fish for the woman's name and receive a firm handshake as she gives me her name.

"Nicki Adams, we spoke on the phone. Nice to meet you, Detective. And you must be Miss Davidson." She reaches out to shake Alysia's hand, and I can see my little kitten breathe through her anxiety.

"Just to be clear, what's the aim for today?"

Nicki smiles at Alysia's question and indicates we should sit for a moment.

"We need to replace your passport." Her accent is typically British, the kind I expect to hear reading out the news. She's certainly got that newscaster look. "We'll do all the paperwork here; we have access to your old passport and documents confirming your identity already. We did take the liberty of checking your passport and driver's licence image, and I am satisfied that you look to be the lady in the images. Now, we just need to make up the passport."

"And ye'll do that here?"

Nicki nods in response. "Yes, we will."

"No three week wait?"

Nicky scrunches up her face. "Oh, goodness, no. We came with all the equipment we needed."

"So I could go home on the next flight?" Alysia's voice is sullen and heavy.

Nicki smiles gently. "You could, but I strongly advise you wait for the FBI to do what they need to do and tell you that you can fly commercially. I am simply under instructions to get your new passport to you sooner rather than later and to ensure you don't have to travel to Washington DC for the privilege."

Alysia pulls in a huge breath and nods. "That's good to know. So, what do you need from me? Anything?"

"Just a new photograph, then we need about two hours. Our flight back to DC is booked for half-past four."

"Where do you want me?" she asks, and I try very hard to remain silent and keep things professional.

We leave the bureaucrats in the capable hands of Caroline and Linda. Jason has come in to ensure that two people are on the front desk at all times, and I smirk as Linda's accent turns "British." Guiding Alysia away with a smirk is the best I can do.

"I dinnae realise Linda was a Brit!" She lands on the bean-bag chair as elegantly as is possible, which isn't at all. I need to stop looking at her like I want to devour her again.

"She's not, but I think her family originally came from Yorkshire? She loves the entire BritBox channels we have."

"Ah, that explains it. What did you make of those two?"

"He's not much to write home about. Her? She's in charge."

Alysia smirks. "He's what my da would call a wet lettuce." I grin at her comment, it's accurate.

"Well, they'll be here for a few hours. Now, what did you want to do with this?" I hold up the glue stick and smirk, which makes Alysia's cheeks go pink.

"I just want to use it." She carefully extricates herself from the beanbag and tries to grab the stick from me, but I simply hold it up. She tries to jump for it, but it makes her brush against me.

"Reid!" she hisses. "We're. At. Your. Work." Her punctuated statement brings me back to earth with a bump, and I gently hand over the glue stick.

"Later, kitten," I whisper as she settles back into her chair, and I get on with answering emails. If blushing looks could kill…

$$\cup \cup \cup$$

As Alysia does what she needs to, I find an email from Maggie, asking that I call her when I have a chance—without Alysia being alerted if possible. Picking up the phone, I dial her mobile number.

"It's Detective Flanagan. You asked me to call."

"Ah, yes, Reid! Are you alone?"

"No, ma'am."

"Is Alysia with you?"

"Yes, ma'am."

"Okay, I'll make this brief. Grant Esse flagged up in Germany about three hours ago. I've got German agents trying to track him down, but I do not think the German Federal Police will find him."

"What makes you say that?" I lean back in my chair, wondering why they won't be able to. The German Police are renowned for being hard-asses.

"Because the Italians didn't manage it."

It takes me a moment to respond. "Ah, now that ain't good."

"No, it is not. I'm liaising with the British Police and MI6 to get two officers I've worked with before assigned to the task force. Also, there's going to be a signed-for delivery for you today. Your diplomatic passport is ready."

"Really? Well, that was quick."

Maggie chuckles. "I get you're being vague here so as not to worry Miss Davidson, as I asked, correct?"

"Yes, ma'am, you are correct."

"Alrighty then. Here's the deal. Have a packed bag in the car and keep that with you at all times. I want you ready to travel anywhere if we need to and since you might not get much notice. Now Esse is flagging up, things should move quickly."

"Already on it. I'll ensure I sign for it when it arrives. Thanks for informing me."

"I'll keep you posted, Reid. Keep doing a good job."

"Do you have an update on the other avenues of interest?" I hope Maggie gets my meaning: I'm hoping Alysia isn't the only witness now.

"We do. We have other avenues of success in progress." That means she understood what I was asking, if the other agents managed to turn their scared charges into witnesses. That's a blessing.

"That is good to know. I'll catch up with you soon."

"You shall!" And Maggie hangs up.

I glance down at Alysia, to find her staring up at me. "That was aboot me, wasn't it?"

I grin. "Just my passport coming back to me."

"Oh? Where are you going?"

I lean over and whisper, "Anywhere I need to until I'm told this case is done."

I observe Alysia pull her shoulders back and nod to me. I love her courage and determination.

I get on with a few light duties; Caden and Cody bounce ideas off me that helps them in their plans and enquiries. I even put up with teasing from Matt Bradley. I run a few enquiries for them, giving me something to do while I watch Alysia. Halfway through the day, Samantha comes in with a laptop.

"Henry came by. Said you'd know what to do." She shows us the town's website, and Alysia beams.

"Aye, I do. Is there Word on here? Or Google docs?"

"There is Word on there, yes."

Alysia nods and thanks Samantha, then I have another issue to resolve. There's no spare chair here, and Alysia needs a desk more than the gaming-bag for a chair. It takes me five minutes to get one rustled up and just as I do, Linda asks us to go and see the bureaucrats.

"Is it all done?" Alysia asks, and Nicki hands Alysia her passport almost as soon as we enter the conference room.

"It certainly is, ma'am. We've cancelled the previous version and updated the systems with this image and passport numbers. I've also sent across your paperwork to the DVLA; by the time you get home, a new driver's licence should be waiting."

"I never thought aboot that!" Nicki smiles at her warmly.

"It was on the list of verification platforms, so it made sense to get it updated at the same time. I hope that's okay?"

Alysia nods. "Aye, it's a good idea, thank you."

"You're welcome! Well, we'd better get to the airport. Detective Flanagan, thank you."

"Thank you both." I shake their hands before Alysia does, and it seems that Theo has a little more backbone this time, his handshake far more confident.

I assist Linda in escorting them to the front reception desk to sign out. When they're gone, I advise our front desk that I'm expecting a package that I'll have to sign for, so they'll need to call me when it arrives. Then I head back for Alysia. When I get to the room, she's thumbing through her new passport.

"I can go home," she whispers.

I go and pull her into a hug. "You can, when Maggie says it's safe for you to do so, so don't fret until then. Do you wanna call your folks?"

Alysia nods. "Aye, please. Do I tell them about this?" She waves her passport a few times, and I note it's blue colour. I have no idea what colour mine is going to be.

"If you want. Or you can say it'll take a week or two."

Alysia nods, and I smile. "Let's call them, get it over with," I suggest, but she shakes her head.

"I'd rather call them tomorrow, please? I dinnae want to deal with them and this in the same day."

"Okay, kitten, we can do that. But we will be calling them tomorrow. Are we agreed?"

She looks at me with her chin up. "Yes, sir." Damn if that doesn't make me twitch.

We head back to my office, and there's a chair opposite my desk with the laptop in place before it. With a smile, Alysia settles into reading the town's website, making notes, and all I can hear is the clicking of her fingers on the keys.

"Reid? I'm quite hungry."

I check the time and kick myself, but I am glad she spoke up. "Darn, darlin', I'm sorry. I didn't realise the time. Let's secure that, and we'll head off to grab a bite." It takes her thirty-two seconds to save her work, lock the laptop and secure it in my cupboard before we head out.

There is a light breeze as we walk out of the station, past the Firehouse and over to Brewed Awakening. The coffee stop has at least a different selection of food than Jo's, and while I love Jo's, there's something that's come to mind that Alysia is going to need. With that in mind, we grab our lunch to go, a wrap for Alysia and two for me.

"Yer no gonna eat two?" she declares when she sees what I've had on it. Lou, the deli owner, grins and adds in more stuff.

"Oh, darlin', this is just usual for him!" She wraps them up, and I pay before Alysia can object. She doesn't because she's bought a box of sweet treats to go with it.

"I'm buying dessert." She smirks. I can't tell her that I want her to be my dessert, so I just raise my eyebrows. She purses her lips together; kitten knows exactly what she's doing.

Outside, we walk around to Pig Tails and find a bench to sit at, starting on our wraps.

"I've had a thought."

"Oh, aye? Regarding what, exactly?"

"How you're going to get all these clothes home."

She scrunches up her face. "I'll no want to take them all back."

Now it's my turn to wear a confused face.

"I wanna come back. A lot." It takes me a moment to understand.

"A lot, a lot?" I clarify, to which she nods.

"And for you to come out to Scotland. That is, if ye want to. If you want me to come back, I mean." She's starting to go pink, look at the floor and rush her words. I kinda like her being flustered like this.

I lean in, trying desperately not to kiss her senseless right this moment. "I sure do, kitten." The smile she gives me tells me that she feels the same way. *Thank God for that!*

"So what was yer idea?" she inquires as she takes a small bite of her wrap.

"You'll need a suitcase," I state, finishing off my first wrap before picking up the second.

"Aye, I will. Where would ye get one from here?" She takes small bites, looking me directly in the eye as she does so.

"Bessie's, which we can visit after work, or there's the two thrift stores just here, or maybe Fred's," I point out, which makes her smile. I can only follow suite as she stands and starts walking, eating as she goes, heading back the way we came towards Twice as Nice.

Twice didn't have anything she liked the look of. To be honest, with my duffle bag, I don't need a case, but Maggie's words do go around in my head. We head into Unique Boutique, and she finds something that she likes, with wheels. It's in pretty good condition, and I have to say, it's the pinkest, hardest case I think I've ever laid eyes on. The fact it has a baby case that can go into the cabin with her is a bonus.

My work phone rings, which can mean only one thing: dispatch. "Dispatch to Squad 32."

"Go ahead, dispatch." I love how Alysia smiles as she hears the word "dispatch."

"Squad 32, I've been told to tell you that there's a package at reception, and the courier needs you to sign for it directly. No one else is allowed to sign for it."

"10-4, dispatch, we're on our way back."

With a grin and Alysia dragging two pink suitcases through town that Barbie would be proud of, we head back to the station via the car park and my squad car.

Alysia is with me when I get to the reception desk. Linda motions to a very non-descript man in shorts and a tee sitting there, a package on his lap. I head on over, and he stands, accepting my handshake with firmness.

"I'm Investigations Lieutenant Reid Flanagan. Sorry to keep ya waitin'."

"I was asked to give you this, sir." He hands me a white padded envelope.

"Do I need to open it here?"

He nods. "I'd appreciate it if you did, sir."

I rip it open and take out the black passport that's inside, checking through it.

"Fabulous, sir, I'm told to remind you to keep it on you at all times."

I nod. "I have my instructions."

He grins. "Yes, sir, don't we all. Thank you for your time." With a nod to the girls, he heads out, gets into an SUV and drives away.

I grin at Alysia, and when we're back in my office, I let her look through it.

"You've got diplomatic immunity?" she whispers, looking at me. "Like James Bond?"

I chuckle. "Ain't sure I'm James Bond, or even Felix Lighter. But, yeah, for this case, I do."

"Wow," she breathes, sitting down on the chair as I put my passport in with my documents and pull the laptop she is using from its hiding place. In minutes, we're back to work, and I catch up on the French lady and the report from Maggie with all the fingerprints from that container. Some of them are from women who have been missing for ten years or more.

I spend the time working through the files Maggie has shared with me. I try to keep my reactions down to a minimum with some of the information I'm reading. Fingerprints from the container match missing persons from a decade ago, or more; most women are international.

My blood boils, and for some stupid reason, memories of my uncle come unbidden to the forefront of my mind.

"Reid?" I glance up to see Alysia looking very concerned. "Are ye okay?"

"Just reading something that's brought forth a memory I didn't want to remember."

She glances around. "Do you need a hug?" she asks, and I grin.

"Later, kitten. Are you going to be okay for five or ten minutes? I need to go and call my brother." I stand and lock the computer, knowing she won't be able to unlock it.

She nods and smiles. "I'll be right here. I have water, something to do, and I promise, I'll no faint on anyone."

I grin and refrain from pulling her to me and kissing her. With a little "good girl," whispered to her, I head off to my squad car. Beyond Noah, he's about the only one I can talk to about my troublesome uncle.

I settle into the driver's seat and reflect for a moment about how I'm going to talk with Brayden about Gary. I hit call on Brayden's number and wait for him to pick up.

"Hey, bro!" I greet him as the call is answered.

"Hey, Reid! How's it going?"

I pull in a sigh. "That…" I chuckle.

"Ah, what bothers ya?" Big brother knows me well.

"Gary." The silence back on our corrupt uncle's name makes me think he's hung up.

"What gives you cause to recall his sorry ass?" I hear a door slam. "I've stepped outside the gym; no one can hear me."

"Details of this case that I'm caught up in. It just made me think of him."

"It was thirty years ago. Your case goes back that far?"

"Not quite, but enough to bring him to mind."

"He's rotting in jail. Not one of us has been to visit him. He hadn't married, and as far as I know, he hadn't fathered kids with those girls."

I pull in a breath. "You were older. Did you ever hear him explain to Mom and Dad why?"

"No. And please, for the love of God, do not call to ask."

I chuckle, which shows my nerves. "I wasn't going to."

"Good! So I'm only gonna guess that this case is to do with girls being kept somewhere out of sight."

"Something like that."

My brother chuckles. "Okay. Since you can't talk about it, what did you want to talk about?"

"Just wondering if you knew *why* Gary did it?"

Brayden sighs. "I recall Mom asking Dad the same back then. You were just about three years old, so you weren't up until late. I did hear Mom say she was glad we had both been boys."

"In a way, I am glad I was."

"So am I. He never messed with boys, but the girls, he did. I heard one was from New Jersey." That's quite a distance from down here in Texas.

"I just don't get the mentality, and I wondered if there was an insight you knew."

Brayden sighs again. "I wish I could help you. But I know little more than you do as to what happened, and as for why? We're in the same boat."

I pull in a breath. "Okay, thanks, bro. I'll let you get back to running your gym."

My brother snickers. "What ya benching these days?"

"I'm sticking with about 135," I reply, guessing that to be about kitten's weight.

"So low?"

"Ain't how low you go," I tease.

"I'm sure there's a hidden meaning in there somewhere, Reid. We'll catch up soon!"

"Let me call you though, yeah? At least until this case is over."

There's a moment of silence. "Why for?"

"I might need to go out of the country, and I ain't talking Canada."

Brayden chuckles. "Okay, I think I understand ya. Take it easy!"

"You too! Give my love to Mel and the boys, okay?"

"Will do! Be safe!"

We hang up, and I contemplate a little more about my mother's brother. Before I can alight from the squad car, my father calls.

"Hey, Dad!" I can only guess Brayden called him.

"Hey, son, how's it going? We've not spoken with you much since you got promoted!"

I kick myself. "No, I'm sorry, Dad. I got a huge case when I came back to Falls, and it's taking some time to get through it. Still ain't resolved it."

"Some of them you don't, son. Your brother just called."

"Oh?" My stomach sinks. "What did Brayden say?"

"That you wondered why Gary did it? I wish I knew, son."

"Does Mom know you've called me?"

"She will, but she can't know why, well, not the main reason." I sigh but feel happier. "Her brother never told us; although she did ask. Your mom, she couldn't go to the court and listen. I did. Every. Single. Day. I heard what he did to them, how he scared them, tied them up, kept them hidden. She never knew he was ill in the head like that."

"Was he diagnosed as being mentally unwell?"

"Son, no one who does that to little girls is right in the head. I honestly wish that one of their fathers had managed to shoot him. He's sick. And if you're after men like that, remember that, son. They're inwardly sick. Sick in a way you cannot tell from the outside. Don't you go trying to fix them. His excuse that he was abused didn't fly. That testimony from your mom was enough to verify that."

"I know, I recall her being so closed off when it went to trial; I think I was four? I wasn't going to try and fix anything. Just, I read some stuff on this case, and he came to mind. Then, I just wanted to know that, but not ask Mom."

"Wise that you didn't call the house. I'm outside, on my mobile, your momma can't hear me. I'll tell her you called."

"That'll be great, Dad, thank you. I miss you both. Tell her I love her!"

"We miss you too! Take care; we'll catch up soon."

"Sure thing!" I hang up on Dad and contemplate his words as I head back to my desk.

There are a number of reasons men like my uncle like children in a sexual way. I could write a whole psych paper on why, using every excuse he tried to explain it, to justify it. The fact is, Grant Esse is likely of the same mentality, and so are the others who have done this over the years. They'll scurry to ground, like a Texas lawn insect, when they're threatened. The trick, if there is one, is to catch them in the act.

Or find out their hiding place. I walk back to my office to find Alysia ain't there. The laptop is locked and the door had been closed. Her drink bottle isn't there either, and as I turn around to go find her, she bumps into me.

"Ach, Reid! Are you okay?" I hug her, pulling her close. I can't hold onto her for too long, otherwise I'd be taking her over my desk. And that I cannot do, not here. I breathe in her scent a few more times, using it to ground me and calm my racing emotions.

"I am, thanks for asking." I let her go, and she smiles.

"Did you talk with yer brother?"

I nod. "I did. And my father. It was good to gain some clarity."

"On my situation?"

I shake my head. "Sorting my own head out, darlin'." I check the time. The UK is six hours ahead, which means that her folks will be up and possibly eating their evening meal. So it's technically tomorrow for them, which was our agreement.

"Do you wanna settle in, and we'll call your folks?"

Alysia shivers. "Ye did say we would. I was hoping you'd forget."

I laugh and shake my head. "Sorry, kitten, that ain't how I work."

"Elephant," she sasses, and I lift her chin so she has to look at me. I love how her eyes go wide when she realises I've heard her, and I address it there and then.

"Excuse me?" I raise my eyebrows a little.

"You never forget, the same as elephants."

"Too right. Don't be sassy, kitten."

"Why, will ye spank me?"

I lean in, hoping she doesn't see my pants jump at the very idea of smacking her lily-white, freckled ass. "Are y'all asking me to?"

Alysia shakes her head and bites her lower lip. "No. No, I'm not."

"Good girl. Let's call your folks." Her pursing her lips is all I get in response. And I love it.

Chapter Sixteen

♡ Alysia ♡

"Hi, Dad!" I greet my father as his 'hallo' bellows around Reid's office.

"Alysia, honey, how are ye? We miss ye," he states, right before he bellows for Mum. I roll my eyes and mouth *'sorry'* to Reid, who just grins and shrugs at me.

"Alysia, hen, how are ye?"

"I'm good! I'm resting lots, enjoying the heat." I grin, looking right at Reid. I am. I'm loving the Texan warmth.

"Are you using sun-cream?" Mum asks.

"Aye, I am!" I lie, and Reid raises his eyebrows, then makes a note on his phone. I can guess he'll get some at Bessie's later.

"Good lass! So, what's new?"

"I'm meeting with the passport service people, so I'll be getting paperwork to help me get home as soon as the Feds say I can." Reid nods at my white lie.

"That's braw! So you might be home in time for your birthday?"

I shrug. "Oh, err! I hadn't thought about that. But, we can celebrate when I'm back, aye?" I remind her, thinking fast. I doubt I'm going to be home for my birthday, which is in early May.

"Aye, we can do that! Double celebration to have ye back!" Mum's voice is jovial, but not as much as I expected.

"Is everything okay?" I scrunch up my face and glance at Reid.

"Well, it will be. When yer home."

"What's going on?" I demand. "What's happened?" Her tone tells me something's occurred. Perhaps because I've not heard her voice for so long, I'm more in tune with it now, as if I have fresh ears to listen with.

I can hear Mum pull in a breath. "You've been gone for months, hen. Yer landlord…" she pauses, long enough for my brain to catch up.

"He kicked me oot?" I glare at Reid, as if the poor man is responsible, but he's not.

"Aye. We've grabbed all yer stuff…" I bounce back in my chair, unable to listen to what else my father has to say. Reid taps his ear and points at me, then rolls his hands, as if to repeat. He's telling me I need to hear it again. "Sorry, I didn't hear ye. Where did you say, again?" I wait, looking at the phone with my eyes as wide as saucers.

"I said we've moved ye, to yer Nan's hoose."

"Billie's there."

"Billie *was*." Reid puts a notepad down. He's written *'Billie?,'* and I scribble that Billie is a cousin. And an arrow to say; drug user.

"Was? What happened?" I turn my attention to the phone, as if it were a video call. I can only imagine the looks my parents are giving each other.

There's a small, pregnant pause. I can't imagine what nonsense he's pulled now. "Jim and Tony caught him stealing from Mum. Set cameras up when she moaned at them that things weren't right."

I feel my jaw tense. "Good for them. Did they beat the crap outta that worthless bawbag?" I'd love to give Billie a bloody nose myself; I detest him, he makes my skin crawl.

"Aye, but he'll no press charges. He pawned a lot of stuff, but we've gotten most of it back."

"I'm glad for that! I'll bet Nana is too." I pause, trying to process the news about Nan. I can't, so I switch subjects, hoping for a reprieve. "As for when I'll be home, I don't know when the Feds are going to let me. And I like Texas," I make that statement looking at Reid. "It's much warmer than Scotland."

Dad laughs. "Scotland's no in the Pyrenees, lass! But, we hear ye."
I pull in a breath, wondering what else can happen to my life before I get
home. Which is fast becoming the last place I want to be.

"Aye, true. If Jim or Tony see Billie, hell, even if Sorcha or Kirsty
see him first, gi' him a bloody nose for me, will ye? Stealing from Nana
like that makes me so damn mad." Reid is smirking, but I don't care.

"Alysia, where's this fighting spirit coming fae?" Mum asks, her
voice holding a note of confusion.

"I'm just fed up of being told what to do, by everyone. I ran from
that container because I was told to. I stayed in the hospital because I had
to. Everyone's busy making plans for me, but naebody's asking me."

"We couldn't, sweetheart," Dad says, his tone defensive.

"Aye, I ken. But, nae more." I hear nothing but crickets from
Dad's side of the phone for a few moments too long. "Are ye still there?" I
ask, clarifying that they've no hung up on me.

"Aye, we are. Just, we're a wee bit stunned."

I grin, but I make no other sound. I can't deal with them like this;
this is why I moved out. "Well, I've gotta go. I'll call ye when I get flight
details, or in a couple of weeks, whichever is sooner, okay? Tell Nan and
everyone I was asking for them; I'll no doubt see ye all soon."

"Aye, we'll pass the message along! Take care, sweetheart, we'll
see you soon!"

"Bye for now!" Mum says, and I hang up.

Before Reid can say or do anything, I jump up, head for the door
and head to the service yard where the cars are. Reid takes a moment to
catch up with me, then he opens the door with his fob, and I head out into
the sunshine, before looking at the sky and screaming my heart out.

I'm sure I scared a few birds, not to mention Reid, but it felt good
to just scream. Billie has always been someone you needed eyes in the
back of your head for; that he stole from our grandma and then pawned
what he stole, is just low.

I turn, and Reid is leaning against his squad car, a wry smirk on his
handsome features.

"I'd say it was either that, or you found a brick wall."

I nod. "Something like that," I seethe, pulling in a big breath.

"Good girl. Now, let it out, slowly." I do as he tells me, and as I go to take another breath in, he raises my arms. On the breath out, he makes me lower them.

"Why the arm movement?" I inquire after another one of those.

"It helps you get more air into your lungs and makes your brain focus on the breathing to match the arms."

"Oh. I had no idea. Verra clever."

His coy smile returns. "How about we head out tonight?"

"Where to?" I ask.

"The best restaurant in town." He winks as my brain catches up with where he's suggesting.

"Aurora Heights? When did you book that?" I question, knowing he couldn't have today.

He grins. "I asked Caden to make a reservation and let me know. I wasn't sure how much time we'd have left together, and, darlin'," he steps towards me, encasing me in his arms, "I need to make every moment we have left count."

I smile and snuggle into his embrace, hearing his heart beating, feeling his warmth surrounding me. It's a sound I want to hear regularly.

We finish up with our work and head to the car, gaining a grin from Caden as we leave. As far as looks go, he's okay. Dark brown hair that I'm sure needs a brush through it, but there's an air of arrogance around him that I find off-putting. Maybe it's just me, but Reid seems to get on with him.

After work, I want to suggest we walk back to his, but the car is here, and it's a little sticky already. If we're going to Aurora Heights, I'd rather not be a hot mess, in the literal sense, when we arrive there. I sit and watch the town pass by, lost in my own head about nothing in particular.

"Are you doing okay there, kitten?" Reid asks as we pull up to his loft. I blink to bring myself back to reality.

"Aye, I'm doing okay. It was good to exercise my marketing brain again." When I don't get a reply, I glance across to Reid. His smile makes the lines on his face show, and I find I like him smiling. "Why are ye looking at me like that?"

He chuckles. "You learn about your cousin stealing from your grandma, you'd like your siblings to give him a bloody nose when they see him, 'cause you know they will, and yet, your focus is on doing something useful for someone else."

I shrug. "Nothing I can do about Billie, but I know Jim or Tony will take great pleasure in smacking him into next week again. Stealing from a relative, especially an elderly blood relative? Low life. And he knows it. The town website? I can do something aboot that while I'm here."

Reid nods. "Then let's go get ready so we can deal with the hunger before it sends me into a frenzy." I chuckle but wait as he gets out and comes around to open the door for me.

"And we cannae be havin' that, can we?" I sass as he helps me down from his squad car.

"No, ma'am, we sure can't." His face is serious for a second, then he grins, and all is right in the world.

"You go shower first, kitten."

"Ye dinnae want to join me?" I'm hoping he does, but just as I ask, his phone rings. The number doesn't come up on screen, but his expression becomes serious, business-like.

"Work," he tells me, pointing to the bathroom. "Officer Flanagan," he says into the phone. I can hear a woman's voice ask if he's free. Well, shoot.

"Give me a few," he says, putting the phone onto mute. "Alysia, kitten, I need to take this. I'll be downstairs." I give him a nod and close the bathroom door behind me. Starting the shower, I imagine what that dress I bought the other day would look like. Then I remember I need to bring the cases up from the car too.

I don't rush, but I don't dally either. It feels good to have the warm water plaster my hair to me, and I enjoy the sensation. Though I am sure having Reid wash my hair would be far better. *I wonder if he would?*

By the time Reid comes back from his call, I'm in the bedroom and have shut the door. I hear a knock, but I don't want him to see this outfit. Not yet.

"Dinnae come in for ten minutes? Please?"

"I do need to get some clean clothes, kitten."

"I'll be done when ye come out of the shower, ye can grab them then, aye?" I cross my fingers that he agrees and after a moment, I hear him walking away. I breathe a sigh of relief; thank goodness for that!

I'm slipping on some nice sandals when I hear him come back up the stairs and out of sheer fright, I crouch behind the sofa, keeping my head over the back so he can see me and not panic.

When he does, he chuckles, and I can feel my cheeks blush. He's carrying the cases and hardly flexing a muscle doing it.

"Okay, kitten, I'll see you in ten, okay?" I nod, and it's only when he's encased himself in the bathroom, do I emerge from behind the sofa and quickly finish getting ready.

I stay hidden in a corner until I hear him emerge from the bedroom, and what I see, makes my breath hitch. The dark blue chinos hug his legs and the button-down shirt has the sleeves rolled up just a little, to above the wrists—enough to make out he has tattoos, but not what, specifically.

"Wow, kitten, look at you." I glance down at me and don't realise he's made his way over to me. Lifting my chin, he can't hide his smirk. "You look more beautiful than ever."

I feel my shoulders pull back and my chest stick out, taking his compliment and preening from it. No one else makes me want to look good all the time. I'm glad I found this flowery ruffle dress. "I'm glad ye like it."

"Come on, before I feast on *you* and not food."

With a smirk on my own lips and a swagger on my hips, I let Reid escort me to the restaurant, via an Uber.

At Aurora, we're shown to a table out on the deck. It's a beautiful night, the many stars that I normally wouldn't see at home, sparkle brilliantly in the night sky. The candles on the tables flicker gently with the breeze, but once we're seated, and I look at Reid, I don't notice anything else.

"What would you like to drink?" I flounder at the waiter's simple question, not sure what I want to drink.

"A beer for myself and some sparkling soda for Alysia, please, thank you."

The waiter nods and heads off. "Thank you." I smile as Reid hands me a menu.

"You'll need to pick what you'd like, kitten. And you'll need to tell him too."

I pull in a breath and nod. I can't tell him that he's the reason the cat got my tongue; again.

We order, and this time, I find my voice, settling on the steak Reid says is worth my time.

"I know you think your family are a pain in the butt," he begins once the drinks have been topped up. We even have fancy breadsticks to nibble on while we wait. I shrug, but he's right, I do think that. "However, they love ya. They moved you when you couldn't do it for yourself, they care."

"I guess," I relent. He's right, I know he is, but damn, I just want to live my life. And here. In Piper Falls, Texas.

"I know you better than that, kitten. You know I'm right."

I can't hide the smirk from him. "Aye, I do. They just drive me bonkers though."

He chuckles. "I'd give anything to have my older brother drive me bonkers again."

"Tell me aboot him," I request, and Reid does. From antics when they were bairns, to him moving away from Piper Falls with his girlfriend, who is now his wife. When the bottom fell out of the construction industry, he teamed up with some other construction workers and built a gym that the three of them manage. From Reid's description, he's doing well.

"Brayden was always a leader, someone you could rely on to come up with a plan. Him turning a downturn into a business, that's just who he is. And he and the guys were fit from doing construction anyway." He sips his beer. "They fell in love with New Mexico, so they moved out there."

"And his wife?"

"Mel? She's fabulous. Her folks were from Austin originally, but they moved away for a quieter life. Melanie, she wanted the bustle of the city, but on the edge, not in the middle. It suits Brayden to a tee. And my nephews are a hoot."

"Tell me about them," I encourage as the main course is served. My steak looks and smells amazing with the tiniest new potatoes, green beans and peppercorn sauce that knocks my senses awake.

Reid shakes his head as the waiter leaves us to eat. "I don't want to talk about them, not tonight. Tonight is about us. Tell me about you. I have no idea what your favourite food is, though I guess anything chocolate for dessert is a certainty." I chuckle at that, because he's right. Yet again, I've ordered a warm chocolate-orange bomb with ice cream.

"There's not much I don't like. I love Chow-Mein, anything with chicken and noodles is my go-to. I love cakes, puddings and sweet things. But beyond that, I miss my yoga, especially hot yoga."

"What on earth is hot yoga?" Reid asks, nearly choking on his food. I can only smirk.

"It's yoga done in a warmer than normal environment. Say, with the heating up. The best one, was at a Tai-Chi building that was like a sauna."

"Do you not get faint or light-headed?" he questions, and I shake my head.

"No, but I was a proper hot mess when I came out. My hair was clinging to me, I was sweaty, and the Scottish air isn't often warm, not like here."

The look on Reid's face as I describe myself as a literal hot, dripping mess makes me squirm in my seat, and I want to tease him some more. "I think we could all have knocked someone's eye out." I grin, pulling my shoulder back a little. Reid doesn't react how I expect him to.

"I only wish I'd been there, kitten." His voice is low and husky, his eyes wide. It makes my breath hitch, and I realise, teasing him like this maybe wasn't a good idea.

♡ ♡ ♡

I reduce the innuendos and the teasing for the remainder of the dinner and just enjoy the meal, his company, the views. While a thunderstorm marked the end of our date at Tangled Knotts, tonight, the air is calm, but still, I'm wracked with anticipation.

When dinner is over, we head to another part of the deck, which is more of a viewing area than an eating area.

"Do you get to see this many stars back home, kitten?"

I look up and see hundreds of them, then shake my head. "Perhaps, if I were up high, but not on the estate where I lived. Or will live. The streetlights will prevent me from seeing this many."

I feel Reid walk up behind me, pulling me to him, my back to his rather firm front. He raises an arm up and points to the stars.

"Do you know what Cassiopia looks like?"

"I do." I follow the way his arm is pointing and see the familiar W in the sky. "That I often see." I hear a grunt of satisfaction from him at that statement.

"When we're apart, because we will be, look up, and know we're both beneath the same big sky."

I settle back into his embrace, breathing in both him and the warm Texan air. Somehow, tonight feels significant. When he shifts, he leans in, and in a low, sultry voice, asks me to hold my wrist out. Trusting him, I do, and he turns my hand over so my palm is to the sky before he deposits a box into it.

"Reid?! What's this?" I ask, taking the box with the other hand. It's too big for a ring box, not that I think he'd propose, this is still too new, but jewellery?

"Open it." I obey, and inside is a beautiful Pandora like charm bracelet with a few things on it. "That's a Texan Bluebonnet flower," he says, pointing to one charm. "A rose, because of the yellow rose of Texas, one police car, and I managed to find a thistle too."

There are four charms and pretty separators that I'm stunned he thought about. "This is a special bracelet, kitten, and I need you to understand this. If you get into trouble, even when you're back home, press the sirens on the police car."

I look at him as he takes it out of the box and motions for me to hold out my wrist.

"I'm still in trouble, aren't I? Can I no stay here until the danger's gone away?" I look at him with eyes wide, pleading, hoping to extend whatever stay I have here. I don't want to go home.

Reid chuckles. "You have to go back when the Feds say it's safe, but know I'll get an alert and find ya, somehow."

I wait until he's fastened the bracelet around my wrist securely, and he shows me how to press it, then shows me the alerts on his phone.

"I need to get one of them." I smile, meaning a phone.

"You do, kitten. But, for now, you're on my radar." I look up at him, and one look into his eyes makes my breath hitch. "Come on, let's head back." He holds his arm out for me, and I snake my arm through his, content to let him guide me.

Reid is the perfect gentleman, helping me out of the Uber as we make it back to his. The night is quiet, I can hear the crickets chirping in the grass, an owl hoots and gets an answer, and as Reid opens the door, I feel content. With the door closing, I slide off my shoes.

"Kitten." Reid's voice holds a note of something…dangerous? I turn, expecting to see something terrible, my mind immediately wandering to there being an intruder, but before I can react, he's pushing me up towards the wall so fast, I can only move. I go to push against him, though I realise too late it's of no use. He grabs my hands and raises them above my head.

"I didn't tell you to take the shoes off, kitten." I suck in a breath seconds before his lips find mine. "You've enjoyed teasing me all evening, darlin', and that just won't do."

It's obvious he's aroused, that bulge in his trousers can't be anything else. The kisses are hot, then they turn bitey, and he pulls on my lips before he pulls back and grinds into me. "I want you so bad, darlin'. I can't promise to be gentle or nice with ya tonight." Desperation pours off him in a way I've never seen or felt before. "So if you want me to be a gentleman, tell me to stop now, before I show you just how dirty I want to make you in my bed sheets."

"Don't stop." I have no idea where this wanton hussy comes from, but I want Reid to be rough with me. I'll happily take him at his worst, if this is it.

He pulls back a little, giving me a quizzical look, but I nod. Seconds later, he's kissing me roughly, one hand holding my arms above my head while the other slides the dress up my legs. His fingers find my hot core, and in seconds, he's pushing aside the thin fabric of my knickers to bury his fingers deep inside.

"What have we here, kitten? What did you do, huh?" I blink, unsure what he means. "Keep those hands there, darlin'," he instructs, and with two hands, he lifts the fabric. "Well, you trimmed yourself out, darling!" He grins. "I'm liking it."

I smirk and then throw my head back as his dirty mouth clamps itself to my core, licking and sucking. I don't get time to think or to ponder as his fingers join in, making the sensations I'm feeling build faster and hotter.

"Reid!" I call his name, panic suddenly taking control, but he doesn't stop. In seconds, I'm shaking and unable to stand. Just as I think I am going to fall onto Reid, he catches me. The pleased smirk on his face confuses me. "That was…" Intense? Unbelievable? Not enough. I'm not sure what to feel.

"Fantastic," he says, pushing me back into the wall as he unbuttons his trousers. In moments, he's lifting me up. "Wrap your legs…that's it!" He gives out a huge sigh as he slides into me.

"Amazing," I utter, being unable to form any more words to describe how full he's making me; the sensations I'm feeling are unlike anything I've had with him before. Slowly, he thrusts into me, keeping my arms above my head, his kisses get harder, bitier, intense. I don't know what to feel first, or at all. I'm his to be played with, and I like that I am. I can feel another wave of emotions building, waiting to crash and drown me. With Reid to hang onto, I know I'll float.

Seconds later, I'm doing just that, pulsing around him as my body convulses in a way I didn't know it could. Reid's hips slow, but his kisses build up.

"Good girl, you're taking me so well." He still has me pinned to the wall with my arms above my head. His mouth teases and assaults mine as the waves die back, then his hips find their rhythm and thrust into me. All I can do is kiss him back and let myself feel and moan through every sensation his body is making mine react to. His grip on my wrists tightens, and he bites my lips as his trusts threaten to push me through the wall. I can't object, I haven't the energy for that, and then, he explodes, taking my body, heart and soul with him.

Reid finally lets go of my hands when he leans into me, the wall supporting us both. For a few moments, we just exist. He and I, in his darkened flat, exhausted, sated and content to just be with the other. With a gruff sigh, he pushes himself back off the wall and looks at me.

"You have no idea how amazing you are, do you?"

"I'm not," I begin. He leans his head against mine, his body becoming rigid for a moment before he relaxes. Then, he leans back and looks me in the eye. Even in the low light, I can see the veins on his neck. I dare not speak.

"You are. And you need to change how you talk to yourself, darlin'. Anything short of you being amazing every damn day is doing yourself a disservice."

I can't answer him; I don't see what he sees. When I don't respond to him, he pulls away, leaving me empty. Then he's shucking off his trousers, lifting my feet to take off my knickers and leading me to the shower.

The shower runs, steaming the bathroom, making it nice and warm. In moments, he's got me naked, and then he's shoving me into the steamy shower cubicle. I let the water cascade down my head before I turn, wondering where he is. Then, he's there, his tattoos on full display, his stubble showing his firm jaw. As he closes the door, I wrap my arms around him, grounding myself.

As the water cascades over us, I take solace in the fact he finds me attractive enough to pounce on me, and I smile.

"I'm glad you're smiling, kitten. But, ya need to explain why."

I take a moment to form my words. "I just realised something, that's all."

"Hm," he says, cradling me. "And what is that?"

I close my eyes and squeeze him. "That you find me attractive enough to pounce on me."

He pulls back and stares at me. "Attractive enough?" His voice is high and tight, and I drop my head.

I've done it again.

"Oh, kitten, that ain't how I am." That statement makes me glance up at him and wonder what he sees with those whisky-coloured eyes. "You're more than beautiful enough. You're *more* than enough. I do think that you're too good for me though. What's the song that's doing the rounds right now?"

"I'm not sure…"

"You're too sweet for me."

I chuckle. "I'm Scottish, I'm anything but sweet."

He shakes his head and turns me, grabbing a silver cloth and some soap and begins washing me gently. "You are sweet. You're enticing, like cinnamon. Feisty, like a bunch of thistles." That makes me chuckle. "See? You're anything but 'enough.' You're more than enough, girl, and I need you to remember that, you hear?" I nod, but that's not enough for him. "Need you to use some words here, kitten. Do you understand me?"

I nod. "Aye, I do."

He leans in. "The phrase I need to hear, is 'yes, sir.'"

He looks at me like my father would when I'm being a brat. And I can't deny him. "Aye, sir." He relents; it's close enough.

We enjoy washing each other, content to just be. We hardly talk, but I don't feel we need to. Then we're off to bed. Reid's left out a new cute set of pyjamas, and I dress quickly before dashing under the comforter, enjoying the heaviness and softness of it. By the time Reid comes through, I'm half asleep.

It's only in the morning do I realise why he came through so late. The cases are up, and the flat was tidied. I don't recall making a mess when we came in, and I wonder suddenly if someone did break in that we didn't check for when we got back.

Feeling vulnerable in my thin clothes, I look around for something to wear over it all, but I don't have anything. I never saw a dressing gown in town. Being wary, I head to the kitchen, add water to the kettle and turn it on as I set the mugs down. All the dishes have been washed and dried, then put away.

I jump when huge arms are wrapped around me. "Morning, kitten!"

"Reid! Good morning!" I turn and see his smile. "Did we make a mess last night?" I ask as the kettle whistles.

"No. It was a little untidy, but I thought to mop the floor after our altercation in the hall. Told ya, I was looking to make you and my sheets dirty."

I giggle, not wanting to think of the mess we'd left in the hallway. "Oh, did my dress get ruined?"

Reid shakes his head. "It's a Saturday, so why don't we go get some laundry done and enjoy the town?"

I grin in response. "That sounds like a fine idea."

Happy that there's nothing weird to worry about, we get ready for the day.

We enjoy the town; the bakery and cafe are very busy, so we head to Brewed Awakening. The breakfast bagels are amazing though, it has to be said. I chose to wear a light denim skirt that blows in the breeze, and

I'm glad Reid opts for us to sit inside. There's a few chairs near a bookcase, and as we wait, I browse the shelves, reading who is there. Someone must like the authors from the cabin, they're here too.

"Reid?" I point it out to him; seeing them makes me rather nervous

"You're sure?" I nod. "Okay, I'll get it checked out."

When Louisa, the owner, comes over, Reid asks.

"Oh, there's a lady that comes in from the library. She gets asked to stock indie authors, but she's been told she's *'not allowed,'* so she gets them sent to her and has been stocking them in the little free library too. I added a few to the stack here." She smiles. "People love it! They come in, exchange a book when they're ready, have breakfast, then get on with their day. Wouldn't be the first time someone started a book and stayed for lunch!" She chuckles and heads off after checking we don't need anything else.

"That settle your mind, kitten?"

I nod and follow Reid's strange gaze towards the door. He's looking curiously at a couple just walking in. At least I think they're a couple.

"Well, I'll be damned." I frown at Reid, not quite sure what I am looking at.

I lean across to Reid, and his grin turns wolfish. "What's going on?"

"Jack just walked in with someone. Thought he was still hung up on his old partner." Reid takes a sip of the coffee. "He's a bit of a renegade."

I turn and look at them both while trying to appear to not look at them. I can hear Reid chuckling. "He'll have seen ya lookin', darlin'. He ain't gonna miss something that obvious." I can feel my cheeks becoming hot and turn my attention back to Reid. "Nice try, though, I do like your effort. Nine out of ten for attempt, but an F for execution."

I stick out my tongue at Reid, intentionally being a sassy brat. He just winks at me, and I have to grin back. *Why do I have to go back to Scotland?*

We take the long route back to his, via the gardens in the town where the park is. It's just nice to walk around without dancing in the rain. We come to the dog park section. and a few dogs are in there, playing with their owners, fetching things or doing training. None of them are Buster, and I smile wryly, missing that fluffy hound.

"What goes on in that head of yours, kitten?" The dog nearest us reacts, its ears prick up, and he looks around. I mouth *'sorry'* to the owner and nudge Reid.

"Dinnae call me that when there are dogs aboot!" I motion to the spaniel-type dog that heard him, and because it can't see a cat, it returns to the training.

"Yeah, okay. But, what were you thinking?"

I chuckle, and when we're out of earshot of the dogs, I tell him. He shakes his head at me before we return to his.

The Sunday passed with Reid playing more of his cello and me enjoying the view of it sitting between his muscular thighs for nearly an hour. We cooked, we ate, I napped and let him get on with some work. I awake with a start, having dreamt that I was going home tomorrow; knowing that it is far too soon! It takes talking with Reid about it before my sullen mood shifts.

Before we've finished clearing the breakfast on Monday, Reid gets a call. I can hear the man's voice from where I am, and I know who it is.

"Good morning, Mr Montgomery sir. How can I help you?" There's a pause from Reid as he looks directly at me. He's not looking worried. "Yes, sir. We'll be along very shortly, sir, thank you."

Reid smiles at me. "I think your annulment is through, kitten. We need to go and see Justice Montgomery before we head into the station."

Somehow, the stress I was feeling lifts more than I thought it would.

I can only nod and smile. I'm one step closer to going home.

Reid guides us through the Court House and back to the office of the Justice of the Peace. Mr Montogomery comes out and checks for us, smiling at us.

"My secretary isn't in yet; she's dealing with some kerfuffle at the school. Sorry if you've been waiting."

The truth is, I'd just sat down in the leather chair, so I hadn't had a chance to take in more than a breath before he called us through.

"We hadn't, sir. Thank you for seeing us so early."

The old man chuckles. "You're always polite, Lieutenant Flanagan."

I look across to Reid, noting his chest is puffed out a little more than usual, his shoulders are pulled back, and there is a wry smile on his handsome face.

"My momma made sure of it, sir."

He nods to Reid. "She sure did! Now," Mr Montgomery turns to me, "please take a seat, young lady. This won't take long." We sit as instructed, and I keep eye contact with the older man. "I have here your annulment. I'm also told that the Feds aren't willing to send you home quite yet. I've been asked to start some legal paperwork to allow you to stay during this crime investigation, which could take three months." I try and fail to hide my smile. Three months more? I'll take that! The old man chuckles. "I see that idea appeals to you."

"Aye, sir, it does."

He nods with a smirk. "Then I'll get on with that. Backed with the evidence from the Federal Bureau, it should go through uncontested. Now, I do have to check, is there someone you can stay with? I understand that you're living with Lieutenant Reid here."

I nod and look at Reid. *How much do I tell the auld man?* "Aye, he's been very generous with his time and his home, sir. I'm grateful for all he's doing and has done. And I've made a few friends here too."

James Montgomery smiles. "And who might you have made friends with?"

I grin. "Abi Charmichael and her husband, sir. There are a few others who have helped, Aly the nurse being one." The chuckle stops me from reeling off any more names.

"I see! You'll be in good company then."

"Aye, sir, I am sure I will be."

He checks over his paperwork. "Have you spoken with your family back home?"

I nod. "Aye, we spoke yesterday. My folks are in good spirits." He smiles at me with his eyes sparkling.

"Family is precious."

I begin to agree, but then I think of my cousin. "Not all of them, ye cannae choose your family."

He sniggers. "You can't choose the one you're born to. You can choose the one you make." He hands me a slip of paper, folded three times. "This will help you be able to choose." I grin and open the letter, seeing it's my annulment papers. There are a few reasons cited as to why this paper is legally binding, *"divorcing"* me from my *"husband."* The use of drugs, coercion, threats and intimidation and the marriage ceremony was unwitnessed are just a few reasons my eyes can read. I also notice the incapacity reason.

I look up at Justice James Montgomery, and I can just see him through the sudden blurriness. "Thank you, very much, sir."

He nods and offers me a box of tissues. "Please, go and have a happy life."

I stand and offer the man my hand, grateful I chose to wear the waterproof mascara Abi gifted me with the clothes. "I intend to sir, thank you."

With a handshake to Reid, we leave the Justice's office. I'm free!

As we step outside, I look up at the Texas sun. It's warm, there's a breeze, I can smell the fragrance of the flowers, and I can't be bothered to remember the last time I stopped to smell them.

With a grin on my face, I turn and wrap my arms around Reid, the feel of him pulling me into him, squeezing me in a reassuring way and then just holding me, makes me happier. He was there, sharing this moment with me.

"I take it ya happy, darlin'?"

I chuckle into his chest, listening to his heart beating strongly.

"Aye, more than I thought I would ever be!"

"Well, I'm glad! Young, free and single."

I look up at him, seeing how his eyes are stormy. "I'm wi' ye." I can't be the first one to say those three wee words. Reid just grins down at me.

"Ya are, darlin'. Let's get a coffee to celebrate, shall we?"

I nod, and as he takes my hand in his, I can't think of anywhere better to begin celebrating.

Chapter Seventeen

♡ Reid ♡

I wish I had the courage to tell Alysia what I want. But she's my duty. Hell, I shouldn't be bedding the girl, never mind pinning her up against a wall in my home and rutting into her like some Highland Stag. I can't get enough of her though, no matter how much I try to avoid or even deny it.

I can't stand to see her hurting, and I wish I wasn't the cause. The way her body reacts when she climaxes is bliss and like a drug; I want my next fix. The positions I have in mind to get her into are depraved, certainly X-rated and not at all gentle. I find I don't care. What I do care about is that she's stopping herself from saying those three little words. I can't blame her, I don't want to say them any more than she does.

With a grin, we buy coffee and three large trays of donuts before heading into the office. I'd wondered why she bought a few smaller ones too. When she sees Linda and Caroline, they thank her and dive into the treats just as Alysia reminds them that one is for Jason.

For some reason, she insists on going to the bull-pen with the first tray.

"Why do you wanna go there?"

"Ye keep going there, and I dinnae get why." I chuckle, and we head to where the uniformed guys are gathered. Somehow, they keep their comments under wraps, though the grins on their faces suggest they'd like to tease her or me. With a smile from Alysia, they dive into the treats she's brought.

"Well, thank you, ma'am."

I lean into Ethan, fake whispering why the baked goods are being offered around. "Alysia had some good news, so she's celebrating."

Alysia throws me a look. "*We* are," she sasses. With a wink, we head around the offices, starting with Caden. Usually, he won't touch this much sugar, but today, he does. Given that I've seen him running around the town with a lady I don't rightly know, but he clearly does, and he looks happy with it, I don't give him any sass. I don't think I recall him smiling like this before.

"Enjoy!" Alysia sings out to various people as we tour around the offices. She insists on taking one to Preston, as well as Harry and Peter. No one refuses them, and in no time flat, they're all gone. We head back to my office and set up for the day.

"Now I feel like we didn't celebrate alone." She beams and reminds me of the blonde sorority chicks from college. Only, Alysia is being genuine, and I doubt those other girls ever knew what that was.

We settle in, and I get a message to call Maggie. With a word to Alysia about where I'm going, I find the conference room the bureaucrats used, slide the engaged notice across and head into it, closing the door behind me.

"Maggie, it's Lieutenant Flanagan. I'm alone, and Alysia is safe. What's happened?"

There's a long pause from Maggie's side, to the extent I think she's hung up. "Sorry, I had to process what was in front of me. Esse's left Europe, flew out on a private jet. We have him landing just outside Washington a little while ago."

"DC or State?"

"DC. And we lost track of him at the airport. What's surprising is that there's a young man with him. We're working on identifying him."

"So he's trafficking boys now too?" The reasons as to why run through my head, like a freight train. "What age? Alysia mentioned that the word sophomore came up, but she can't recall where. Just that she'd heard it a lot. I'm thinking that it's the target age range for these girls."

"I'll dig around. Alysia is above that age, but some of the girls weren't, so they'd fit the sophomore age range. As for him trafficking boys, I don't think so. This boy was guided, standing, and coherent. If he was being trafficked, I doubt we'd be seeing his face."

"So what's the plan?" I sit on the desk, one leg touching the ground as the other bends to help take my weight.

"I've got people looking, watching. The issue is this: Esse knows how to hide from the Feds. He knows I'll be watching out for him."

"He knows you'll alert me and the others too. This young man might be more important than we think he is."

"I'll be happier when *I* know who he is. We're tracking through flight plans, but as you know—"

"Yeah, they can take a little while."

"Exactly. Until then, your instructions are still the same. Keep her safe."

"Are you in Texas?"

I hear a snort, kind of a laugh. "You know I can't tell you that, Lieutenant. I'll call you if anything new comes up."

"Why do I feel like I'm being kept in the dark?"

"You're right, you are. For now, it's necessary. I need you to trust me, please." I sigh, letting my frustration show, but appreciating her softer tone and candour. "The less you know, the less you can share if anything happens. This is to protect you just as much as you're protecting her. But, I am advising you to use caution. Deadly force *can* be used if necessary; that right is always yours." I don't need the reminder, but I'll take it.

"Don't like the feeling I've been played."

"Reid, I promise you, I'm *not* playing you. Everyone else is having to try as hard as you as you're setting the bar high. They're in the *'dark'* as much as you are, for their own safety too."

"I'd like to believe that!"

201

"When this is all over, trust me, you'll get the chance to compare notes. The briefing is going to be extensive."

"Yes, ma'am."

"Okay, good. I'll let you get back to it. Oh, courtesy of the United States Government, there's an International compatible mobile phone heading your way for Alysia. The British Government have installed tracking software on it that we have access to."

"That's a good move." I hold back that I've placed a personal tracker on her. If the need arises, I'll share that information. "When is it due to arrive?"

"Tomorrow. It's unlocked, so she can take it home and use a British SIM."

"That's good to know! I'll be sure to tell her."

"Thank you. You go and have a good day now."

"Yes, ma'am, and you!" We hang up, but it takes a few moments before I can leave this office.

When I get back to my desk, Alysia is working through the same page she was when I left. There are screens open, notes scribbled on the pad, and she's editing a line and reading it aloud.

"I like the second attempt at that, kitten." She jumps, and I chuckle; clearly she didn't hear me walking in.

"Ach, ye made me jump."

"Yes, I did, didn't I?" I tease, and she sticks out her tongue at me. I lean down. "Kitten, unless you want me to repeat the other night in this office, you need to keep that tongue in your mouth."

She goes to sass me but thinks better of it. She quickly pulls her tongue back into her mouth and turns to face the screen. Only, her fingers do not move across the keys. Unsettling her is my new favourite hobby.

I sit down at my desk and open up an email from Maggie, showing me the young man who travelled to the USA with Grant. The note attached says he hasn't gone through customs, so he's here illegally, not that Grant gives a hoot about that. In that email is confirmation of the phone and my instructions as well. As if I needed reminding. Discreetly, I look across at

Alysia, who has gone back to work. The keys tap under her fingers and the pad slowly fills with notes as she utters out new ways to say what's on the page. Copyrighting can be a bitch.

We stop for lunch, but we don't dawdle in Knautical Grill. We pick up our food and eat in the truck at the park, where I can see people coming and going. When we get back, I'm barely at my desk when Matt pops his head around the door.

"Reid?" He motions for me to step outside, and within sight but not earshot of my office, he opens his hand. "This was on your squad." The tiny device is a tracker.

"How the hell?" I look at him and then at the device, taking it from him.

"No idea. You came back into the yard just before me, and I parked next to you for a change. Saw this as I bent down to pick up a dime I'd dropped."

The damn tracker is about the size of a dime. Still holding it, I head back to my desk. "Fancy having some fun with that?" Matt calls, the mischievous grin that I know is his asshole-self coming forth.

"Yeah, I wanna know who put this on. And who's watching."

Matt winks at me and holds his hand out for it. I hand it over and watch as one of my life-long friends heads out of the station to the yard. I just hope I haven't set him up to meet Noah.

I send an update to Maggie when I unlock my laptop. I find it frustrating that I can't just call her, but the reason why any of this is happening, Alysia, is blissfully unaware of it, and I would like to keep it that way for as long as possible.

Alysia glances up at me, and her face changes. "Things okay?"

I smile and pretend like it's all roses, when it's far from it. "Just police work, darlin', I'm just thinking", I drawl, hoping that I sound normal as I tap my temple. I'm anything but right now.

I wonder what Matt's up to, when he appears again about twenty minutes later with a wicked grin on his face.

"You might want to check your files," he states, grinning at Alysia's laptop before coming past. In moments, I have the images of who went to collect the tracker. It's the same young man Esse was guiding through the airport.

"What the hell?" I didn't see Alysia come and look over our shoulder, and I click away. "Naw, put that back. I think I know who that is. But, he should be back in Scotland, no oot here."

I glance between Matt and Alysia. "Alysia, please explain."

"That's my bawbag of a cousin, Billie. The one who sold my Nan's things. The one my brothers beat up. See his black eye? That's him. The wee gobshite."

It takes me one whole second to pick up the phone and call Maggie. Things just got mighty interesting.

With Alysia's cousin known to be around the Piper Falls area, it doesn't take long for Preston to call a meeting. I asked Caroline at reception to keep an eye on Alysia and let me know her whereabouts if she leaves the station. Everyone is disgruntled as they file in, moaning about the inconvenience of it all.

"Okay, ladies, time to sit down, shut up and listen good." There's still some moaning, until Preston whistles through his teeth. That shuts everyone up. Then there's a projection of Maggie on the wall.

"Evening, everyone. I'm driving down to Piper Falls as I speak, so I'll be brief. The witness under your protection seems to be in more danger than we thought, and that danger might well be imminent. Lieutenant Reid, I'll let you brief your team. I'm a few hours out, and I won't be coming in alone."

"We understand, Special Agent Forrester. We'll see you soon."

As soon as Preston cuts the video connection, I stand and prepare to present the case as I have it to the team. I've never needed their help as much as I do right now.

I take Preston's place front and centre, looking around at everyone who has gathered. In moments, I have Grant Esse's image up on the wall.

"FBI Agent Grant Esse," I state, garnering sniggers from the crew. "Yeah, he lives up to his name. Went AWOL after these two tracked Alysia and I to the Rangers' cabin half-an-hour out. He was supposed to be on site with Maggie, but he didn't show. One was shot by Maggie," I pull his picture up, "Turns out Alysia recalls him and not in a good way. I believe he was one member of the gang that drugged and raped her. This was his accomplice." I switch to the other image. "He was found dead in his cell, thankfully not ours, the following morning."

I go on to explain where he was being held before I switch the image to Billie, Alysia's cousin, and explain to the guys who he is to Alysia and his background.

"So, her cousin got into the country with Esse, he's put a tracker on your squad, and he was seen trying to follow it. Who gave him the shiner?" I grin at Matt's question, though he has more of an idea of what's going on than anyone else in the room, even Preston.

I chuckle. "Alysia's brothers. Seems Billie here likes taking advantage of older people, sold their grandmother's stuff to a pawn broker. Her brothers found him, gave him a hiding." That gains a few noises of agreement. "I don't know why he's in town, but if he's with Esse, the chances are he's here to lure her out."

I turn as Caroline comes in. "Oh sorry! Erm…Reid? Alysia just went out, said you knew? We tried to stop her—" I nod and run out, following where Caroline yells at me the way Alysia went. I just hope I'm not too late.

I run down the street, trying to find where she's gone, and as I run to the corner, I see her in the coffee shop, buying an iced drink. Without thinking, I march up to her and lean down to whisper in her ear. "Alysia, I ain't happy you left the station."

She turns and smiles, until she sees my face. "I only went to get an iced tea," she explains, as if that's going to be a good excuse.

"Thanks, Jo." I nod to Jo and refrain from grabbing Alysia's arm and marching her back to the station. Instead, I lean down. "Your cousin is in town. How do you think he got here?" It takes her a moment, then her face falls. "Exactly. Who do you think he might be here with?"

"I didn't think—"

"I know. Let's go. Now." She picks up her drink after paying, and we head back. All the while I'm watching our backs.

In my office, I shut the door and let my temper rise. "Now what the hell were you thinking?" She slumps down into the chair and doesn't look at me. "If they are following you, which is now entirely possible, they might well have just been able to grab you again."

"I'm sorry." She doesn't sniff or look up. I move and sit on the sofa, desperately trying not to lose my calm and rant at her. It takes her a moment before she lifts her head up to look at me.

"You're still in danger. You can't go doing things like that, do you understand me?" I clip my words, annunciating them clearly so she cannot misunderstand them or my meaning.

"I do."

I hold her stare, desperate for her to say "yes, sir." She doesn't.

"I do!"

I keep silent, my jaw hurts, and I'm in two minds as to how to lay down the law. I pick the softer option.   "Stay in this room. You can visit the bathroom, but do not leave this station or even go out into the vehicle yard. Am I understood?" She nods, moments away from tearing up, but I don't care. "I'm going back to this briefing, about keeping you safe. So stay put." I leave and shut the door behind me. It doesn't take much force to rattle the blinds or the framework.

Back in the briefing room, Preston turns to me. Everyone else but he and Matt have filed out. "Did you find her?" he asks and sighs in relief as I nod.

"I did. She'd gone to get an iced tea, of all things." The gapes from Preston and Matt tell me all I need to know. "I know. Not laid into her yet. I forget that she's still a kid at times."

"She's twenty-two, nearly twenty-three. Hardly a kid."

I look at Matt. "Her mentality tells me she's not quite grown."

Matt shrugs. "Hard to tell with women. Hopefully, this will put some sense into her head." I snort at his comment. I want to tear Alysia a new one and wrap her up in a huge hug at the same time. Both are sitting on even odds about what I do. For now, both ideas have to be parked up.

"Speaking of sense," Preston comments, making me turn to him. "Maggie will be here soon. I've got dispatch and officers checking CCTV and patrolling."

"Esse will work out quickly that we know he's in town. Especially if he sees Maggie at any point."

Preston nods. "Keep your wits about you." With a nod to Matt and me, he leaves the room.

"Where are you going to sleep tonight?"

"My place. I can't be putting anyone else in danger."

"Caden had his Joker grin on when he came by earlier. Said he's cooked up a few surprises for whoever your guests are." I'd roll my eyes, but the idea of surprising any unwanted guests is enough to have me grinning like Caden.

I go back to my office, but before I enter, I collect my thoughts, trying to rein in my emotions. When I open the door, Alysia is there, curled up on the sofa, and she's been crying. I can guess why and hope the fear of what might have happened has been processed.

"I'm sorry. I didn't think. I didn't realise Billie was here, in Piper Falls. When you spoke with that FBI agent, I thought you meant here as in the States."

I look across at her; seeing her crying slowly melts my resolve. I like and dislike her ability to get past my defences so easily.

"I'd have preferred that you asked."

"I know." Her sullen reply tells me that she's done nothing *but* think about it. She snaps her head up and goes to ask me something. The minutes creep by, and all I can hear is the ticking of the clock in the hallway. "You're no yelling at me."

I lean against my desk and fold my arms. "Would it help you understand just how scared and angry your actions made me?"

She shakes her head slowly, her voice still low. "I already ken that."

"As much as I want to yell at you—because, darlin', trust me, I do—it ain't gonna make any difference now, is it?"

She shakes her head again. "Naw. But you might feel better if ye did."

I shrug. It might, but so would a good gym session. "Perhaps, but I have a better idea. Pack your stuff up, we're done for the day."

I pick up my phone and text Abi, hoping that the lady can help as I briefly explain why. When her confused but compliant reply comes through minutes later, I grin.

♡ ♡ ♡

Abi's in the reception area when I get there with Alysia. She looks between us both when she checks out the bag Abi hands her.

"I've never done anything in the gym…" She looks at me with wide eyes, appealing to Abi.

"Yer getting nae sympathy ootta me, hen. Ye ran off. Best let the man get his frustrations out on the curls, aye?"

"I just went to get an iced tea—" Alysia whines, but the look from Abi shuts her up.

"Ye put yourself at risk. Ye've not been telt it's safe, that this nonsense is over. And we've no bust its chops. So, until we have, ye need to keep yer wits aboot ye and be wise." Alysia goes to make a comment. "Nae excuses. Yer twenty-two, no two." It makes Alysia pause, and if looks could kill… However, Abi's not troubled by it. "Build a bridge, learn from it, get o'er it and level up, lass. I ken ye can." With a nod and a smile to me, she stalks out of the station, meeting up with Nick and her dog. She doesn't glance back.

In the gym ten minutes later, we're dressed and ready. There's just her and me in the police gym; no one else is around.

"Do you know how to warm up?" I ask, but she shakes her head. "Jumping jacks?" I demonstrate in the hope she did some at school.

She smiles at me with a small nod. "Star jumps."

I chuckle. Same thing, different name. "Okay, about thirty of those. Stair climbers?"

"Ach, I hate those." Okay, she knows what *they* are.

"Hate them or not, twenty. Race you." I begin, and she quickly catches on. "Do what I do for warmups, as best you can."

She nods, and we get on with working out my frustrations. The view I get from the tight active leggings and crop top makes her leaving the station for an iced tea a thing of the past.

An hour later, after working out on incline bench-presses, weights, rows and abs, I'm done. Alysia gave up about ten minutes ago and has been watching me via the mirrors. I catch her watching me a few times, but she doesn't interrupt my flow.

I stop when Jason appears with a package in his hand and gives it to Alysia. Taking the towel, I wipe the sweat from my neck and face.

"What's this?"

"Open it and find out." I watch as she slowly finds the edge of the box and opens it. Her eyes go wide.

"It's a new mobile phone?!" She is so excited, she lays it down and then comes to hug me, even though I'm a sweaty mess. "Reid, why? How?!"

I shrug. "Maggie and the British Consulate did their thing."

She grins and holds the phone to her. "Thank you."

"You're welcome." I love that genuine smile from her lips. "Now, go shower, and we'll get on with getting food, okay?"

Alysia nods, and I watch as she heads for the showers, happy as can be.

$\heartsuit \heartsuit \heartsuit$

We head out, and I check the yard, aware that Billie and Esse are likely watching, but I don't see a thing, and nothing new is on the squad. As we head out, I get to thinking about what is still in the flat for us to eat, and I have to admit, it likely ain't much or fresh. Watching my six, I head to Bessie's.

"I need you to stay close, kitten."

"We're going shopping?" I nod at her question as I pull into the parking area and park as close to the doors as I can, throwing her a wry grin.

"We do need to eat." At that mention, her stomach rumbles, and I shake my head. "Exactly my point!"

With a grin, she unbuckles her seatbelt, and I go around to help her down. Grabbing a basket as we head in, she sticks close to me as we walk around. There are a few things she picks up, checks out and sets back down. Mostly, cookies. I pick up a packet I like the look of and pop it into the basket. I hear raised voices from the front of the store and turn to grab Alysia, but she's suddenly not anywhere near me. I glance up and just see the warehouse door swing shut.

I drop the basket where it is and run to the warehouse door. When I get into the delivery area, there are staff tied up, and the back doors are wide open with no van or truck backed up against the grate.

The staff groan and fidget, taking my attention and need away from Alysia's now unknown whereabouts to them.

"Some large guy came in with a gun, tied us up, and this young kid that was with him stole my shirt!" I untie one young lad who is about the same build and height as Billie likely is.

I sigh and call Maggie.

"Maggie, it's Reid. They got her."

"Fuck! Okay, I'm in Piper Falls. Does she have her phone with her?"

I think for a moment, recalling Alysia putting it into her side pocket. "Yes, ma'am, she did when she left the squad."

"I'll start tracking it. Meet me out by the gas station."

"Yes, ma'am." I hang up, check Alysia's personal tracker and call dispatch.

"Squad 32 to dispatch."

"Squad 32, go ahead."

"Inform Squad 7, 37 and 4 that the cat was taken out of the bag. I repeat, she's been taken. Also need units down to Bessie's to interview the staff."

"10-4, 32. Backup's on the way."

"10-4."

As I get into my vehicle, my temper rises, and I see her bag on the seat. I check it, just to ensure the phone isn't there. It isn't, and I aim the car towards the gas station. I just need her to activate that tracker, and if I ever needed a prayer to be answered, it's then and there.

Maggie's waiting in her car when I get to the gas station, and I jump into the passenger seat. "Walk me through what happened," she demands as the door slams shut behind me.

I take Maggie through what occurred as she watches the screen. Seconds later, my phone lights up with an alert and a beeping.

"What's that?" Maggie nods to my phone, and I figure it's time to come clean.

"I installed a personal tracker into some jewellery she's wearin'. Figured Esse wouldn't look that closely for a tracker, he'd likely go for a phone."

Maggie's eyes go wide, then she grins. "Okay, good call. When were you going to enlighten me?"

"Not until I needed to, which is right now." I motion to the phone. "Is her location matching her mobile?"

Maggie compares the two and nods. "For now, yes. You know where that is?" I watch the blips as they slow and stop down a track several miles out. Then, mine starts moving, but the phone doesn't move.

"I sure do," I stare at the screen, "And they've worked out the phone is tracked."

"He has. Fuck."

I grin. "He ain't aware she's awake, or that she's got a tracker around her wrist."

"Thank the heavens above for that! Where are they going?"

I watch as a coldness seeps into my core. "Fucker knows my history."

Maggie gives me a questioning look. "How so?" She starts the engine, and I quickly grab some kit from the trunk of my squad car.

"I'll give you a quick version of my dirty-cop uncle as we drive. I can't believe that place is still standing."

Chapter Eighteen

♡ Alysia ♡

It hurts to move, and it's pitch black, but I can tell my hands are bound together with just enough movement to activate that tracker. It takes a few attempts before I manage it, then I relax, letting whatever it is they subdued me with to go through my body. I feel so rubbery, and the air smells of almonds; I try to move away from where the smell is the strongest. The vehicle slows and stops, a door opens, then closes again a few moments later, and we slowly pull away.

I can tell the car speeds up but doesn't go overly fast, as if the driver is obeying the speed limit.

I can hear muffled voices, and I work out I'm in the boot of a car. I manage to try and feel for my phone, but I can't. I'm guessing my new toy is resting somewhere at the bottom of a puddle or the river. I curse my cousin, vowing to hurt him in some way.

The car slows, then jostles and lurches as it carefully makes its way over whatever terrain it's being driven over. I listen; I can't hear any gravel crunching under the tyres, and the car feels sluggish. I try to recall how Billie separated me from Reid and wonder if he knows where I am. I check the tracker again, watching it closely, hoping to see some sort of light come from it. But I don't see a thing. That disheartens me, but I just hope that I did it right and it reaches Reid.

The car jostles again, then there's a lot of cursing about avoiding muddy trenches and that no one would think to look out here for me, seeing as it was still in the district of Piper Falls. That alone gives me hope that Reid will find me. And that I get to kick Billie where it hurts, though I personally doubt he's got anything there to damage, the wee scroat.

The vehicle finally comes to a stop, and the engine is turned off. I close my eyes and feign that I'm still asleep; at least I'll get a chance to maybe see where I am if I behave as if I'm still incapacitated.

The boot opens, and the rag that I smelled is removed.

"Dae ye think she's still oot?"

There's a grunt, and I'm hauled up as if I weigh nothing. I try to act limp, but when he puts me over his shoulder, I huff, groan. "She's in the process of waking up. Let's get her into the basement."

I can see my cousin following, but I try not to let on I'm awake. My captor turns. "Go and hide the car." He tosses Billie the keys. My cousin couldn't catch a cold if it was stitched to him, never mind a set of keys. I try not to laugh as Billie drops them, making the ape holding me grunt and shake his head as best he can. Then he turns back towards the building. I swear if I sneezed, it would fall over, like a house of cards.

The walls shake as the door is finally wrenched open, and the stale air hits my nose. I try to continue my charade, but I think the game is up. My captor drops me onto an old, dusty, crusty smelling chair that even the moths have long since abandoned.

"So, you *are* awake."

I decide to continue to act groggy and look up to stare at the man who's captured me. I take in every one of his features: the broken nose that never got set straight, the droopy eyes and the thinning hair, the total opposite of his gut.

"Kinda."

"You ain't fooling me, princess. You've been awake a little while. Knew that worthless shit of a cousin couldn't do it."

I hold back a second or two, not quite holding my head up before asking, "Couldn't do what?" I take my time to speak, so that it looks like I am still struggling. The fact is, I know I won't get far if I try to run, so I need to eek this out, give Reid time to find me.

"Knock you out properly. Guessing your side got all the brains, huh?"

I don't answer him, not that his statement needs an answer. The truth is what it is.

"Well, don't matter none. We'll be out of here by dark, and your shit-for-brains cousin can take the blame." My mouth doesn't want to work, but it seems my face does all the talking. "I can see you like that idea." From his back, he pulls out a gun and waves it at me. "Move. Down the stairs."

He opens a door and waves me onwards. He pulls a cord, and a light pops on. There are cobwebs everywhere, and I freeze; I hate spiders.

"Move!" he growls at me and shoves me down. I just about manage to not fall head-first down the stairs when he shoves me, but seconds later, it doesn't matter. The door is shut, and I try to open it, only to find it bolted. I sit down, annoyed that I'm left with a crappy light, a basement full of spiders and a stairwell full of cobwebs.

I wake with a start, hearing angry hushed voices outside.

"You got rid of the phone, didn't you, boy?"

"Aye, I did! You were there when I left it by the road."

"So how do you think they found us?"

"Why the hell should I ken?" I can hear my cousin's tone get shorter and snippier in seconds. "Dinnae be askin' me. I did what ye telt me to."

"Doesn't matter. We need to get her out of here. Where are the keys?"

"Right here," he says, then I hear a faint "Oh, shite!"

"What?"

"I dropped them, and they went doon that hole."

"You dumbwit! That goes to the basement."

"And how do we get to that?"

There's a boom sound, I'm not sure what, then there's a sound of wood breaking.

"What did ye hit me for! You're off yer heid." I snort; trust my stupid cousin to finally get the memo—when it's too late. "Ye can go and get her yerself." I can hear someone stomping away.

"Oh, Billie?" I hear the American man say, right before I hear the sound of a gun going off. I jump and hold my breath; I don't want my cousin dead because of this bawbag.

♡ ♡ ♡

Far too long later, which might truly have only been minutes, the door opens, and I get yanked out, first by my hair, then my arm.

"Come here!" the American man is growling, and it's dark now. So very dark. The light cord is pulled, and I can't see for a few moments. There's a hole in the floor that I am guided around, and I can't help but wonder if Billie is down there. The car is there, running, but I don't know how he got the keys, then the hole in the floor makes sense. All too quickly, I'm near the car, and I pull against him, putting all of my weight to the ground as quickly as I can.

He pulls me up, and I yell, then there are lights all around us, and a very familiar voice calls out crystal clear into the night.

"Freeze!"

Reid!

♡ Reid ♡

We watch, hidden by the shadows as Grant finally emerges from the cabin my uncle once called home. Finding the phone they'd tossed on the main road reminded me about this road and the only building in the vicinity; Alysia's little GPS backed it up. Maggie has Caden and the others positioned about twenty yards out, all prepped for the second wave, but for now, it's just her, the other Federal agent I met earlier, and me. I don't intend on letting Caden or anyone else get a shot in.

"Ah, there he is. The boy scout." Grant sneers at me as he hauls Alysia up by the arm, and the coward uses her as a shield before backing up against the car. He's as much of a coward as I thought he would be

216

"What's wrong, *Esse*? Got to use a little lady as a shield?" I need him to get annoyed with me, to do something foolish. He's a Fed, a bad one. I also now know his real name.

Grant snorts at my comment but doesn't say anything in reply. That gun is too close to Alysia to make a move just yet, but I can see her looking at my hands. I signal for her to just wait.

"Ah, ah, Flanagan. No hand signals to my little wife here."

Alysia fights, twisting, but his hold on her tightens, and he waves the gun in her sight, making her freeze. "Yer no my husband, ye skanky bawbag! The Judge took care of that."

He leans in and sniffs her while looking at me, a ploy on the Joker grin Matt often entertains. He's wanting me to react, and I'm trying my damn hardest not to.

"Did he now? We'll just have to fix that back to her being mine, won't we?"

"Don't think for a second that's gonna happen. We know who you really are." I curse myself for responding, but I see Maggie getting into position, and she nods.

He laughs, pulling Alysia to him so her back is to his front and his back is firmly against the car.

"Do ya now? That's interesting."

"Stands to reason you'd follow in *that* mangy dog's footsteps. Does the poor bastard even know he fathered a child?"

Grant is a few years older than me, the same age as my brother, and while Grant is his real name, the Esse isn't; it's a play on his mother's name: Estelle. His father? That would be my uncle, which makes this mangy dawg my cousin.

Alysia holds her ground, not leaning into Grant, who just laughs at my statement. "That worthless old man? Not a chance."

"What would you say to him? If ya could."

Grant's face gets sneery, spiteful, and it's an ugly look. "Nothing that would be useful. He didn't care what he did, and I get that now." He sniffs Alysia's hair again as he holds the gun in front of her.

"No, he didn't care that he destroyed not only his life, but that of his family too."

"So you're going to play the '*family*' card, are ya, boy?"

"Sure ain't answering '*sir*' to y'all. Not that you'd understand what the word '*family*' means."

He snorts. "I know plenty, Momma told me that."

"Pity you didn't listen to her."

"Hard to. Drugs took her when I was eleven, and I was in the system." He pulls Alysia closer, and she yells out, but I signal again to wait.

"You had a choice," I remind him. "You chose the wrong side, the wrong way. Yeah, you were a victim, but you didn't have to stay there. It wasn't your final destination."

He chuckles. "Who says I was a victim?"

"Who said you weren't? You were, just as much as Estelle was. You could have reached out, asked for help. Found out the real meaning of family, tested that idea"

"To be turned away?" he sneers. "Momma wasn't going to give your '*family*' that level of satisfaction. Family was when it suited them."

"We didn't know; she never asked. It's hard to be involved and give a helping hand if you don't know that someone needs help." I thank God I was quickly able to call my brother and father to find out what they knew.

"Aww, what's wrang? Yer pride get in yer way?" Alysia hisses, pushing her shoulder against Grant, but he hauls her closer still, using his weight to restrain her, the big yellow-belly.

"Stay still, wife," he commands, his voice low.

"She ain't your wife. She did tell ya the Judge fixed that. Tell me, did you have someone stand in for her? Or did you just fabricate the whole thing?"

He laughs, but he doesn't let go of his grip on her. "She was there. Not that she was upright. It's amazing what people will do for some nice, copper-filled pussy, ain't it?"

I lift my gun, ready to shoot the mangy dawg. "You ain't a real man. You had to drug her; bet you can't get it up otherwise."

He sniffs her. "I can tell she's been plucked recently. Was she good when she was awake, boy?" I clench my jaw as something behind him snaps, and he turns to see Maggie, her gun steady and level. I give Alysia the signal to wait, and she gives me an index finger. Good girl understands. "Ah, my partner in crime!"

"Old partner, and never in crime. I'm under instructions to bring you in, Grant, preferably alive."

He shakes his head. "Now, that's not gonna happen, is it?"

Maggie gives a non-committal shrug. "That's down to you. Where's the boy?"

"He's in the hoose! Likely dead, I swear I heard this bawbag kill him." Alysia looks at me; a sadness fills her eyes at the mention of her cousin.

Grant leans down and snarls in her ear. "He was a useless associate."

"Aye, he was. Doesn't mean he gets to die because you're a narcissistic arsehole," she spits out. I love it when my little kitten shows her claws.

Grant kicks the back of Alysia's knee in anger, making her scream, but she isn't giving in. When he hauls her back to her feet, she stomps on his foot and drops her weight, rolling like I taught her. I take aim, and Grant reacts, trying to stop her, and they fall over each other, the gun flying out of his hand as she makes them both drop. In seconds, we're on them, and my gun is trained on Grant; I'm telling him to freeze. Maggie is saying the same. From his pants, he pulls out a large knife with one hand as Alysia tries to continue escaping, and my finger pulls the trigger as the arm with the knife arcs up. Maggie and her associate shoot too, and in seconds, my cousin is dead, but there's still screaming happening. *Alysia.*

I put the safety on and holster my gun.

"What's up, kitten? Where's it hurting?"

"My leg!" She turns to look, and I do too. The way the leg is angled now ain't natural, and I know in a heartbeat, it's broken in more than one place. The next sound I hear is her vomiting, and I pull her hair back away from her face in time. Maggie and Michael carefully remove Grant's limbs from around hers so we can move her. My paramedic colleagues swarm in, but in my mind, they can't get her to the General Hospital quickly enough.

Hours later, I've given my badge and gun over to Maggie, at least for now. Maggie found Billie's deceased body in the basement, something I haven't had a chance to tell Alysia yet. When she got loaded onto the stretcher and taken to the hospital, we started clearing down the site, removing the two dead bodies and then debriefing. My head is still numb from the revelations Maggie threw at me after Grant got Alysia: his real name, birth parents, his relationship to me and how long he'd been shipping girls around the States. He'd come across them as part of his case load but would cover up what happened, or change the evidence, so colleagues were sent on a goose-chase.

It's taken Maggie all this time to find out who was helping him, and the triumphant look on her face a little while ago means she was successful. We made the call to Billie's parents together, telling them that he was in the States and that they needed to come over. Alysia's parents, I believe, are on their way too, which is going to be interesting.

I do have a "hall pass" to be at Alysia's bedside, and I'm under instructions not to leave town under any circumstances. Not that I would. I'd be in the operating room at the hospital if I could, but they won't even let me watch, which might be wise.

Now, I'm sitting on the chairs in the waiting room on the post-surgery floor, waiting for her to come out of surgery. I'm told that Doctor Klaus Monroe insisted on doing the operation himself when he heard. Doc Candy is in there too, so the break must be awful.

"Reid, go home." I shake my head at Aly's advice. "Ain't ya picking up her parents and her uncle from the airport?"

"No, I aint. I can't leave town, but they've only just got to the airport on their side. They'll be another twelve hours yet, at least. Maggie has that in hand."

"So will Alysia. They'll want her to sleep it off; they're having to pin the leg in four places."

I wince but nod, then I rub my hands over my face. "I wanna be here." I don't want her to wake up without her knowing I'm here.

"You'll need your rest."

I smile at Aly but shake my head. "No point. I won't sleep here any better than I would at home." Aly looks up, and I turn. I see Abi and Nick walk in, Abi leading the charge. In a second, she's hugging me, and I take that embrace. Man, I need it.

"We heard what happened. Is there anything we can do?"

Aly laughs, hugging her friend. "Get him to go home and sleep!"

Abi snorts in response. "No likely to happen. So," she turns to me, "How about an air mattress and a pillow with a blanket?" She unrolls the camping mattress and hands me a pillow.

"You're not seriously encouraging him to sleep here?" Abi turns to Aly with a grin.

"If it were Luke being operated on? Or Essie? Jason? Sakura?" Abi's head tilts, and Aly relents.

"Yeah, okay. I just hope you don't snore. I don't need the complaints."

I chuckle, knowing that I don't. With thanks to Abi and Nick, who at least leave me with a thermos of good coffee and a blanket, they head off with the promise to be here tomorrow at some point. I nod; they're aware I don't want her to be left alone. I lay the mattress out so that I'm facing the way Alysia will come up from recovery, and I rest as best I can.

At four am, I hear the bed being wheeled around, and I wake up, focusing on Alysia. She's breathing normally, but her leg is in a cast from foot to hip and held up slightly in a sling.

Santa squeezes my shoulder as does Candy, then they leave, and I pull the bedding Abi gave me and place it on the floor alongside Alysia's bed. I just need another few hours.

I hear voices that are similar to Alysia's, and thinking it's Abi, I groan as I turn over, asking her to keep it down.

"Oh my goodness! Who the hell are ye?"

I wake up, finding myself staring at an older lady with hair as coppery as Alysia's and smile lines around her eyes and a man who is very salt-and-pepper in the hair with a decent amount of stubble. I scramble to my feet, hoping I don't smell like a sewer.

"Lieutenant Reid Flanagan, Piper Falls PD. You would be?"

"Freya and Hamish Davidson." Her dad's voice is clipped, but he extends his hand out for a shake, and I take it, noting how firm that handshake is. "We weren't sure who was picking us up. We were told you were waiting for Alysia here. But we dinnae realise you'd be this close."

"Reid?" Alysia's faint voice calls out from behind me, and I turn, smiling at her. "Oh my God!" She reaches her arms out for a hug, and I oblige; forgetting her parents are watching, I kiss her stupid.

"Hey, kitten. Welcome back!"

"You found me!"

I place my forehead on hers, breathing her in, even if she doesn't smell like she usually does.

"You did good, activating that tracker like you did."

She eventually moves, and I pull back so I can see her face, which looks sad. "Is he gone?"

I nod slowly. "The devil came to Piper Falls and took him."

"Huh?"

"Ain't you ever heard the song 'The Devil Came Down to Georgia'?"

She throws me a quizzical look. "This isnae Georgia."

"Which is why the devil has come and claimed his own."

It takes her a few minutes before she quietly asks, "Billie's dead, isn't he?"

"I'm afraid so, darlin'. Nothing you can do about that."

She starts crying, and her parents are suddenly at her other side. "Ma! Da!" They hug her for a moment, and I back away, unsure of what to do. When I turn, Maggie is there with a soft look on her face, Aly and Doctor Klaus right behind her.

"Miss Davidson, I hear the surgery was a success?" Maggie walks into the room, confident but kind.

Alysia looks at her leg. "Aye, but my leg bloody hurts!"

"I'll let the medical staff do their thing. I need to ask you some questions which will take an hour or so, then your parents can sit with you, that work for ya?"

"Does it have to be now? They just got here."

"The quicker I get a statement from you, the quicker they can come sit with ya." Maggie's giving off this whole *'let me do my job'* vibe, and I get it.

"It needs to be done while it's fresh, kitten. I'll take your folks to the Cozy Bean, and we'll be back in an hour, okay?"

"Reid?" Maggie's voice has a note of caution, but I know what she's going to say.

"Yeah, I know. Town limits." She nods, and I guide Alysia's parents to the Cozy Bean.

Alysia

For too long, this Federal agent has me walk through what happened when Billie kidnapped me at gunpoint in Bessie's to when Reid, Maggie and someone else shot Grant dead. From him trapping me in the basement stairwell to shooting Billie about the car keys, then him falling on me when he was shot, everything that was said or occurred, we went over. Twice.

I am tired by the time Reid and my parents come back, and Reid looks like he's swallowed a wasp. Despite my parents trying to engage me in some conversation, my eyes are heavy, and I can't keep them open.

When I open them again, Reid's not around, neither is my dad, but Mum is.

"Oh, hiya," I greet my mum, who looks like she's been crying. In a moment, she's hugging me, and it's the best feeling, having her here. "I'm alive, Mum, thanks to Reid."

Mum's jaw clenches and moves, so she's likely going to ask me something I'm no going to like. "We heard about the tracker he put on ye."

I nod but don't try to find the bracelet. I know it was removed for the surgery, and I was told I'd get it back. "It was how he found me." She smiles. "It was, wasn't it?" Mum shrugs. "What dae ye know?"

"That the Federal agent that got ye, he was that copper's cousin."

I shiver. "No way!"

Mum nods. "Swears he didn't know until he'd got ye, then he was following you."

"I was his duty."

Mum cocks her head to the side. "Ye looked like far more than that!"

I swallow. "He is. To me, he is a lot more than just a copper who saved me. He's made me realise a few things, let me grow, take things in my own time. Reminded me that I had a life afore all a' this."

"And?"

I swallow. "I wanna stay, but I can't, can I?"

Mum shakes her head. "Not right now, no. But, I've seen how he looks at ye, how ye look at him. Yer taken wi' him."

I pull in a breath but nod. "Aye, I am."

"He's taken wi' ye anol. That Federal officer telt us ye need to come home when yer well enough to travel. Ye cannae stay here. But, ye can come back. This time, of yer own free will." I nod; I get it. It hurts, but I understand. I'm not allowed to just stay here, as much as that hurts and as much as I want to.

My mother becomes blurry, and she shoves a tissue into my hand. "And the thing is, I think ye wanna see how it goes, aye?"

I shake my head. "I already know how it goes, Ma. I want that. I want him."

"Yer only twenty-four."

"And ye were married with a bairn on the way," I remind her, but she shakes her head, chuckling.

"Jason was already born. I was pregnant with Anthony only a few months after having Jason. Found out a few months after my twenty-fourth birthday."

I dry my eyes. "I know what I want. I just want to know if he wants me too. Getting to live out here, I need to see how that's done. It's been done already; I just need to ask her how she did it."

Mum's hand is entwined in my own. "Who has done it already?"

"Erm…Abi Charmichael."

Mum's face scrunches up. "Mary Whitlock's lass?"

I shrug. "Maybe? Her dad was a firefighter here," I add, making Mum nod.

"Aye, that's Mary's lass. Well, if anyone can show ye what ye need to do, it'll be her. Mary wasnae pleased she's moved out here. I can guess why—but, honey, I'm gonna tell ye what I told Jason, Anthony and Sorcha. Follow yer heart."

Epilogue

♡ Reid ♡

It took a few weeks before I could go back to work, and I offered Alysia's parents my apartment for a while when Abi offered me her spare room with Alysia to help keep their costs down. It turns out the Scots are just as family-oriented as us Texans. Alysia's parents knew Abi's momma, so that made a connection.

Billie's parents flew home with his remains when the coroner had concluded his examination. Transpires that the gunshot didn't kill Billie; breaking his neck in the fall to the rotten floor due to the gunshot was the cause.

There's some strain now between Alysia's parents and Billie's, but that ain't something I can fix, especially when I know what he was doing to their grandmother. There was a lot of shouting about blame out in my garage one evening between the brothers, but I didn't intervene, which was hard. I did make sure the guns were locked away when they moved in for a spell, just in case.

I grin as Alysia uses the crutches like a pro, moving around like she'd been doing it for months, not days. Doc Klaus and Candy told her that they weren't letting her out until she'd mastered them. So, she mastered them.

Buster even knows that she has a bad leg; he walks up to her with a calmness I've never seen him display with anyone, except her. I know Abi gets the inquisition from Alysia, and she's able to answer all her questions about immigrating over here, what paperwork is needed. Alysia thinks I don't know that she's asking all this for, but I do. Nick briefed me on a dog walk; Abi just asked me outright if I wanted Alysia here. Then she told me to tell her that I do. I haven't been brave enough to utter those words yet, though I don't get why; I'd live with the girl today, now. *Hell, I followed her when she was my duty, and now that she isn't? I'd still follow her.*

"Reid?" We've got the house to ourselves. Abi and Nick had an incident with a house fire where the hydrants failed because of low water pressure and the house and pets couldn't be saved. It happened on Abi's shift, and I can tell she's kicking herself about it. Nick's taken her and Buster out on an overnight hike, meaning they'll hike, camp, then come back the following day so Nick can turn in for his shift.

I turn to Alysia as I cook; her face is sad and serious. "Yeah, kitten?"

"Dae ye want me to move out here?"

I look up from the light meal I'm cooking, nearly dropping the fried egg.

"Kitten, know this: I don't want to be without you for a day."

She lifts her chin, holding back tears. *Where is she going with this?*

"But do you…" She leaves the sentence hanging and swallows a lot. "I think I love you more than you love me." She grabs her crutches and jumps down from the bar stool.

"Hang on." I'm at her side in seconds, the plated food now cooling for a few moments. "You love me?" I imitate Joey from *Friends* and use hand-gestures to ensure I understand her meaning. "I didn't…"

"I'm fed up of waiting for ye to say it." She looks at me expectantly, then the tears begin. "Thought so…" She turns.

"Youu thought what, kitten?" I stand in front of her, and she tries to move around me. I step in front of her, determined to get her to say what she's thinking. "That I don't love you back?" That makes her stop. "It scares me so much that I feel this way. That you'll fly back to Scotland, and any plans you have on immigrating out here will fall flat. That you'll find some nice Scottish guy, and you'll go with him because he's closer than I am, which by the way is four thousand, seven hundred and sixty-five miles, give or take a few." I reach out and cup her face. "I want it all." Then I kiss her, determined to show her that she's the one for me. "But I don't want to hold you back."

"Stop pushing me away."

I rest my forehead against hers, and I sigh. "I didn't realise I was, kitten. I don't like the idea that I'm coercing you into anything, especially a life with someone older, like me. Not after what you've been through."

She chuckles. "Aye, yer aulder, but that's because you're mature, wiser. I need a man, no a lad."

I nod in understanding. It's time to follow through.

Later on, we go through some of her immigration documentation. The stuff Nick says he helped Abi with, I'll likely have to help Alysia with. Before she returns home, the basis of Alysia's immigration and support is submitted. All she needs now is a job here in Piper Falls.

Alysia

Finding a job in Piper Falls that fits the criteria of immigration isn't easy. Abi had a transferable skill; I don't. While my leg heals, I look at the jobs here in Piper Falls, but none of them would be enough to fulfil an immigration reason.

I didn't finish the town's website re-write, and I'm bored of reading. Don't get me wrong, I love to read, but my brain isn't stimulated. Abi takes me along to the gym at the fire station, just so I can get out of the house. I insist on 'walking' with the crutches, but she won't hear of it and tells me to jump in the car. I do as I'm told because the weather is humid; she's been like a big sister to me and another lass, Olivia, here in Piper Falls. She has the air-con on for Buster, and he's laying on his back on his cool-mats, living quite the life when we leave.

I get a comfy chair from the break-out room brought to me and a stool to place my leg on while I do some research, or try to. Abi lends me her laptop, and I take a quick look at the town's website, but nothing has been updated. When Maggie left town, she gave me back the phone Grant had tossed out of the car. They were able to track it, so they found it. I'm told that the software has been deactivated, but I am not that sure. I have given that number to Mum and Dad, so at least I can talk with them.

I check my emails again as I'm waiting on an answer from my company about whether or not I still have any sort of job. As I do, I'm surprised when my mum's number comes up on screen. I answer in a heartbeat.

"Hiya, Mum!"

"Hey, sweetheart, how's it going?"

"Meh," I reply. "Bored. Trying to find something to keep my mind occupied while my body heals. Got any suggestions?"

"Sorry, honey, I haven't. Just wanted to let you know a few things."

I lock the laptop and lean back in this comfy chair. "Oh, aye?"

"Aye, Billie was buried today. Yer gran had a wee word wi' yer dad and uncle about Billie."

"Did she miss her target?" My gran would have given her boys hell for how they've been acting to each other, and I'm sure my uncle and aunt would have had a few home truths about how they raised Billie.

"Naw! Dae ye expect her to?"

I chuckle. "Naw! So, what else is new?"

"That's why I'm calling. What was the company you worked for?"

"Wallace House Digital. Why for?"

Mum sighs. "Thought so. They got closed down by Companies House today; the police were in attendance too, armed officers everywhere. The two owners were arrested."

"Arrested?" The image of my blond boss swims across my eyes. "Why for?"

"They were into trafficking girls, apparently. You weren't the only one."

It takes me a moment to answer. "Bloody hell! Seriously?"

"Aye, that's what yer da and I thought."

"So the company doesn't exist?"

"Not anymore, love, no."

Well, shite.

♡ Reid ♡

It's been three months now since Alysia left Piper Falls. Three months of me just existing for the next video call, the evening and good morning text messages. Today is just another day without her. The Fourth of July came and went; she didn't get back for that, a lack of funds being the reason. Without a job either side of the pond, she just can't afford it. I can't yet afford the flight for her to be here for six weeks, though I'm close to having that saved.

Maggie and I worked out who in Chicago helped get Alysia out of the hotel and cleaned her room. I watch via CCTV as that avenue is closed. Three staff at the hotel and a duty manager suddenly found themselves at the other side of Maggie's interrogation skills, leading her onto bigger fish in that murky pond.

Matt pops his head around the door. "Hey, man! You got a minute to talk? Need someone to listen regarding Amber and Katie. I could use a sounding wall."

I nod, grateful that my friend trusts me enough to just listen. The other, I'm still upset that he left town and didn't even come back for Noah's funeral. Griffin might be in town now, but we've got a ways to go to rebuild that bridge. We go through what Amber and Katie have been up against, and while I get Matt's reluctance to not get serious with Amber, I can't help but wonder if she'd grieve as hard anyway if he, too, died while on duty.

I let Matt sound out his ideas and come to his own conclusions, giving him some things to think about. When he's gone, I check my phone again, waiting on a message back from Alysia. Nothing.

I go through the day, caseload by caseload, determined to call Alysia this evening. Matt comes by again, this time with Griffin. That gets my interest.

"You've been a sour-puss for months. You missing the girl?"

I look at Matt, not wanting to air things out with Griffin right at this moment, though I feel that moment has arrived. "Hard not to. She's not told me how that interview in London went, and I expected to hear from her by now. She's six hours ahead, so I'll wait up and call her around midnight."

"Come and have beer with us, in Papi's."

I look at Griffin; our relationship still ain't healed. I come around to their side of my desk and sit, glaring at Griffin the whole time.

"Before I go for a beer with you two, we need to talk." Matt sits down, and Griffin sighs. The time has come to clear the air.

"You fucking left us high and dry. All the times Noah was there for us during school, with Lyndsey, Amber." I stand and square up to Griff. "How the hell can you not even come to his funeral?" I flex my arms, trying very hard not to just punch his lights out in the station, while on duty.

"I was at the funeral."

I take a step back. "You what? No you fucking weren't."

Griffin squirms. "I was. I snuck in at the back of the church and left before everyone else. Same at the cemetery."

"Why the fuck would you do that? And why are you here?"

"I'm back because of Dad, you know that."

"I mean here at the station, dressed as you are." That's an interview suit. What the hell is he interviewing for?

"I can forgive you for not knowing, you've had your head in your cases. You better tell him." I look at Matt, then back towards Griff.

"I'm dating Mallory."

"You what?!" I stand, exploding, but refrain from smacking him in his nice suit. "Does she know you're a cop?"

Griffin nods. Of the four of us, he was the shortest. Noah was the redhead, Matt was the football star and I was the musician. "I'm taking over from Bill Camden."

That shuts me up. "Well, fuck me gently."

"No, thanks! We'll leave that to your little firecracker of a Scot."

Griffin grins at Matt's comment. "What's the joke?"

"I had the pleasure of meeting Abi Charmichael earlier. Is Alysia anything like her?"

I laugh. "Pleasure, huh? Did you piss her off?" Griffin goes red. "Oh, fuck, what did you do?"

"I might not have realised there was a fence between the yards now, and I drove into the station. Her and some big brute gave me a hard time when I asked them to just swing the gates open."

I laugh. "Sounds like Beau. You meet Estrella too?"

He nods, his cheeks going redder, and I laugh.

"Why didn't you say you were at Noah's funeral?" My voice is less harsh. Griff often needs a direct question, and knowing what to ask him is key.

"Pride. My own stupid ego, that's what. I left; the family, the farm, Carla, it got too much, and I didn't want that expectation to fall on me as I didn't want it. If I stayed, I wouldn't have become a cop in Waco. I knew it would stifle me, hold me back. I felt that if I did come back, I'd be back in that cage."

My jaw unclenches. "You know you've always held the key to that cage, don'tchya?"

Griff shrugs. "Learning that," he admits. I extend my hand, welcoming back one of my best friends to the town and the station.

With a firm handshake, we smile.

"Please tell me you've spoken with Carla?"

Griffin nods his head, his jaw locking. "Oh yeah, we've spoken."

Thank fuck!

Several hours later, we're in Papi's. I went home and changed, washing the conversation with Griffin and Matt away. I get why Griff didn't want to come home, but he needed to. We needed him, and tonight, I finally told him how I've been feeling since Noah died. My anger towards him was to my mind justified, but to learn who he's been seeing and what's going on with Mallory, set me off.

I sent a message to Alysia. It gets sent, but remains unread. I check the time; she's likely sleeping, if her interview in London went well. If she's back home. There's too many "ifs" concerning her right now.

I grab a beer and listen to the karaoke, and some of them tonight, ain't bad. As one song finishes, the DJ comes back on.

"Now, I'm told that I can't use this lady's name, but the man in this 'ere room will know that this song is meant for him."

I don't turn around, preferring to just listen. Then, *'Cheap Thrills'* comes on, and I can't help but recall the last time I played this. Alysia was there. Matt nudges me and motions behind me to the stage.

I turn, hurting from the words and when this song last hit my ears. Standing on the stage, singing about not needing dollar bills to have fun tonight, is Alysia. She's grinning as she sings and dances. I don't care about anyone else anymore. I grin. My girl…my kitten. She's more than a diamond, certainly more than gold. She's here.

As the song ends, she jumps down off the stage, and I catch her as she runs up to me. I spin her around before kissing her senseless. My girl is home!

♡ Alysia ♡

Seeing Reid's face when he realised it was me singing, was a picture! I told Reid I had an interview in London, but it wasn't happening in London. It was here, in Piper Falls. Richard Parsons invited me to come for an interview. The town web designer stepped down, apparently upset that the website was being updated without their knowledge or consent. Richard and Henry soon put the young guy in his place, being reminded that the website belongs to the town, and informed him that his services were suddenly no longer required.

They put an advert out for a social media marketer for the town. Piper Falls relies on tourist trade, and Henry loved how I had re-written the pages I had managed to get through and showed Richard.

Back in Scotland, I had a few temporary roles, contracts to see me through, to keep the money coming in; doing that with website infrastructure I hadn't understood, but I learned, fast. Thankfully, it was under one agency umbrella so on a CV, it's going to look okay.

Living with my gran wasn't ideal, but it turns out to have been the best thing. I could work from home and help her around the house. Then, Abi sent me a message, asking if I'd contact Richard directly and why. I was quite happy to, and at midnight my time just four days ago, he offered me an interview.

Others have also interviewed for this post, but none of them have done the level of copyrighting and webwork I'd set out. When I handed that laptop over to Henry again, I hadn't expected him to look at the document I'd started compiling, or to start asking for it to be implemented.

Richard is sorting the paperwork so I can be here on a three-year work-visa. News I get to tell Reid. All my clothes and things are currently at Abi's. She picked me up yesterday, kept me hidden and took me to meet Richard. I even visited Doc Candy and Santa, letting them know how I was healing, thanks to their medical expertise.

I know I might have to go home for a few weeks, but I'm here to acclimatise to Texan life. My goal to surprise Reid was a success.

When he finally puts me down, it's to cheers from colleagues that I know, Abi and a few others, and plenty I do not.

"You kept that quiet, kitten."

I grin at him. "I'll make some noise later," I tease.

He pulls me to him, and I can feel his heart beating under that shirt and in his hard chest. "You sure will, darlin'!"

I grin as he introduces me around to a new guy named Griff, then Matt and many others, including Ethan and Caden. I love that his arm is forever wrapped around me, making me feel like I'm home. And I am.

The End

Piper Falls: Station 28 Series

Available Now

Embracing My Duty by Melony Ann
Torn By My Duty by Kayla Baker
Against My Duty by Anneke Boshoff
Defying My Duty by D.L. Howe
Leave Of My Duty by Nikki A. Lamers
Fulfilling My Duty by Havana Wilder
Following My Duty by Louise Murchie
Replete In My Duty by Stacy Kristen
Accepting My Duty by Darley Collins

Other Books By Louise Murchie

Piper Falls: Firehouse 49 Series

Available Now

Ignite My Fire by Melony Ann
Regain My Fire by Kindra White
Playing With My Fire by D.L. Howe
Fight My Fire by Darley Collins
Against My Fire by Anneke Boshoff
Relight My Fire by Louise Murchie
Harness My Fire by Ayana Lisbet
Quench My Fire by Havana Wilder

Soulsong Duology

Available Now

True Colours
Time After Time

Standalone

Available Now

The Storyteller

Tango Down Duet

Available Now

Dionadair: Our Defender
Trodaiche: My Fighter

Let's Be Friends

Follow me on

Instagram
@louisemurchieauthor

Facebook
https://www.facebook.com/louisemurchieauthor

Tik Tok
https://www.tiktok.com/@louisemurchieauthor

Visit my website and subscribe to my newsletter!
https://louisemurchie.com/newsletter

Acknowledgements

For my ever supportive husband and my fabulous kids. To Tina and my British Chit Chat
group (Nat, Annie, Billie, Lizzie, Linz, Jen, Aisling, Ellie and Mel).

My Carxander family (Nick, Cody, Mel, Laura, Nikki, Darley, Stacy, Alyssa, Kayla, Lauren,
Samantha and Billie).

My absolute fabulous Street Team: I noticed ALL the shares, trust me.

My close family and the friends who I consider family; other family members who genuinely
know me and have helped me write another romance; thank you!

9 798227 553294